My Father's Ears

Also by Karen Goa

One Flat Coyote on the Centre Line: Cruising Canada in a classic Chevy

Bitten by the Bullet: Motorcycle Adventures in India (co-authored with Steve Kryzstyniak)

My Father's Ears

Karen Goa

GoaNotesNZ

First printed in 2015 by GoaNotesNZ, Auckland

This book was written with assistance from Creative New Zealand through the sponsored mentorship program administered by the New Zealand Society of Authors (Pen Inc).

A catalogue record for this book is available from the
National Library of New Zealand.
Goa, Karen, author. My Father's Ears/Karen Goa.
ISBN: 978-0-473-33587-8 (paperback)
ISBN: 978-1-311-468939 (ebook)

GoaNotesNZ
13 Calman Place, Chatswood
Auckland, New Zealand 0626
www.karengoa.com

Cover design: Alchemy Book Covers www.alchemybookcovers.com
Printed in the USA

Author's Disclaimer

This novel had its origins in part in the author's fictitious short story *Flight,* broadcast on Radio New Zealand National. The novel is a work of fiction inspired in part by such true historical incidents as Italian immigration to North America, American orphan trains, the Ontario Petawawa Internment Camp, Rocco Perri and the Canadian mafia, and the world of carnivals. Otherwise, the characters, incidents and dialog are products of the author's imagination and are not to be construed as factual. Some liberties have been taken with the time frame of actual events. Any errors are the author's responsibility.

For Ken

with love

always

Acknowledgements

Special thanks to Sue McCauley for her wise and prescient mentoring. Without Sue, this book would still be a millstone around my neck.

My gratitude also to Steve Danby, Eva Radich and other drama producers at Radio New Zealand, for their encouragement and support of my fiction.

Many thanks to Antona Wagstaff and Janet Lewis for their insightful comments, and to my many friends who prodded me along over the years it took to write this book.

Loving thanks to Kathleen Wheler for being the best mother ever, and for her help with the Italian side of things.

And always, to my darling husband, Ken Goa, thank you for your love and faith and for always coming up with the funniest lines.

Chapter 1

Lou drops a bombshell

I have a brother.

His name is Alex.

This is news to me. It's also news to my father. Maybe to my mother too, but we'll probably never know.

"Tell me again, Lou." I set an espresso in front of my father, mint green tea for me, and sink into a battered vinyl chair. "A man you know nothing about calls you from out of nowhere and claims he's your long-lost son."

Lou twitches like a fox terrier with a burr on its bum. He twirls the coffee, scratches at the chipped red Formica, mines his hairy left ear for waxy pickings. Lou's ears, both of them, are unusually hairy. They are not just old-man hairy, sprouting tufts from inside; they're also covered with long fuzz on the tops and the edges, like miniature silky pets attached to both sides of his head. As I wait for Lou to explain himself, I realize I've sat at this table staring at Lou's ears for more than four decades, waiting for him to listen to me.

"Not nowhere, somewhere. New Zealand." Lou juts his jaw. That's never a good sign. "He call me from New Zealand. Last-a week. Tuesday." Lou sounds flattered and impressed, as if he didn't know that telephones could dredge up voices, better yet unknown missing sons, all the way to Canada from the Southern Hemisphere.

"New Zealand. That's a handy place to hole up. So he calls and tells you he's your son. Why didn't you tell me this on Tuesday? Why do you believe anything this conman says? Why would you think you have a son?"

"*È mio figlio.*" Lou fiddles with his coffee cup. "I know this. I know."

"How do you know, Lou?"

I wait, and wait. The cuckoo clock on the kitchen wall strikes seven. The cuckoo flies out, dangles drunkenly on its spring, howls seven demented cuckoos and snaps back smartly behind the little wooden door. When I was two I accidentally ripped the little wooden door off the clock, looking for the Mamma and Papa and sister and brother cuckoo birds I was sure were hiding inside. Lou was not pleased. He is more adept with a garden trowel than a screwdriver.

I contemplate the ridiculous clock with its mended-with-duct-tape door, the ancient television blaring on the kitchen counter, the stippled ceiling where a urine-colored stain the shape of Australia claims more of the paint each spring. On the other side of the kitchen wall Lou's neighbor, Mrs Wooschuk, is speed-yelling in Ukrainian at somebody or, more likely, nobody. Only a mostly deaf eighty-five-year-old could live here.

"How-do-you-know?" I press him, louder.

"Don't-a yell, Sophie. I know because he know things," he says flatly. His jaw lifts another inch.

"Things? Like what? Your birthday? Anyone can find that out."

"Private things." Lou, I swear, is smirking. It's not attractive in an elderly parent. "Things nobody knows."

"Private things? What private things? Shoe size? Which brand of underpants you wear?"

Lou probably doesn't know that particular private thing himself. I buy Lou's underwear for him, serviceable cotton pants, all of them white, so Lou doesn't have to make a weighty decision about something as trivial as underwear. Fruit of the Loom, size S. Not so long ago it was size M. Lou's never been a hulk, but without my mother to cook for him and cajole him into eating he's shrinking all over at an alarming rate.

"Private things," says Lou, mysteriously. "You don't know." He leans across the table and whispers, "Not even Rosa know."

"What are you talking about? What doesn't Mamma know?"

"Alex is coming for visit. You see. Soon. What you cook for dinner tonight, Sophia?"

"Hold on, Lou. Forget about dinner. You say this man is coming to visit you here? In Saskatoon? Five minutes ago I didn't know this person existed and now you're already putting out the welcome mat. Isn't that a little hasty?"

"You so suspicious, Sophie. Yes, Alex come soon, he say. Maybe a couple of weeks. He know things," he says, again.

I try all kinds of interrogative and sneak-up tactics. "What things? You have to tell me now, Lou, for your own good" and "What city did you say Alex lives in?" I cannot pry one more word out of him. Lou can be as stubborn as a team of teenage mules.

It's Thursday, so Lou's dinner is half of the lasagne I baked this morning. I shove it in his fridge beside a shriveled carrot and a half-full carton of sour milk. Lou refuses to eat supermarket vegetables — taste like dead things, he says — even when the only other choice is a wrinkly carrot survivor from last summer's garden. Throughout my childhood and teenage years, Lou owned a fruit and vegetable shop selling his own almost indecently bountiful crops. His green thumb is legendary among Italian vegetable sellers. Even this early in the season, his Roma tomato plants and romaine lettuces sprout in pots in the postage stamp-sized courtyard behind my parents' townhouse. It's a spring frenzy of new green bravely sprouting away, despite the one hundred per cent chance of a killing frost.

Usually I stay on Thursdays to eat dinner with Lou, but today his twitchy smirks and non-answers are driving me crazy. He barely notices

3

when I say goodbye. I steer my elderly Toyota out of Lou's street, which for reasons of thrift (his) and sanity (mine) is as far across town from my own house as possible while still remaining within Saskatoon's city limits.

I have always wanted a brother, to stop Lou grumbling about the disappointment of girls, namely me, the blemished and only fruit of his loins. My mother often told me, of course your father loves you. You're his daughter, his first-born (his only-born). Even as a child I suspected it was a lesser, cut-price love than the Cherished Son of Lou would have got. From the age of five, when I understood the potential for siblings, I wished for a brother, to set me free to be Sophie the Darling Daughter instead of Sophie the Disappointing Non-Son.

Be careful what you wish for.

I have wished to lose a few annoyingly persistent pounds after an all-inclusive Cuban holiday and was granted food poisoning (annoying pounds gone). Worse, I have wished for my mother to live after her stroke and was granted a mute vegetable who doesn't know me. Now here's Lou, slobbery as a puppy with a freshly butchered bone, yelping about a mystery son.

What's this Alex up to? It's a long way from New Zealand to the middle of Canada, and for what? If this is an internet con, it's a poor one. Lou is an unlikely target. He won't so much as touch a computer keyboard, for fear of setting his hair on fire or making his dodgy heart beat funny. He is as anti-tech as it gets. Bad for men's business, he grumbled once, when I mentioned buying him a cellphone in case of emergency. What emergency, Sophia?

Being burgled, I suggested. Having a heart attack. Falling off a ladder. Lou was having none of it. No cellphones. Bad for men's business. We left it at that. I don't care to know what 'men's business' means to Lou.

If Alex is after money, he's got the wrong Luigi Sanzari. Lou doesn't have a dime to his name. This is not Lou's fault. He worked hard all his life.

He just made some bad decisions, with the aid of a financial adviser now handsomely domiciled in the Dominican Republic.

Questions I should have asked Lou pop into my head on the drive home. What's Alex's last name? How old is he? Married, children? There are useful clues to help me track down the imposter online, the better to expose him as the fraud he undoubtedly is before this gets completely out of hand. I unlock my door, walk straight to the phone and call Lou. He doesn't answer. I listen to Rose's quiet voice on the answerphone asking me to leave a message. Lou and I both know he should record a more up-to-date and Lou-like greeting.

Pronto, you speak to Luigi Sanzari, waddaya want?

Neither of us can do it. Neither of us can erase this piece of my mother politely inviting friends, relatives and cable TV salespeople to leave a message. Sometimes I call Lou when I know he's not at home, just to hear my mother's voice.

I heat up my half of the lasagne in the microwave and eat it straight out of the dish in front of the TV. Rose would be horrified. Living alone has done antisocial things to my table manners. Ten minutes later I'm bloated with lasagne and anxiety. The 'to-do' list on the refrigerator begs for my attention. I ignore it. Lou's bombshell has shoved such boring tasks as buying plants for the deck and stocking up on cat food for Sass into the 'later if you're lucky' category. Sass meows round my ankles, threatening to pack her catnip mouse and depart for a more attentive household. I pick up the phone again and dial.

"Hi Dixie, it's me, Sophie."

"Of course it's you, Sophie," says Dixie, snappish. "No-one else would call me when t'Street is on."

"Oh. Sorry." I'm not, though. No-one else I know under the age of seventy watches Coronation Street. "Can we talk? It's important."

5

Dixie heaves a gusty sigh down the line. "It better be. Give me a minute." There's a clunk in my ear as the phone hits something hard. Not for the first time I wonder about finding a new best friend, someone less luminous so the rest of us could shine a little, too. There is only one Dixie, though. She's shrewd and smart, still the brightest spark I know.

"Okay, Soph, I'm back. Sorry for snapping at you. My hormones must be acting up. Crack away, lovey, let it all out."

I tell her about Alex the Evil Imposter Son from New Zealand and Lou's intractable gullibility and what am I going to do about it.

Silence.

"Are you listening?" I wouldn't put it past her to shut the phone in the refrigerator while I'm pouring out my woes. It's happened before.

"Listen, Sophie," says Dixie in a thoughtful, grown-up voice I haven't heard for a long time, "you've got to give people a chance. Give this Alex a chance. Maybe it's true. Stranger things have happened, hon, you know that. Find out his story. Lou's a tough nut. He can take care of himself."

I'm speechless. Stranger things have happened, yes, I know that better than anyone, but this is not the answer I expected from Dixie. She's fond of Lou, even though Lou refuses to say one word to her since Derek disappeared from my life. He forbids me to speak her name in his presence. Lou holds Dixie solely responsible for the divorce (he's right about that) and my parlous finances.

More than anything, he will not forgive Dixie for Rose's stroke, which claimed my mother's brain while Dixie and I rattled around Turkey celebrating the End of Derek, if you could call it a celebration. I cried the whole time. Dixie smoked a truckload of nauseating Turkish cigarettes and spent money she didn't have on a giant brass hookah and a full-length red deerskin coat with a Russian mink collar. Lou blamed Dixie for luring me to the disreputable East. He blamed me for being incommunicado on the other side of the planet when Rose fell ill.

Dixie is still prattling on about Lou's happiness and opening my mind to the idea of Alex. This is not what I want to hear.

"Thanks for the support, Dix." I bang down the phone. There's a heel of Australian shiraz on the kitchen counter. I pour it in a glass and down it in one hit. The phone rings.

"Don't drink alone, Sophie, it makes you maudlin." Click.

Caught again. I don't know how she does it, spying on me all the way from Vancouver. At least I used a glass this time. I drop the bottle in the recycle bin, eye up a full one in the wine rack and decide against it, not because of Dixie's long-distance finger-wagging. With Alex on the prowl, I'll need all my wits about me.

Over the weekend I busy myself whittling away at the 'to-do' list. I buy plants for the garden and cat food, although I forget to water the plants and they shrivel melodramatically in the garage, and I absent-mindedly buy the kind of cat food Sass doesn't like, roasted lamb morsels with mint. She licks at her dish before stalking off to throw up lavishly on the expensive Turkish carpet Dixie bought me as a 'please-get-over-it' bribe, made less expensive by her strategic lash-batting at the carpet seller.

Lou phones Friday, Saturday, and Sunday to remind me about Alex's impending, as yet unscheduled, Grand Visit. In the space of an overseas phone call he's become a man possessed; as wound-up and wired as if the Pope were planning to drop in for some cucumber planting. Reason and rationality were never Lou's strongest points. Now they're bagged up like last week's soup bones and tossed out the door.

This son-brother business should please me. This is the very thing I wished for as a child, on the twinkliest stars in the sky, when blowing out birthday candles year after year, on dried chicken wishbones, on pennies dropped in wishing wells, crossing my fingers as the coins sank through the water like small copper suns. Those times are past. I am not pleased. I am well and truly over wishing for a brother. I think about calling Dixie again. No, she would not forgive two t'Street interruptions in one night.

Instead I flip open my laptop and bring up the color samples PaintMe sent through this week. Of the twenty-five colors in the PaintMeKidz new range, I've only managed to name three. This year's theme is Pirates for boys; Wizards are apparently having a rest. There's a jaunty blue-red I've called Swash yer Buckle, and an inky black touched with purple is Captain Hook's Hat. For girls it's Fairies, again, no surprise there. It's usually Fairies for girls, or sometimes Princesses, or Mermaids. There is a pretty soft pink-grey on the screen. Mouse Princess? I Dream of Mousie? Cripes. This is not where I thought a diploma in interior design would lead.

On Tuesday I drive across the 25th Street bridge to see Rose. The nurses' aides know that I show up every Tuesday like clockwork, so Rose's hair is washed and she's wearing the white-with-pink-roses organic cotton nightgown I bought her for Christmas last year — as if my mother would care whether her nightie had roses or garbage trucks on it. Sometimes I think about popping in unannounced, to see if her hair is stringy with grease and her nightgown has been slipped onto somebody else's mother who's getting a visitor that day. That would be unbearable and would only prove what I already know: this is not the place for Rose.

My mother looks exactly the same as she did the last time I saw her, and the time before that, and a year of Tuesdays before that. Her eyes are closed. She's breathing. That's all.

"Sophie's here, Rose," says Melanie. She gently lifts Rose's head to straighten the pillow. I like Mel. She doesn't pretend things are any better than they are. She doesn't press my hand like some of the other nurses' aides and whisper suggestions to pray to indifferent higher powers that might repair my mother's brain or relieve her suffering. Is she suffering? I don't know. No-one knows. At least she's not wandering around outside in her slippers knee-deep in snow. It's a harsh world out there in winter, whether you're a pea plant or a seventy-year-old stroke victim.

"Any change?"

Mel shakes her head. I hand her a bouquet of lilacs cut from the bush Rose planted when she and Lou moved into their house, the house I now own. The lilacs are fat and dark as grapes and heavy with old-fashioned perfume. They smell of spring, many springs: the spring we moved into the little white stucco house when I was six, the spring my parents gave me a nearly-new red bicycle when I was eight, the spring two years later when my mother got so sick and was taken to the hospital by ambulance and nearly died and after that there was no more talk of sisters or brothers for me to play with.

After Mel leaves I take Rose's hand in mine. Her fingernails are manicured (thank you Mel) but her fingers have lost so much flesh they're no thicker than sparrows' bones. Rose, my gentle Mamma who would never hurt a living thing, breathes, in, out. Heart pumping, lungs moving like bellows. In, out. She looks peaceful, and somehow younger than she did before the stroke.

I shake my head and clear my throat. "I have something to tell you, Rose." I take a deep breath and tell her about Lou and Alex. I confess my fears that Lou, or somebody, or everybody, will get hurt. I confess fears I haven't admitted even to myself.

What if it's true?

"Do you know anything about this, Rose?" It's a pointless question. I ask anyway, if only to pretend we're having a conversation.

Whatever the 'private thing' is, Lou would have told Rose, I'm sure of it, despite his denials. He would have pressed the words into her ears, whether she wanted to know or not. Lou and my mother are — were — so close. They went everywhere holding hands. How do you find a love like that? How do you compete with it? I have envied them my whole life. It's caused endless problems. Rose, I'm convinced, is the reason Lou never really wanted a daughter. There is only one Rosa.

As I watch my mother do nothing, an image pops into my head from one of the few holidays our family could afford on a vegetable-seller's earnings. It was late autumn. We stayed at a lake, in a small, cold cabin scattered with squirrel turds and reeking of the previous renter's bacon grease. One moon-bright night we set out along the lakeside, rustling through the brittle drifts of leaves. Next to the lake, there was something I'd never seen: an outdoor stage set up for Saturday dances. Rose and Lou stepped onto the empty stage and swayed under the stars, holding each other close, their shoes shuffling soft on the wooden boards. If a bear had dragged me away shrieking into the bushes, they wouldn't have noticed.

Rose cannot tell me if she knows about Lou's 'private things'. My mother, trapped within her flooded brain, doesn't twitch a lip, much less utter a word. Maybe that's a good thing. The more I ponder the whole Alex mess, the angrier I get. Lou is too old to hear more bad news. Rosa's stroke nearly killed him, too. I do not wish ill upon my aging father (although I have in the past). I don't know what this man Alex is up to, but this is not a game.

Rose breathes, in, out. My eyes prickle with tears. I kiss her forehead.

Mamma. Can you hear me?

In, out. In, out. The cotton gown barely moves.

Chapter 2

When Sophia was born

This is the story of my birth, according to Lou's sisters Carmina and Margherita, the keepers of the Sanzari family secrets, of which annoyingly few are known to me. Once a year these two elderly widowed ladies, my beloved *zie*, lock up the brownstone townhouse they share in Toronto's Cabbagetown and chauffeur their pampered labradoodle Benson to a pet hotel. They fly direct from Toronto to Saskatoon, never stopping in Winnipeg or any other place of unnecessary diversion, always on a Friday afternoon in the first week of July. They arrive immaculate in floral frocks, neat white gloves and dangly rhinestone earrings (the small pert hats were given up, reluctantly, a decade ago. Too hard to find a decent milliner these days, says Carmina). My aunts, who are prone to thrilling exaggeration, shamelessly shore up their failing memories with livelier versions of events I've heard before, while Lou sits in his chair grumbling and rolling his eyes. True or not, the story of my birth is accepted family lore.

Months before I, Sophia Luigina Sanzari, was born, my pregnant-as-an-elephant mother Rose Ethel Sanzari walked six miles to the Greatest Ever American Midway and Carnival, which had set up a ferris wheel and a roller coaster and tents within which they trotted out pickled two-headed calves and fat ladies with arms rounder than piglets. On this summer afternoon, so hot the asphalt in the street melted and stuck to Rose's canvas shoes (the Sanzaris being too poor to afford leather), Rose walked all the way to the dust-blown edge of town in secret, to consult a fortune teller about her impending baby. The walk was worth every sticky step. The turbanned and faintly moustachioed gypsy palmist confidently foretold Lou's greatest wish. Rose would bear a healthy, strapping boy.

This was momentous news indeed. After two miscarriages and a stillborn infant — a perfect boy — Rose's impending baby was again a boy. This happy news (made real by nothing more than the gypsy's canny ability to cash in on a hopeful face and the twist of nervous fingers) was taken as gospel by the normally rational Rose, who desperately wanted to make up for the previous failures. Rose knitted booties in robin's egg blue wool and sewed a tiny sailor suit striped in navy and white. Lou, who would rather poke sticks in his eyes than spend money on frivolous novelties, squirreled away a few precious dollars for a box of cheap blue-ribbonned cigars.

After the carnival had packed up and gone and the trees shed their autumn leaves and the first snowflakes skirled through the city streets, on a cold grey October morning Rose gave birth. Her endless night of huffing and puffing and groaning was all for naught. The longed-for boy was a girl. Her blue eyes and wispy blonde hair and lack of a tiny boyish spout shocked and mystified her parents. They had already chosen a name. Antonio. They should have known better.

Una bambina non un bambino. A girl not a boy. Rose clutched the baby to her swollen bosom and wailed. The baby wailed, too. We both knew what the score was, even then. Lou howled at the shocked nurses to bring him his son, demanding to know who had stolen him. When he threatened to punch a doctor he was escorted from the corridors of St Paul's Hospital by two burly orderlies and forbidden to return.

It took a month for Rose and Lou to think of a name for their inexplicable daughter, who they called Baby until a fed-up Carmina ordered Rose to name the blameless infant Sophia, after seeing Sophia Loren in

Marriage Italian-Style at the Sunday matinée. In a guilty twist Rose added Luigina, for Luigi, my father. (In my teenage years I told anyone who discovered this shameful secret that I was named for that other screen siren, Gina Luigina Lollobrigida. No girl wants to be named after her hairy-eared dad.)

The next August, Rose plucked up her courage to visit the Greatest Ever American Carnival once again, this time carting her female changeling dressed in the navy blue sailor suit. Trembling like a birch leaf she demanded her money back from the fraudulent palmist, or at least someone in a headscarf and jangly earrings that looked like last summer's gypsy. The woman crossed her eyes and spat vile things, terrible things about Rose's soon-to-be-barren womb and Lou's twisted seed. Rose fled, her blonde hair standing on end, the stripy toddler howling in her arms.

In this, at least, the gypsy foretold the truth. I was their one and only child. Rose blamed their inability to have any more children, let alone Luigi's missing son, on the fortune teller's curse.

"We both loved you anyway," said my mother once (not catching herself before the 'anyway' slipped out). "You were such a sweet baby girl, with perfect, pink (she meant hairless) ears." Much later, Rose confessed that after I was born the second thing she looked at (after the lack of tiny spout) was my ears. A boy with hairy ears, she could accept. A hairy-eared girl would have been another type of failing altogether.

Uno bambina non un bambino. It's as intractable and moody a lament as my Italian father, who's never been to Italy, can utter. Lately, Lou has taken to dropping even more frequent hints about his sorrowful lack of a proper male heir. Had I, his daughter Sophia, been a boy, or made a different, better, choice of partner he, Luigi Giuseppe Sanzari, would now be somehow wealthier in his advancing years. Even more poignantly, he wouldn't be the last viable male leaf on the Sanzari family tree, or at least his tiny shopkeeper branch of it.

13

This is the crux of the problem. Lou is the last of his line, and his father's line, and his grandfather's line, and many Italian ancestors before that. I remind him, as I have countless times, that my last name is Sanzari, too, and I am perfectly capable of ministering to him in his old age (which, as a matter of record, I do, at least weekly). When I point out that, in theory, I am also able to pass on the Sanzari name, should I ever find a more suitable mate than Derek to mingle genes with he gasps and mutters, as if I'm offering him his own last-of-line family jewels in an onion bag. The truth is, it's getting a little late for me to think about finding a suitable mate, never mind mingling genes with unpredictable results.

On more charitable days I feel sorry for Lou. He has one daughter, me. His sisters Margherita and Carmina had many daughters, my cousins Suzie and Sarah and all the rest, too many to count. None of the sisters have sons. Ours is a genetic freak show. It's as if the entire Sanzari quota of Y chromosomes had been mislaid or given to some other, more persuasive, Italian family. It's not an easy job being Lou's only offspring, and female, and a failed vessel for producing a suitable heir to the Sanzari name and fortune, not that there is one.

There was Antonio, of course, but nobody talks about Antonio. After all these years, Lou still will not utter his brother's name. Antonio is a clanking set of bones in what is beginning to look like a full-to-bulging Sanzari family closet.

Chapter 3

A message from downunder

There is a pile of photography books on Lou's kitchen table. I pick up one with a glossy cover. *Wild Places of New Zealand. Lonely Planet Guide to New Zealand.* There are a few more with similarly outdoorsy titles. These are expensive books. Lou's too tight with his money to buy anything as sleek as these. He still rations toilet paper to three squares per visit (four if absolutely necessary, not that I want to know). He must have borrowed these books from the library. Lou is not a reader. I'm surprised he knows where to find the library.

"What's this?" I wave the *Lonely Planet* around. "Are you planning a trip to New Zealand?"

Lou ignores me. As far as I know, Lou has never traveled anywhere except to Toronto once with Rose, to visit his sisters when Margherita turned forty. That summer I stayed behind, pouting and furious, with my English grandparents. Rose's elderly Presbyterian parents had no idea what to do with a spoiled eight-year-old, other than to warn me against the wickedness of sloth and to quote the *Bible* as a foil to any prepubescent evils I might be hatching. 'The Lord lift up his continents upon thee' was a particular deterrent; I envisioned all of North America, rocks, trees, lakes, upending and tumbling down upon me. It was many years before I understood my error.

Lou nearly wept at the state of the wilted lettuces and drooping tomato plants I had promised to weed and water but forgot about during the hottest week of the year, the week I spent reading a summer's worth of books by lantern light amid the shelves of dill pickles and mustard relish in my grandparents' cool root cellar. I felt guilty but also vindicated that the lettuces ended up as willfully neglected as I was. If I had been a boy, would Lou have taken me along to show me off? He'd gotten off lightly with just a few dead lettuces, I reckoned.

I sigh and sit down beside him.

"What have you been looking at, Lou? Can you show me?"

Lou flips me a flinty look, but he carefully cracks opens *Wild Places*.

"So beautiful, New Zealand, see Sophie."

This faraway country is so skinny that two entire New Zealands could fit inside our province's borders. It's captured page by page in unnatural neon greens and soft misty greys and rare blues so shamelessly clear they dazzle the eyes. There are volcanic mountains, bloopy boiling mud and everywhere a shining sea poured out like liquid steel. In our prairie city we could not be any farther from any ocean if we tried. From long-ago visits to Vancouver I remember rock, and strewn logs, and mountains, lovely to look at but claustrophobic to a prairie girl. This New Zealand is a different sea, with sandy beaches the color of old gold and ferns the size of trees.

"It's beautiful, but that's a lot of books to get through. When do you need to return them?"

"Return where?"

"To the library. When do you have to take these books back?"

"Not from the library. From Alex. These-a books, come today. And wine, *sei bottiglie*. A man in a van, he bring them." He waves at half a dozen bottles of wine standing on the kitchen counter. How did I miss these?

Lou hands me a note. The note reads, "To Lou, *kia ora*. See you soon, cheers and best wishes, Alex." The handwriting is bold and black and confident.

Blood rushes to my face. So. The bribery begins. The courier must have cost a fortune. But if there's a courier there's got to be a courier bag or box with a return address. Sure enough, there's a large empty white box with a DHL sticker on it set neatly by the recycle bin. I casually stand up, take my tea cup to the sink, rinse the cup and run my eyes all over the box. I spot a rough patch where a return address sticker once was. I turn around. Lou is watching me, and there's that smirk again. He's smarter than I thought.

Outside, the temperature has dropped a good ten degrees. There's a killing frost in the wind, maybe snow. I should go back inside and tell Lou to cover up his plants. He's an old-time gardener, though. He, like his mother Maria-Therese, the Italian grandmother I never met, has the gift for reading the skies. He probably smelled the snow before the snow even knew it was coming.

Snow it does, for an entire week. In June. This is not the spring I remember from my childhood. Something has happening to our weather, and not in a now-we-live-in-the-steamy-tropics way. The mini-blizzard brutalizes the tender leaf buds and batters the lilac bush's dark petals off the branch. They stain the snow the color of old blood. After the snow comes a shower of grape-sized hail pinging like crystal off the windows. For the next week I turn up the heat and set foot outside only for my scheduled parental visits.

I used to love snow, the fluffy, drifting flakes, the wet, heavy snowball-making kind. On warmer days Rose swaddled me like a foundling yeti in a snowsuit, boots, hat and mittens. I remember peering through a gap in my woolly scarf at a snowman twice as tall as I was. Even then, aged five or so, I wore the air of a midget sceptic. This isn't Frosty the Snowman, I sneered, it's three whopping snowballs topped off with a limp carrot and two chunks of coal for eyes. The top lump had a wrinkly watermelon rind for a mouth. Lou or Rose must have stored that rind for months, just so my snowman could wear a melony grin. I whined for a coal mouth, like the other kids' snowmen had.

When Frosty's attractions waned I ran at him like a linebacker, toppling him into snowy mounds. I re-formed him into snowballs perfect for tossing with wild inaccuracy at the fence, the house and, once, the mailman, who rang the doorbell and demanded to speak to my mother. Say you're sorry, my mother chided. Sorry, I said to the grumpy mailman wiping snow off his chest, but I wasn't.

One December day we awoke to a diamond-bright world. Rose stuffed me into my snowsuit and belted herself into a long blue wool coat. We dashed into the nippy air. Rose cracked long spears of icicles off an elm branch for us to suck. We flung ourselves down into the pristine powdery whiteness and flapped our legs and arms. Flying low on our backs we made snow angels, one woman-sized, one child, their wing tips touching. Minutes later a blizzard howled down from the north, sending us scuttling into the house and erasing our angels in seconds.

Day by day the June snow melts, unveiling trees bare of leaves against a brittle blue sky and brown roads slushy with winter's dregs. The spring snow-sludge is not only messy but camouflages winter's worst secrets. My eavestroughs leak. There are holes in the road deep enough to swallow a cyclist or break a car axle if you hit it wrong. The sidewalk gently steams with thawing doggy doo. From the size of it, I suspect the german shepherd next door.

I wrap myself in a scarf and woolly hat, kick the doggy doo into the gutter and set off for the river. Sass presses her face to the window. She begs to be let out, just this once; she promises she'll leave the birds alone, meow meow. I feel so sorry for Sass. She's got the spring scampers. She lived the merry hunter life of an outdoor cat before the city's 'lock up your killer cat' law came into force. No amount of fake scratch 'em trees, feathered cat toys or demented dashes up and down the hall can appease her. She is, though, a true escape artist and a proven bird menace. You'll end up in cat jail yet, or worse, on death row, I warn her. I promise to take her out on a leash when I return from my own walk. She stares at me with unblinking disgust.

Everyone in the city plus their friends and relatives has surged outside to soak up some sunshine. I share the bridge with cyclists and joggers and a shirtless yoof in goofy shoes doing a kamikaze skateboard run among the noonday traffic. Looking over the railing to the river gives me a short, giddy thrill. The water tumbles and surges, steam rising along the banks. At the other end of the bridge I trot past the band rotunda, skirting the park.

The lower path meanders through birch trees and saskatoon berry bushes thick with frost-nipped buds. The river is running high, gorged on spring snowmelt in the Rockies. The air smells of mulch and earth and river spray. There's a rustling in the bushes. I stand perfectly still, hoping it's not a bad-tempered skunk waking from its winter nap. It's not a skunk, it's a fat, shiny beaver bundling across the path toward the river. He glances at me but waddles on, his sleek coat gleaming, and his paddle tail dragging behind him. I haven't seen a beaver in years. I can't help grinning. Winter's over.

It may be spring, but PaintMe is already giving me the hurry-up for the autumn/winter range. They want to launch in three months, on the grand occasion of the Province of Saskatchewan's Centennial Anniversary. Andy the marketing boffin expects provincial pride to galvanize the entire population into leaping to their paint tins on the first day of September, enthusiastically splashing The Elf King's Throne (a lustrous gold; not exactly Pirates but maybe they won't notice) and Merry Fairies (strawberry pink with cranberry undertones) around children's bedrooms from Uranium City to Moose Jaw.

They've also asked me to name a special hard-wearing, green-toned outdoor paint to mark the 100th birthday of our province. It's suitable for exteriors, decks, balconies, and other house parts destined to endure the prairie winter. Andy's marketing bumf says it's 'a complex, multi-hued color, medium green with hints of darker green (for the northern pine forests) shot with a mellow yellow (for the bountiful canola fields)'. My offerings are: a) How Green is My Province, b) Saskabush, and c) Pine'n for Grain. Not quite what we're after, chides the return email. We're looking for something patriotic yet jazzy. Please try again. I slam the laptop shut and grab my car keys.

In tune with his vegetable-seller instincts, Lou has dragged the entire potted veggie garden into his tiny kitchen before the snowstorm struck. We drink our coffee and tea amid a miniature forest of tomato plants, beans, and whiskery carrot tops. Thyme and oregano festoon the kitchen counter, next to the taunting bottles of New Zealand wine. Lou is either saving the bottles for a special occasion or making a shrine out of them. He notices me eying the bottles and sighs like a steam train.

"What's the matter, Lou?"

"Nothing, Sophie, nothing you worry about," says Lou in a tone that means, 'my worry is your worry, multiplied by ten.'

"Tell me, Lou." I watch him weigh up how much of today's worry he will choose to tell me versus how much I will have to pry out of him.

"I have a pain, Sophie. Here." He leans back in his chair and lightly thumps his chest. Alarm bells bong in my head. "Where, Lou? Tell me where! How long have you had this pain? I'm calling an ambulance." I shoot from my chair, clutching at the phone on the wall. Lou shoots after

20

me, surprisingly quickly for an elderly man having a heart attack. He pulls my arm away from the phone.

"No no Sophie, sit, sit. Not that pain."

"What is it then, Lou? Where does it hurt?"

Lou thumps his chest again. "*Il mio cuore.* My heart, Sophie. My heart. No, sit! My heart, she hurt not from attack. No, I have pain in the heart because you, Sophie, say bad things about Alex."

I'm so dumbfounded it takes a minute or two for me to even speak. "What are you talking about, Lou? I haven't said a word about Alex since I got here."

"Yes, you see? Who do I talk to about this important thing? Not my poor Rosa. I talk to Rosa, I tell her things, but she not talk to me. *Signora* Woloschuk, she want to know everything about everything, she ask and ask what come in that box that the red van bring, but I don't tell anything. She so snoopy, like a raccoon. But no, not you. Not my daughter Sophia." He sighs again, and flutters his eyelids shut.

It's the worst kind of melodrama. Complete eyeball-rolling rubbish, but with a sliver of truth jabbing me from inside. 'Not my poor Rosa' hits me in a spot so tender it feels like a punch. I don't want to talk about Alex. If we don't talk about him, maybe he'll disappear.

"Lou," I say carefully. "I'm your daughter. I want you to be happy. I don't want you to get hurt or have pain in your heart. But if Alex is your son, and I'm not saying he is, then I have a brother, sort of. Have you thought about how I might feel about that?"

Lou's eyes pop open. "Happy, Sophia. You feel happy. Why you not feel happy if you have a brother?"

I bite off my answer. What can I say? 'I don't want to share my last remaining conscious parent, even my grumpy standoffish Papa, with some Alex-come-lately' is what I want to say. Even in my own mind that sounds petulant and selfish.

21

Later it occurs to me that Lou might have been thinking about his own brother, the lost Antonio. He might even have talked about him, had I given him the chance. I know nothing about my mysterious uncle, only that Antonio arrived after Carmina and before Luigi and Margherita in the Sanzari family birth order. Something unspeakable must have happened for Lou to erase his own brother, his only brother, so completely.

Chapter 4

The coming of Alex

I'm in the garden plucking chickweed from among the newly-sprung daffodils when the phone rings. I can tell by the shrill, 'pick-me-up-now' ring that Lou is on the other end. He's so excited he's squeaking. Alex is-a come today, for the lunch. Alex is-a come. I, Sophie, am to bring the lunch.

"Pepperoni salami, pastrami and ciabatta. Maybe some olives, black, nice and fat. Fresh, not from the can, they taste like the dead mouse. Also *pomodori e insalata*, very fresh. My own *verdure* not ready yet. Some Valpolicella, *sì, due bottiglie*, no, *tre. Ciao, bella.*" Click.

Lunch with Alex. Alex is-a come. I had no idea Alex had even left New Zealand. There has been plenty of time, weeks even, to think about how this meeting will unfold. Still I'm caught off guard and surly because of it. I consider buying a greasy lump of baloney, a loaf of Wonderbread, a bag of wormy lettuce and a bottle of vinegar to feed Lou's unwelcome guest, but I am not a rebellious fourteen anymore, despite the way Lou treats me. Instead I choose the freshest pastrami and crustiest ciabatta from Lou's favorite deli on 3rd Avenue. It takes trips to three different liquor stores to find the miserable wine.

When at last I arrive at Lou's townhouse, a brand new black BMW with rental plates is flaunting itself in the only visitor's parking space. It looks like something a drug-dealing undertaker would use as a getaway car when not toting bodies around in the trunk. I park halfway down the block and huff up the front steps hauling the lunch bags.

More of the brown paint has flaked off Lou's front door since I visited last week. A daughter's job, says Lou, is to cook, not paint. There is no son, so there is no paint. The last time Lou climbed up a ladder (to spring clean the eavestroughs, he said, but really to prove he could still climb a ladder), he fell off and broke his right ankle (prompting my offer of a cellphone). I brought him dinner every day for a month. It nearly killed both of us.

From behind the door I can hear Lou laughing his 'I'm having a really good time' laugh. Haw hee haw a haw haw haw. I haven't heard Lou laugh since Rose's stroke. This is so surprising and so infuriating I don't even knock.

"Sophia! *Vieni qui*! Come, meet Alex! He just arrive!"

Lou waves at me from his usual chair at the head of the table. His grin creases his face in two. The man sitting at my father's kitchen table has the grace to look abashed. I appraise him, coolly, searching for genetic giveaways. Alex is mid-50s, at a guess, maybe older but lean and as athletically built as a gymnast. He's pale-skinned, with greying hair the color of winter wheat (Lou's hair was almost black before turning a startling snow-white). Gooseberry Green eyes (Lou's are as brown as the dirt he digs in) I scan the Ears of Alex. They're hairless. (Gotcha! Maybe). Alex is trying not to stare at the Ears of Lou. They're quite a sight. Without Rose to clip them, Lou's ears have gone feral. Lately he won't let me near him with a sharp object.

"I'm Alex," says Alex unnecessarily, springing to his feet and extending a long-fingered hand. He's wearing pressed cream slacks, a striped green polo shirt, white shoes. He is tall, very tall. This man cannot be Lou's son. Lou and I are circus dwarves beside him, even taking into account Lou's dwindling frame. I manage a smile. His hand is still sticking out. I take it and squeeze, meaningfully.

24

"Sophia Sanzari." I lean heavily on the Sanzari. "I didn't catch your last name."

"Mironescu. Alexandru Mironescu. Alex Miron these days."

"Alexandru Mironescu," I frown. "Is that Hungarian?"

"Romanian." He pauses. "My mother was Romanian."

"Sophia, where is the lunch? Let's eat! *Andiamo a mangiare!*" cries Lou, before I can say another word. I plonk the bags on the table and arrange the meat and bread on the plates Lou has set out. These are Rose's best china plates, Royal Doulton English Rose. Lou bought an entire eight-piece setting for Rose on their tenth wedding anniversary, with matching cream jug and sugar bowl. After all these years the set is still complete, not counting the dinner plate Rose threw at Lou when I was eight. It was the only time I ever saw her lose her temper. The plates are pretty if you like that sort of thing, gilt-edged with roses in pink and yellow and tiny blue flowers, maybe forget-me-nots, entwined round the edges. I remember Rose crying softly when she opened the box. I thought she, like me, had asked Lou for something special (in my case, a pony) and was bitterly disappointed yet again.

"You say your mother was Romanian?" I hold out a plateful of salami and bread to Alex. He wraps his fingers around the plate. In his hand it's the size of a drinks coaster.

"Why you ask these things now," Lou cuts in. "Eat! Drink wine! Sophie, you pour, *per favore.*" I pour the nasty wine, a big dollop for Lou and Alex, a dribble for me. A swallow too much of that stuff can strip out all of your internal organs.

"To Alex!" cries Lou. "*Salute!*"

"*Salute,*" says Alex, smiling.

Cheers. I lift my glass, nod and sip. There are many questions I want to ask this man Alex. With uncanny prescience and nifty timing Lou cuts me off every time my lips shape a word he doesn't like the look of, like 'why' or 'how' or, especially, 'who'. Instead, we talk about nothing much.

Lou: "You like-a Saskatoon?"

Me: "How long are you staying?"

"I've only been here since yesterday, but I like what I see." Alex smiles, twirling his glass. "I don't know how long I'm staying. Nice little city. I'm staying in that hotel by the river. The Bessborough. Lovely old place. I'm thinking of taking a walk along the river later."

Despite my own exhilarating riverside walk a couple of weeks ago, I'm quick to warn him of Saskatoon's spring terrors. This is another Year of the Worms. I explain, in juicy Hitchcockian detail, how platoons of brown worms swarm over every green thing, nibble it to death and then dangle on strings from the defoliated trees. They drop onto unsuspecting pedestrians and cyclists, onto hats and shoulders and heads. They are a squirmy insect curse. Alex just laughs. When he laughs, his whole face joins in. A bit like Lou's.

I frown and try again. I mention the garter snakes sunning themselves on the riverside trails. "You don't have snakes in New Zealand, do you?"

He shakes his head and looks, I'm gratified to see, mildly alarmed. "Are these ones poisonous? Like Aussie snakes?"

Lou jumps in. "Not poison. Nice-a snakes. Eat-a the rats."

When we've exhausted talk of nice snakes and nice spring weather, Lou allows me to ask a few more penetrating questions. What I do find out is not much. Alex is fifteen years older than I am. He has lived in "many places," including New Zealand for the last ten years, which explains his muddled accent. He owns an import business in Auckland.

"What do you import?" I get in quick, while Lou's munching a mouthful of ciabatta and salami. Alex crosses his arms and shifts in his chair.

"Nothing interesting. It's a small business."

I've watched those 'catch-criminals-by-their-facial-twitches' TV shows. He's hiding something. Blood diamonds, I'm thinking. Heroin. Methamphetamine. Eastern European women forced into prostitution. That would explain his taste in cars and shoes, although maybe that's just a Romanian thing. Lou and I both look expectantly at Alex.

"Pesticides," he says, at last. "I import pesticides, organic ones, and other chemicals. For home gardens."

"Pest-ee-cides." Lou rolls the word around in his mouth like a rotten grape. For the first time since this farce began, he frowns. "Pesticides, no good. I grow my own *verdure*, I sell in my shop. Ask me, I know. I plant *aglio* for the insects. No poison." He mutters something under his breath. Lou holds strong views on pesticides. He'd probably be happier if Alex imported heroin.

"Lou had a fruit and vegetable shop for forty years," I tell Alex. "He was growing organic tomatoes and vegetables years before the word was invented."

Alex says nothing. Lou says nothing. Into this silence I slide the first Big Question.

"Why are you looking for Lou — for your father now? Why not twenty years ago?"

Alex sets his plate on the table. The silence lays so thick over all of us it takes on a weight of its own.

"I have a son," Alex begins.

A son. There's a ringing in my ears. My skin feels tight all over. With those two little words, Alex has played his trump card.

Chapter 5

He won't go away

Lou is making a strangling sound. Tears dribble down his wrinkly cheeks. He pushes his plate away.

"*Il figlio, mio figlio.*" Lou is hiccupping and snorting so violently he's making himself sick. This is the first time I've seen Lou cry since Rose's stroke.

"I think you should go now. I've never seen Papa so upset." I move over beside Lou and hand him another tissue, feeling like a fraud. It's been years since I called Lou anything but Lou.

Alex nods. "I'm sorry."

"Please, Alex, can you just go." I stand fierce as a Gurkha guard by Lou's side.

"I'm sorry," says Alex, again. "I'll ring later to see how he is. Or you can ring me on my cellphone."

He lays a business card on the table and stands up. Lou breaks into a fresh fit of sobbing.

"No no Alex, stay, stay, we drink-a wine, you tell me about your son, tell me. I want to know everythings."

To his credit, Alex agrees it's not in anyone's best interests for him to linger. I hear the black BMW start up and prowl away. Lou fixes me with a furious look. I have not seen this look since I told my parents about my divorce. It makes my stomach flip.

"You make him leave, Sophia. Why? Why you make such trouble?"

"You were upset. I was only thinking about you."

"Go away, Sophia," says my ungrateful father.

I clatter down the steps, leaving him dabbing his eyes over the uneaten lunch and the barely-sipped glasses of wine. Mrs Woloschuk sticks her head out her window as I rush past. Her permed hair is dyed a rich Hereford brown, reminding me more than usual of a cow hanging over a fence.

"Who vas dat man, Sophie, who visit your fadder?"

"Nobody, Mrs Woloschuk." I have suspicions about Mrs Woloschuk's intentions toward my father. Every few weeks she tries to tempt him with a batch of home-made cabbage rolls and potato perogies, which Lou detests. He stashes them in the freezer until they crystalize into inedible lumps he can throw away in good conscience.

"Look like somebuddy to me," Mrs Woloschuk calls out, blunt as a stone axe. "Big car. Important man."

Big car, important man. Everything Lou could possibly want in a son.

At home I google 'Alex Miron'. Nothing. Then 'Alexandru Mironescu'. There are authors and philosophers but nobody, *nada*, by that name in the whole internet world who lives in New Zealand and imports garden pesticides. I do discover that 'Alexandru' means 'defender of mankind' in Romanian. I also discover my own name means 'wisdom' in Italian, which must be Carmina's idea of a joke.

I need a plan. I could call Dixie again, but her solutions to life's problems usually involve running off to hot faraway countries or buying diamond earrings, neither of which are helpful or affordable. I finger the little card I slipped off Lou's table. I dial the number.

My usual café on 23rd St is crowded with late lunch-goers. Alex sticks out like a giraffe among pygmy hippos. He nods as I slide onto the bench across from him and sits quietly while I order a tea.

"How's Lou?"

I shrug. "A mess. He won't talk to me. His own daughter." I give him my best death-stare. "Look, Alex, if that's really your name, what's this all about? What do you think you're doing, upsetting an old man?"

Alex leans back and spreads his long fingers on the table.

"As I said, I have a son. He's thirty-five. He lives in New Zealand with his fiancée. They're getting married later this year. Olivia is a doctor. She's curious. They want children, and she's keen to know what's in the genes on my side of the family." He sips his coffee, grimaces, adds two spoons of sugar. "I'd like to know myself."

"Ears," I hiss. "Hairy ears. In case you hadn't noticed. Pinna hypertrichosis. It's linked to the Y chromosome and can skip generations. It's a dominant gene though." I have no idea if this is true. Lou has never said if his father Carlo had hairy ears. Or his brother. I've never seen a photo of Antonio. This is something else to ask the aunts. I've given up hoping Lou will ever tell me anything.

Alex shrugs. "That's not so bad, if it's the only thing."

My shoulders stiffen. That 'only thing' has not made Lou's life easy, I know that much from Carmina's odd hint here and there.

"What does your mother think about this?"

He looks away. "She's dead."

"I'm sorry," I say, and I mean it. I can't help thinking about Rose. At least she's still with us, in a way.

"She died a long time ago. But I'd prefer to tell Luigi, er, Lou, about it first, if you don't mind."

I do mind. I mind so much my heart is beating a battle tattoo in my chest. "You do know my own mother's still alive? How do you think she'll feel, knowing Lou has a — a — bastard son? If you are his son?" A lump swells up in my throat. I push it down with a gulp of tea, burning my tongue.

Alex hesitates. "I understand your mother is — she's —"

30

"She's what? A vegetable?" My tongue hurts. I'm almost shouting. "How do you know? Did Lou tell you? What else did he tell you?" People are turning their heads. One of the waiters flashes me a wary look. Alex is calm, too calm to have one splash of Italian blood in his veins. His strange green eyes harden to grey. Cold War Steel.

"I am Lou's son. I can prove it, and I will, if I must. But not here. Not to you."

I reel back as if I've been slapped. I fight the urge to throw my tea cup at his head. "If that's the way you want it."

"It's what I want. For myself, and for my son."

I don't want to say one more word to this man, but curiosity gets the better of me.

"Your son — what's his name?"

Alex is silent. I wait, tapping my spoon on the table. "My son's name is Luigi Antonio Miron," he says finally. "He's called Tony."

Alex is worrying about nobody believing him when he says he's riding on a giant snail. I say, that giant mollusc there? He nods, yes. I say, What mollusc? Then I laugh. Hahaha.

I wake up to a toxic sun stripping skin off my face. Some malign imp has crawled inside my stomach and scraped it out with oyster shells. The clock chides me; both its hands sit on the 12. Sass jumps on the bed, mewing her 'where's-my-breakfast' reproach. There's an empty wine bottle on the bedside table. I don't remember opening it, or drinking it. I stumble into the bathroom. My face looks like it's spent the night slammed inside a sandwich maker. There's a tide mark on my teeth where too much merlot has come and gone.

This is not good.

Dixie's not answering her phone. I leave a message. Call me. Urgent. Call me, Dix. Please. Twenty minutes later the phone rings.

"What's up, hon? I was in the shower."

I don't want to know why she was in the shower at noon. I start to tell her about Alex and Antonio and Lou and the too-much wine, but my tongue has turned into a felt insole. Instead I snivel, "Can you come, Dixie? Alex is tough. I can't do this by myself."

Dixie sighs. I can tell there's a 'no' in it. "I can't right now, Sophie. I'm really sorry. For the very first time, Jerome is having a little friend to stay overnight. It'll be a zoo around here and he'll be so wound up afterward I could run a generator off him. I might be able to fly out by the end of the week. Can you hang in 'til then?"

I close my eyes. Dixie hasn't mentioned Jerome in months. We don't talk about Jerome.

"Isn't there anyone else you can talk to?"

Mentally I run through a few names. No-one springs to mind. Most of our friends were Derek's friends. After the divorce they fell on that side of the fence, or they disappeared into that void where post-divorce friends go. Not that I blame them. I was a wreck and no fun to be around. I didn't make much of an effort. Derek was always the social one.

I blow my nose, thank Dixie, tell her yes there is someone, now that she mentions it, and ask her to call me if she thinks she can come sooner.

"Okay, sweet." There's an expectant pause. I know she's waiting for me to ask about Jerome, how's Jerome, I could say, just those two words, but I don't. I can't. Dixie sighs into the silence. "Talk to you later then, Soph. *Ciao, bella.*"

Jerome. When everyone around her completely fell apart, Dixie was the only one coping with Jerome's imperfections. She is braver than I could ever be. In the human genetics crap shoot, Jerome lost big time. Take an

XX (mom) and an XY (dad), mix them up and what does Jerome get? A long bony face, a lip split to his nose and a brain that wanders down lonely, unproductive paths.

Siderius syndrome, it's called. I now know more than I ever want to know about X-linked recessive inherited diseases. It is so rare I had never even heard of it until Jerome arrived and rubbed our noses in the consequences. Jerome had a fifty per cent chance of being dealt his unsuspecting mother's faulty X chromosome with its nasty secret. He got the losing hand. Simple as that. It's the same game of chance you play when you flip a coin. Heads you win, tails you lose. Luck of the draw. Luck doesn't differentiate between tiny babies being born with wonky genes or winning the Saskatchewan Boat Raffle.

That's enough about Jerome. There has been so much angst over that little child. Enough to shatter a whole family of hearts into jagged little pieces that will never be put back together again.

When Lou opens his door I hand him a pot of basil as a peace offering. It's a special type of Thai basil, purple not green, pointy-leaved and hard to find this year. He says nothing but takes the basil and shuffles into the kitchen.

"Can I come in?" I say to his retreating back. He waves his hand in a do-what-you-want way. I step inside and close the door. The peeling brown door is now a freshly painted Victory Red. There is a son, so there is paint. Alex is quicker than I thought.

"I'm sorry, Lou."

He tosses me such a sad look I nearly burst into tears again.

"Why you so angry, Sophie? Why you not happy?"

It's a good question, one I have no answer for. I don't know why I clutch my torments to me like bloodied war trophies. "Let's not talk about me, Lou. Let's talk about you. And Alex."

A frown puckers Lou's forehead.

"I mean it. I'm sorry, I've been horrible. Can we start again?"

Lou shrugs. "Alex, he come soon. We all talk together."

"Oh. Okay." I hadn't counted on having Alex in the room so soon as part of my contrition. The imp is back, scraping at my stomach. "We'll all talk together."

Evening has fallen by the time Alex arrives. Alex and I greet each other coolly and formally, like diplomats from warring countries. For Lou's sake, I tell myself. For Lou's sake, keep it under control. Lou leads us toward the living room. It hasn't been used in years. There is dust all over the furniture and something small, dark and hard, maybe mouse droppings, on the carpet. Lou has always been a decent housekeeper. I wonder if his eyesight is going. I backtrack to the kitchen, with Lou and Alex following.

"It's sunnier in the kitchen. Let's sit here."

"There are things I'd like to know," Alex starts right in.

Lou nods. "Myself, I like to know some things, too." He pauses. "About Tatiana."

"Who's Tatiana?"

Alex glances at Lou. "Tatiana was my mother," he says to me. To my father, who looks like he might erupt into another fit of weeping, he says, "Her real name was Olga. Did you know that?"

Lou shakes his head. "Olga. I don't-a know this. I don't-a like this name, is-a name for Fat Lady, not your beautiful Mamma. I think of her only as Tatiana. Is okay?"

Alex nods. "Sure. If that's what you want. But Lou, please. Tell me about yourself. Start at the beginning. There's a lot I don't know about you. We can talk about my mother another time."

34

I scarcely have time to register the words 'Tatiana' and 'mother' before Lou starts gabbling. Now that the long-lost son has shown up, Lou unplugs the cork on his family history and lets it all flow out. I nearly choke on this injustice but I sit, quietly fuming, while Lou spins yarns for the stranger he clearly believes is his own true heir.

Chapter 6

New York, October, 1927

It was snowing the day Luigi's *papá* died, small, mean flakes of icy snow that stung Luigi's cheeks. His legs itched to run the last two blocks home, but he knew if he ran his tormentors would be on him as fast as a tenement dog ripping up a rat. Four of them, big, smelly Polish boys, loitered a few yards behind him yelling insults. "Dago! Wop! Garlic-eater! Monkey ears!"

Luigi had heard it all before, but it still hurt. Papa always said (twisting his ear an extra twist beyond a joke) you're an East Harlem boy, be tough. He wasn't tough. Not like Antonio. He wished his brother would step out from behind that brick wall up there and thump those other boys with a plank or a shoe or even his bare fists. Antonio could do it. Antonio was tall for a twelve-year-old. He, Luigi, was a hairy-eared shrimp.

He hadn't seen Antonio for weeks, not since that night when Papa slapped their mother (again) with his rough ditch digger's hand, slapped her so hard she fell down (again) and Antonio had jumped up and punched Papa in the face. (That was the first time and, as it turned out, the last). Luigi saw fist hit nose, heard bones crack. Then all was chaos. A fountain of blood spurting from Papa's nose, his father staggering and roaring, Maria, I'm-a gonna kill that little bastard, Mamma limp on the floor, little Margherita shrieking. Luigi felt his insides turn to water. Antonio ran down the stairs and out the door.

"It was terrible," says Lou, shuddering. "So bad. Papa was crazy like *un toro impazzito, scusa* Alex, a mad bull."

After Mamma had picked herself up and dabbed at Papa's nosebleed and quietened Margherita (Carmina standing in the corner as still as a wax statue) she whispered to Luigi, go find your brother. Find Antonio.

Luigi had searched the streets. He looked everywhere, in alleyways, by the river, even sticking his head into O'Riley's pub before Mick O'Riley roared at him to get out or he'd get such a thrashing he'd have to pick up his own arms and legs and carry them home in a bucket. He found other dirty-kneed, flint-eyed boys, but he didn't find Antonio. One night he heard one of the boys saying that Antonio slept rough, one day selling matches, shining shoes the next. He hoped Antonio wasn't stealing, not from other Italians anyway. Mamma would kill him herself.

One more block to go. Luigi burst into a gallop. The Polish boys raced after him, hollering bloodthirsty cries, but they stopped at First Avenue. They knew not to cross the line. Something hit Luigi hard, in the back of the head. Luigi picked it up. A lump of coal. From across the street the boys jeered, oogh oogh ugg ugg monkey ears. Safe on his side of the street, Luigi ignored them, fingering the coal.

"My head, it didn't hurt. Only a little. And I had something to give to Mamma."

When he got home their one-room flat was full of people. Mamma's sister, *zia* Constanza, and Papa's sister Frances, scary in her flapping black nun's clothes, and *zio* Marco, and as many neighbors as could cram inside a space that could barely accommodate a family of thin rats. All the people were standing around something on the floor, talking in low voices. Mamma pulled Luigi to her. Her eyes were red.

"Papa." She tipped her head toward the floor.

Luigi pushed through warm legs and hands to see. Papa lay on his back, on a door. Luigi didn't recognize the door. Or Papa. His face looked like someone had stepped on it with big heavy boots. (Later, Luigi found out from the gleeful Polish boys, who'd watched the whole thumping, that quite a few 'someones' had stepped on Carlo. Kicked him in the head too and turned out his pockets looking for the money he owed them. Luigi could have told the men in boots that all they would find was lint.)

After all the people had gone, taking their warm bodies with them, the flat grew colder and colder despite Luigi's contribution of one lump of coal. Lying in the dark squished in with Mamma and Carmina and Margherita on the damp mattress that smelled of mold and pee (not his), he tried not to think about his dead, smashed-up father lying inches away. He hoped Antonio would come home now. Mamma cried all night.

"I think she cry for Papa." Lou shakes his head. "What I know. I know nothing."

After the funeral, which the children were forbidden to attend, Mamma went out looking for work. She took Margherita with her and sent Carmina and Luigi off to school in clothes so raggedy they would embarrass a scarecrow. Every night Mamma came home so tired she could barely walk up the stairs, her hands cracked and bleeding from scrubbing rich people's floors. Carmina stopped going to school so she could do the laundry and cook and scrub other people's floors, too.

Mamma would not let Carmina sell paper flowers on the streets or sing in her high, clear voice for the sailors on the big boats in the harbor. My daughter is not doing those dirty things, she said. It is not for a decent girl to do these things. When Luigi said, I'm the man of the house now, I'm not going to school any more, Mamma shook him by the shoulders. I am not raising another street arab, she hissed. You go to school.

One day Antonio bounced up the stairs and into the flat. He roughed up Luigi's hair and tweaked his ears, gave Mamma some money, kissed his sisters, one dark-haired, one blonde. Mamma threw him a hard look but she tucked the money under the mattress. She did not say, Antonio, where have you been and where did you get this money, for fear of what she might hear. She did not want to hear he had been stealing things. (It was worse. Antonio had been out spreading 'Italian lightning', setting fire to shops whose keepers foolishly failed to pay protection money to his small but brutal street gang.) She said, Come home Antonio, come home to us. He shook his head, no.

Antonio and Luigi walked outside, past the trough in the hallway where they got their water (a dead baby rat floating in it) and the reeking toilets in the alley. Antonio had grown hard muscles in his arms and smoked a store-bought cigarette, not one you rolled yourself. Luigi was braver, or stupider, than Mamma. He asked, Where have you been and where did you get the money. I want to get some, too. Antonio laughed and flicked his half-smoked cigarette butt into the gutter. Stay here with Mamma and the girls. I'll figure something out. It'll be all right.

Antonio was wrong. Nothing was all right. Luigi and his sisters went to bed hungry more days than they had bread in their bellies. Margherita cried from the cold creeping into their bones, Carmina shush shushing and rocking her to keep her warm. Some nights Mamma did not come home until it was light.

Then Mamma got sick and everything changed for the worse, as if the worst had not already happened. Night after night she lay sweating and feverish on the mattress, coughing and coughing, until Luigi finally summoned up a speck of courage and knocked on a neighbor's door. The neighbor took one look at Mamma, crossed herself and called for someone to bring a doctor, Mamma gasping no doctor, I can't pay, no doctor.

The doctor came anyway. He laid his hand on her forehead, listened to the croak in her chest. Then he gathered up Mamma and half-carried her downstairs into a buggy waiting outside. Luigi and his sisters stood on the street watching his mother disappear, the girls clutching each other and wailing, Luigi gnawed by a terror so hard and deep he threw up his breakfast bread on the cobbles, next to a steaming pile of manure fresh from the bony old buggy horse.

"When it get dark, a man and a lady in black clothes climb-a the stairs. They take me and Carmina and little Margherita away."

Chapter 7

Where the truth lies

Lou gently plucks a wilted leaf from the basil plant. Alex is pale and silent. I'm silent for another reason. I do not want to embarrass Luigi in front of Alex but I do want to say, Lou Sanzari, you're making all this up to impress this man.

Instead I murmur, "That's an awful story. Where did they take you? Why didn't you ever tell me?"

"Long time ago." Lou squeezes his eyes shut. "Not good times. I only want happy things for you, Sophia. Always. Only happy things. I don't want tell you these things."

This must mean Alex is manly enough to deal with these unhappy things after barely a day's grace. He stirs in his chair. "Did she ... pass away then, your mother?"

Lou closes his eyes. "Enough speaking for this night. *Io sono stanco.*" Lou does look exhausted. There are deep shadows under his eyes. Lou stands up, kisses me on the cheek, and drops a hand on Alex's shoulder.

"You didn't know?" asks Alex, casually, after Lou's bedroom door closes.

"Not all of it." It would be too humiliating to admit, "No. Nothing at all," and I would be a serious contender for Wicked Daughter of the Year if I said, "I don't think a word of it's true." Luigi has never talked about his childhood. Carmina and Margherita, on the other hand, have led me down a childhood garden path strewn, if not with roses, then certainly not with tubercular mothers, dead rats, and thuggish brothers.

"What happened to your mother? Tatiana? I mean, Olga?"

Alex looks away. "Luigi should know first. I can't tell you now. I'm sorry."

For a while we sit, saying nothing. I get up and start washing the tower of dishes on the kitchen counter. Lou has not lifted a finger in days. As I'm wiping my hands on a dishtowel a phone rings. Not Lou's. Not mine. Alex hesitates, glancing at me.

"I'll take this outside. See you later."

When I step outside a good fifteen minutes later Alex is sitting in the AssassinMobile, still talking on his phone. From what I can see, he does not look pleased. When he spots me he nods, then drops his phone and roars off down the street. It could be nothing. Trouble with his business. Women problems. Missing out on an online auction for a case lot of white shoes. It didn't feel like that to me. If I'm going to cover all bases I need a full-time spy.

Mrs Woloschuk opens her back door. She's either prescient or she's been lying in wait behind her curtains, which are a riotous red and gold to match her sofa and the kitchen chairs and almost everything else I can see from the doorway.

"Sophie! Come in, sit," bellows Mrs Woloschuk over the roaring television. "You eat? I make perogies fresh today, cottage cheese, with fried onions. So good. You like da sour cream?"

I sit on the nearest red and gold chair. She plunks a knoll of rubbery white potato dumplings in front of me. Her round face beams under her nodding stack of hair. Today it's witchy black with a white skunk-like stripe in front.

"Eat, Sophie."

Like Lou, I'd rather eat wallpaper paste. "Thank you, but I'm sorry, Mrs Woloschuk. I've already eaten, I'm full."

She pushes the plate toward me. "You too skinny Sophie, like a boy. No meat on your bones. Eat."

I ignore the insult, although it's true, and prod the fat, slippery pockets of dough around my plate. "Mrs Woloschuk."

"Oksana," she interrupts. "This my name. You call me Oksana."

"Oksana. Okay." It's unnerving to call Lou's long-time neighbor anything but Mrs Woloschuk. It occurs to me that I have never been in her house in all the years Lou and Rose have lived next door. "Oksana, I would like to ask for your help."

"Anything Sophie, anything for you or Lou or your poor mudder, I do it."

At the mention of Rose I swallow, hard. "You know the man who's been visiting my father?"

She nods. "Yes, dat tall man with pale hair, so good-looking, nice shiny car, I try to make some little talk, I try to be good neighbor but he only say hello, only hello then *zup*! In he go to see Lou. Always he bring something for Lou, sometimes a plant, sometimes I don't know, I can't see what he bring. He look so nice, handsome, good suit, best quality, I know, I sew nice clothes for rich people in Kiev."

I put down my fork. "I'm not sure he's so nice, Oksana. I don't think he is who he says he is. I think he's trying to con Lou out of something. Maybe money."

"Oy!" Mrs Woloschuk plants her plump hands on the table. "Who is he, dis man?"

"He's — he claims to be a family friend. I think he's a fraud."

"Tsk. I didn't know, Sophie. So bad, dat is bad. What I do to help?"

I lean forward. "Can you watch him for me, Mrs – Oksana? Can you tell me when he comes and goes, and how long he stays, and anything else you can find out? Not a word to Lou, though." I scribble my phone number on a note pad and push it towards her.

She nods gravely. "I do dat for you, Sophie. Poor Lou! I watch dis man. I say nuddink to Lou. I tell only you Sophie, I watch and I tell only you."

Her eyes gleam behind her thick glasses. I have just given Mrs Woloschuk, snoopy, nosey, irritating Mrs Woloschuk, my full permission to spy on Alex and my father. I nibble a perogy. Only then am I allowed to bid my undercover agent farewell.

Mel is extra cheery this morning. She is usually in an upbeat, if matter-of-fact, mood despite being constantly surrounded by the increasingly elderly and the incrementally dying. Stop it, Sophie, I scold myself. This is your mother you're talking about.

"Sophie!" Mel grips my hand. "Something happened this morning. Have a seat."

I settle myself in my usual chair next to Rose's bed.

"What happened, Mel?" I am stingy with my hopes. There have been false alarms before.

Mel's bony face rearranges itself in a smiley way. "You won't believe it, Sophie. I wouldn't have believed it but Millie was here with me, doing the bed change. Rose opened her left eye. It was only for a second, maybe less, but we both saw it."

My heart rockets around my ribs. "Are you sure? What does this mean?"

Mel shakes her head. "You'll have to ask the doctor, Sophie. Maybe it's something. Maybe it's nothing. In all this time, I've never seen her do this, or anything else."

44

I lean forward, willing Rose to do it again. Look at me, Mamma. Please look at me.

Nothing happens. Not a twitch.

Mel pats my hand. "Don't be disappointed, Sophie. What happened once could happen again."

The trouble with hope is there is such a long, rocky way to fall when the earth caves in. I would like to hope, but I'm afraid of the consequences. The end of my marriage to Derek meant the end of many things, especially hope. It was as amicable a parting as can be expected when the person you love decides it's time for a change. There were clues, I realize now, I just didn't see them or I chose to ignore them. It was not the end of all things, although some vital parts of me went missing for quite a while, like the will to get up in the morning or dress myself or talk to other human beings.

I decide not to tell Lou about Rose's eye flicker until I know something more. If it is just a twitch, and not a sign of anything better, his landing would be even rougher than mine.

"Mel, can you ask Dr Hodges to call me when he comes on his rounds? You've told him about this, right?"

"Of course, Sophie, I told him right away. I got the feeling he doesn't think it means anything, but —"

But it could mean something. It could mean a few perky blood vessels have snapped themselves back together again. There's that little shard of hope, glimmering against the odds.

I find an email in my inbox from Carmina, who is more techno-savvy than Lou despite being four years older. It's a reply to my own email about Carlo's death and Antonio and the Sanzari family's supposed tragic circumstances. I have not told her about Alex. Lou probably hasn't mentioned him either. He won't pick up the phone to call his sisters unless I prod him with the 'you'll-be sorry-when-they're gone' guilt stick.

"*Mia cara* Sophia," reads her email, "we will talk when Margherita and I visit. Love, your *zia* Carmina." Short, unsettling, and infuriating. She has neither confirmed nor denied it. The Sanzaris are slippery characters, the entire fishy bunch of them. "Carmina," I type. "Is any of it true? I need to know. Urgent. Love, Sophie."

I've finished off half of the PaintMeKidz range. Not my finest work, but my mind has been on other things. The deadline for the centennial paint-naming job is in two days. PaintMe has rejected every name I've come up with. Centennial Green. Verdant 100. Gold'n'Grow. They're awful, I admit it. Their marketing guy's emails are testy bordering on hostile. You'd think he was responsible for naming a new nation or an heir to the throne, not a home-decorating product. Adjectives for green tumble around in my head. It's no use. All I can think about is the flicker of my mother's eye, opening like a shutter and closing before anyone can see what's behind it.

Like it or not, I have to be civil to Alex, if I'm to find out the truth about him and rescue Lou from crushing disappointment or worse. Lou says *sì sì* to my invitation to come to dinner tonight, with Alex. "I come with Alex in the big car, he-a bring me, Sophie. Seven o'clock."

Seven o'clock comes and goes. Then seven-thirty. I try Lou's number while stirring the squid ink into the pasta. No answer. If this is an alpha male ploy to annoy me, it's working. I'm about to call Alex when the two of them walk in. Sassy, who has been lurking in the kitchen begging for a shrimp handout, takes one look at Alex's size extra-large white shoes looming at her like a pair of sailing yachts and shoots off down the hall.

"Where have you been? I was about to call the police."

"Everything okay Sophie, you no worry." Lou cradles his right hand. Something green is sticking out of the shirt sleeve he is trying to tug down.

"What happened? What's that green thing?"

"Lou burnt his wrist on the stove," says Alex. "I wanted to take him to A&E but he wouldn't let me."

"Why didn't you call me, Lou? Let me see." I pull up Lou's sleeve. A piece of limp broccoli is taped over a red patch on his wrist.

"Alex was there, is okay. He help me fix."

"With broccoli, Lou?"

"Frozen *broccolo*. Good for burns. Easy to use. Taste good, too. Here, for you." He holds out a bunch of frilly new lettuce.

I laugh. I can't help it. Lou looks so ridiculous with a brassica taped to his wrist. I laugh, and Alex laughs. Lou looks at both of us and smiles. Despite his burn, he looks happier than I have seen him look for months. His hair is combed and his ears neatly trimmed.

"Next-a time, I call you," grins Lou. He takes a brand new cellphone out of his jacket pocket. "On this thing. Alex give me today."

I can't believe it. Alex has once again convinced Lou to do something I've utterly failed to do. "Alex gave you a cellphone? And you took it? What about cellphones being bad for men's business?"

"What talk is this, Sophie? Alex give me this gift, I am happy to take."

"Never mind. Let's eat."

The phone rings as I'm setting the pot on the table. I answer it, still fuming, hoping it might be Rose's doctor, who is taking his own sweet time getting back to me.

"Sophia," shrieks Mrs Woloschuk, "dat man, he take Lou away in his big black car, I get into my liddle car and I drive and drive but I don't see dem and I heff a small crash, I hit anudder car I drive so fast after your fadder, just a small accident a liddle bump, I don't know where dat man take your poor fadder, maybe you call the police, Sophia."

"It's okay," I whisper. "I know where they are. Don't worry. Thanks for your help. I hope your car is all right. Goodbye." I leave the phone off the hook.

The condition I have placed on cooking dinner for Lou and Alex is that we will not talk about Lou's past until after we've eaten. That way I can surreptitiously tape that conversation and confront Carmina with it later, so she can't say, "Sophie, you imagine things."

"How long are you staying, Alex?" I ask, as a subtle opening gambit.

"You ask that before, Sophie," grumbles Lou. "Ask another thing."

So I do. I ask Alex every question I can think of about his life in New Zealand. He answers every pointed question with a relentless equanimity I can't help but grudgingly admire. He lives in the biggest city, Auckland, in a house near the sea where he can swim every day, summer or winter. (A seaside house? There must be a lot of money in pesticides.) The sea is not really warm. It's in the South Pacific, isn't it? Yes, but not the warm part, like Fiji. His business partner is taking care of the pesticides while he's away. (Lou mutters something, and sighs). He has a golden Labrador dog named Duke (where is Duke now? On holiday too, in his favorite kennel. Don't worry, Lou.) New Zealand is small and green, not rich but not poor. There are lots of dairy cows munching grass in green paddocks, plenty of sheep but not much grain farming, not like flat, fertile Saskatchewan. For holidays he takes his campervan to a beach in the north of the North Island where he can fish for snapper and gather shellfish which he calls *pipi* and *tuatua*. That's a surprise. I wouldn't have taken the suave and sartorial Alex for a campervan man.

While I'm clearing away the dishes, I mention my struggle with the centennial paint name. Lou, who has made it clear he thinks my job is a waste of time and talent, is unusually sympathetic.

"You a smart girl, Sophie, you think of something."

"I've wracked my brain. I'm stumped. How many ways can you describe green?"

"How about … mmm … GreenSheaves," offers Alex, the garden pesticide importer from a wheatless nation.

Lou claps his hands. "What you say, Sophie? Alex, he help you. *È perfetto!*"

GreenSheaves. Yes, it's perfect. I bang the pasta pot into the sink.

Alex clears his throat. "Can you tell us more of your story, Lou? If that's okay with you. I'm keen to hear what happened next."

The tape recorder is hidden on my knee, my finger poised over Play. Lou sighs.

"Okay okay, I do this for both of you, *i miei figli*. But Alex, some things better we should leave in peace."

Chapter 8

New York, November, 1927

St Joseph's Orphanage felt like a jail. There were so many rules, too many for an eight-year-old boy to remember. Luigi's hands were always red from getting whacked with a wooden stick. No laughing. No running in the hallways. So many prayers. Prayers in the morning, and before meals, at night, and sometimes just for fun whenever the nuns said so. If he didn't say his prayers or talked when he wasn't allowed to talk, he missed out on the evening bread and gruel as punishment.

"Food, not good," grumbles Lou. "Worse is no food. My stomach she yell so loud it wake me up at night."

Each morning Luigi scrubbed his face in cold water with a hard soap that smelled like poison. Sometimes Sister Joseph came into the room and ordered all the boys to strip and get rubbed all over with something even smellier. Larkspur for the fleas and the crawling, itchy lice that not even kerosene baths could chase away.

His clothes, at least, were better than his old raggedy ones. Never before had he owned a jacket and a tie, and the black felt cap and long johns kept him warmer as winter closed in. The jacket and the shirt, though, were too tight (and whose idea was it to dress little boys in white shirts anyway), the scratchy blue broadcloth pants laid his ankles bare and the shoes pinched his feet.

Luigi missed his sisters. He caught glimpses of Carmina and Margherita in their own new clothes. They looked so clean and neat in their cotton dresses (which Carmina, who was good with a needle and thread, sewed from bed sheets), blue bloomers, black wool stockings (every inch mended, but still serviceable) and white aprons. On Sundays their bonnets and gloves disguised them so much he hardly recognized them. His sisters, one dark-haired, one blonde, had a little more flesh on their bones and color in their cheeks. For the first time he saw his sisters as girls, even pretty ones, especially little Margherita.

One day Mamma came to visit them. It was a cold day, and rainy. Mamma's hair was wet and her bones poked him when he hugged her. She coughed a little, but not as much as before. Luigi looked around to see if any of the other children had noticed their skinny mother in her patched dress. Then he felt bad. He and his sisters were only half-orphans. Some of the children had no parents at all, not even an almost-dead one. The orphans' parents coughed themselves into fits from the disease that made blood come from their mouths, or died from washing dishes in dirty water from the hallway troughs or, like, Carlo, from drinking too much whiskey and making enemies of bad men. Some, like the toughest boy, Luca, were what the nuns called 'foundlings'. Luca had been abandoned like a scrawny puppy on the doorstep and never even knew his Mamma or Papa.

Take me home Mamma, take me home, take me home, pleaded Luigi, Carmina and Margherita. Mamma cried and cried and wiped her eyes. Then she said, No I can't take you home, I have no home and no money. I sleep on the floor with your *zia* Constanza and five other girls in one room, I can't take you home. I swear I will come for you, my darlings, *miei carissimi figli*. Someday soon, I will come for you. *Vi voglio bene, bene.*

The girls cried, We love you, too Mamma, we love you. Luigi took a big breath and squeezed back his tears. Where is Antonio, Mamma? She shook her head, laying her hand gently over his mouth.

Ssshh, no more questions. I have something for you, look. Into their hands she pressed shiny red apples smelling of autumn. When she walked away, waving, the children dropped the apples and ran after her. Margherita howled and choked until she was sick all over her freshly-washed dress. Sister Joseph whooshed in and snatched her away to be cleaned up, smoothing down her sweet blonde curls. Margherita was Sister's pet, even when she stuffed the much-despised mashed parsnips up her bloomers at dinner time. Watching her sister go off in the arms of the nun, Carmina murmured, Luigi, promise you won't let them take her away.

"Carmina and me, we are so scared for little Margherita." Lou is nearly whispering. "We see what happen to other little girls."

Luigi had heard rumors after dark, when the boys lay in their creaky iron beds row upon row whispering the orphanage news. One day last week a man and a woman in fancy clothes and a shiny black car had come to St Joseph's. The woman wore a spotted hat made of some furry animal, maybe a cat. The man and the woman in fancy clothes had taken away one of the prettiest little girls. Luigi and some of the children, pressing their faces against the gates of St Joseph's, had watched Betty being carried away shrieking and kicking and crying for her Mamma. She was yellow-haired, like Margherita. Her Mamma, whispered the boy telling the story, didn't want her anymore. She married a new Papa who didn't want another man's bastard in his house eating his food. That's what he'd heard, anyway.

"I hold my breath, like this," says Lou, sucking up air. "I wait for the boy to be struck down by God for saying a bad word." Nothing happened, which gave Luigi both a big surprise and a creeping sense of freedom. But now he knew what a bastard was, and what happened if you were one.

I won't let them take her away, he said, or you, Carmina.

Carmina laughed a bitter laugh too old for her fourteen years.

I'm dark. Not pretty like Margherita. I look Italian. Dago dago dago. Nobody wants me.

Luigi felt his stomach loosen. Me too, said Luigi. He waggled his ears to make her laugh. Nobody want me, either.

Chapter 9

Dixie hatches a plan

Dixie is on her way. Everything is last minute: I booked a cheap flight darling, Jerome's staying at the home, I can only stay a couple of nights, see you tonight around five, my lovely.

She's late, as usual. I should know this by now. I'm anxious with all Lou's tales to tell her, and cranky, although it's not all Dixie's fault. Dr Hodges' phone call this morning wasn't encouraging. Dr Hodges has been the family doctor for as long as I can remember, back when he was pencil-slim and, I thought, slightly dashing. Now that he's chubbied up and wheezes, he doesn't inspire confidence in his ability to heal anyone else. At least he has agreed to arrange some tests for Rose. An MRI, he says, is the best way to tell if anything has changed. We need a neurologist's confirmation. The waiting list is weeks, not days. I could get Sass in for an MRI faster than my own mother.

Then Mrs Woloschuk phoned to tell me that Alex had come to pick up Lou "in dat big black car" and they hadn't come back for hours. Did I want her to follow them again? It niggles that Alex is out chauffeuring Lou around in grand style, but I can't deal with that now. I had to promise Mrs Woloschuck I'd come for a strategic-planning visit before she'd get off the phone.

I pace my tiny living room. Maybe I've got the date wrong. Maybe Dixie's not even arriving today. Maybe I dreamt the whole thing. As I'm about to put the home-made pork terrine back in the fridge and pour myself a large consoling wine, a car door slams.

Dixie strides up the sidewalk in four-inch platform heels, all six feet of her. If I tried to walk in those shoes, I'd be bum over brains with the first step, both ankles broken. Dixie saunters along as if she was born in platform shoes. Her black mane swings almost to the hem of her dress. Scarlet, to match her nails. Red Sky Dawning. She is gorgeous, raven-haired, sun-drenched. She kisses me on both cheeks, mwah mwah, hands me a bottle of champagne and sinks into my fake leopard chair, my one extravagance.

"Sorry I'm late, Sophie, I ran into an old school friend in the airport, do you remember Howie Dombrowsky? I had such a crush on him in high school. Bet you never knew that. He was sooo divine. Now he's bald as an egg and something ferrety has happened to his nose. He was surprised to see me, I can tell you. How's life in the paint world, Sophie? Oh rack off, you stupid cat." Sassy adores Dixie for the simple reason that Dixie, for all her feline graces, can't stand cats. She nudges Sass away with one red toe.

"Not much is happening there, Dixie. I found a name for the Saskatchewan Centennial paint color." It's not quite a lie.

"Liked it, did they?"

"They loved it so much they gave me a bonus. I donated it to the Street Cat Rescue Program. Can you help me with this? The cork's too tight." I pass her the champagne. She pops the cork effortlessly.

"So what's next? More cunning captions for the color-challenged?"

"Oh lay off, Dixie. Some of us do have to work for a living." Instead of bludging off sad fat cats like The Sultan.

Dixie can't hear this silent jab, but as usual she knows what I'm thinking.

"Sorry, sweetie. Truly, I am. The Sultan is very good to me. He can't help being short and dumpy but extremely rich. Shall I fetch the glasses?"

"I'll do it."

In the kitchen I wonder, not for the first time, if it's worth it. Put us together on the same patch of planet and we spark off each other, laying just the right amount of tinder, striking the flint with deadly timing. The Turkey trip nearly destroyed us. I murder the pork terrine with a blunt knife, slop the champagne into my only two wine glasses and hand one to Dixie.

"Mmm, delish. It's marvelous to see you, Sophie."

It is good. More than good. "It's wonderful to see you too, Dix." To stop myself from another weepy flood I jump up and hug her. She hugs me back, strong and warm. She has always been a prodigious hugger.

"Tell me about this Alex menace."

I tell her everything I can remember, from the first day Alex sauntered into our lives. Dixie listens to every word. She cackles at Mrs Woloschuk's bumbling sneakery. It's nearly dark by the time I stop talking. The terrine is long gone. Two empty champagne bottles loll on the carpet.

"Well, darling, Dixie's here now. We'll have to dig up the truth, no matter how sorry and sordid. Alex sounds intriguing. When can I meet him?"

I shoot her a warning look. Dixie laughs. She's even more beautiful when she laughs, with all that black hair thrown back from those knife-sharp cheekbones and tumbling down her back. A picture of Alex and Dixie flashes through my mind, her dark mane sprawled over his long white limbs, the two of them welded together. Good god, girl. I blink it away.

Dixie is watching me carefully. She rests a talonned hand on my arm. "Don't worry, sweetheart. I'm on your side. I won't do anything you wouldn't do."

Ha.

★

Someone is singing in my kitchen. I don't remember the last time I woke up to the sound of someone in my kitchen. Oh wait, I do remember. Not his name, just his face. Dark hair, pale skin. Looked a bit like Derek. He broke a wine glass in the sink then he ruined the waste disposal unit trying to get rid of the evidence. That was six months ago. Greg, that was his name. There have been no further romantic developments.

"Good morning, darling Sophia!" Dixie is beating up something in a bowl. I can smell toast. "Creamy scrambled eggs with cumin, coming up. The way you like them, right?"

"Right," I yawn. "Why are you up so early? I thought you never got out of bed before noon."

"Plans, we must concoct a strategy. Time is of the essence. It's all too thrilling. But first, you need sustenance, my starveling waif. Have you been subsisting on Sass's leftovers?"

"Sass doesn't leave leftovers. She eats every scrap."

"Exactly. Here, eat." The eggs are perfect. I scoop up every last scrumbly piece. Dixie hums. "How's Rose?" she asks abruptly. I've already told her about the eye flicker. A sigh slips out before I can stop it.

"We're still waiting for the MRI. A specialist, a neurologist I think, came to look at Rose last week, according to Mel. Dr Armstrong – that's the neurologist – decides if Rose can have the MRI. I tried calling his office to hurry them up, but no luck. Don't call us, we'll call you. Nothing else has happened with Rose, not that Mel or anyone else has seen." I look down at my plate. I've been trying to be chin-up and brave about Rose, but having Dixie here is tripping a switch I thought I'd locked down in self-defense long ago.

"I think about her every single day. She's more real to me inside my head than she is lying there in that bed. I remember so many things, from when I was a kid. She was like the fairy godmother on our street. Anyone who came near the house got a cookie and a cup of tea. One day, I must have been about eight, this old guy came stumbling up the front steps and peed on her peonies. He got a cup of tea and a cookie, too, after he's washed his hands under the outside tap of course."

I twist my cup, round and round. "I miss her so much, Dix."

Dixie nods. "Of course you do, darling. I miss her too. Rose is of the Genuinely Good tribe. She's been so, so kind to me, too. She's not gone yet, though. Let's hope for medical miracles from Podgy Hodgy and the MRI."

Dixie's own mother is a shriveled-up, smoking, boozing train wreck (there's a cautionary tale, Sophie). The first time I met Elvira (real name Dorothy, but Dixie didn't tell me that for years), she was slobbering drunk over a half-full whiskey glass at three in the afternoon. The house sagged in a patch of thigh-high weeds. Everything stank of cigarettes, boiled cabbage and a backed-up sewer. Part of the kitchen floor in the kitchen was bare earth covered with cracked linoleum. I could not believe people lived like this.

Give ush a kish, kiddo, Elvira slurred, waving a cigarette in my face. I wanted to run away. Somehow she witched us into driving her to a church a few blocks down the street for Wednesday evening prayers. Why couldn't she walk, I wondered silently. Bad legs, no money for the doctor, she said, reading my mind. You wouldn't know anything about it, you rich girl with your fancy ways. I just stared. Sanzari wealth was news to me.

The little church had been pretty once and would be still, if not for the great chunks of stucco missing from the walls and the stains on the ceiling shaped like dead things. The goat-eyed preacher in a white cowboy hat and snakeskin boots welcomed his congregation: the halt, the lame, the grotesquely fat, the trembling deep-end drunks, all of God's desperate, hopeless souls. Pastor Bob preached against the wickedness of thrift, the sin of stinginess, promising eternal hellfire and damnation for the miserly. After sending around the collection plate, he tossed the coin offerings in the air. Take what you want Lord and leave me the rest, he bellowed. The Lord wasn't in a taking mood that day. We left in a hurry, dragging a screeching Elvira behind us.

Dixie's mother still lives in the same tumbledown shack on Avenue X. She refuses to open her door to Dixie, despite the money Dixie faithfully sends her every month. Elvira can be counted on to squander it on cigarettes, booze and evangelical infomercials. When Dixie phones, Elvira calls her terrible names no mother should even know and slams down the phone. Good riddance, you'd think. But, as Dixie says, your mother is still your mother, even though you'd like to trade her for someone else's mother or even a friendly spaniel.

"What does Lou think about Rose's eye flicker?"

"Oh. Um, I haven't told him yet. I'm waiting for the decision on the MRI. He'll just get excited over something that could be nothing."

Dixie raises an eyebrow. "Don't you think, sweetie, that Lou is old enough to make his own decisions about this? She's his wife. They've been together longer than you've been alive. He's all grown up."

This is not something I want to think about. Lately it feels like I'm the parent and he's the child. I cook (often) and clean (sometimes) and buy his undies (always). Since Rose went into care I've had power of attorney over their estate, modest though it is, in case something happens to my father. Lou is increasingly prone to impulse, like letting strange Romanian-New Zealanders slither into his life. It's as if he's shrugged off his Knight Defender of the Sanzari Family armor and I've had to put it on, piece by clanking piece. I don't like it. It's heavy, doesn't fit well, and feels depressingly permanent.

Still, Dixie is right. Just last week I rescued an elderly man who'd managed to haul himself out of a car but got stuck teetering on the edge of the sidewalk. Please, he'd whispered, help me, pointing a wavering hand to a nearby ATM. I grasped his arm, walked him to the ATM and stood watch while he withdrew some twenties. When we returned to the car a woman in a tracksuit pounced on him. She pushed him into his seat, roaring, I told Dad to stay in the car, he can't do things for himself, I told him to STAY PUT. As if he was a misbehaving six-year-old.

Do I want to become a nag like her? No, I don't. It puts my teeth on edge thinking about it. "Okay." I bite my lip. "I'll tell Lou about Rose."

Dixie cooked, so I clean. I scrape glued-on egg off the fry pan, toss out eggshells, scour plates. Shortly after Greg killed the waste disposal unit, the dishwasher broke and flooded the kitchen. It remains broken but it's handy nonetheless for storing the dinner dishes when I don't want to look at their dirty faces the morning after. The repairman's quote was enough to buy many things more thrilling than fixing a dishwasher. Shoes, a dress, maybe a new watch —

I'm ambushed by another childhood memory, one so shameful that decades later I still burn, even though it was relatively low on my list of childhood transgressions. When I was ten, I stole a watch from Rose. I found it while browsing my parents' dresser for a nickel or, better yet, a dime to slip into my pocket and buy a candy necklace. Rose kept the watch in a small velvet box in her bottom dresser drawer, buried under her winter scarves and gloves. It was the most perfect, beautiful thing, gold with roses twined around the face. I'd never seen Rose wear it.

I couldn't ask my mother about this exquisite watch. That would have exposed my snooping and petty thievery habit. So I took it out of its box and stroked its perfect glass face and peered at the faint inscription on the back. To my only R, love, T. Puzzling over the 'T' (didn't Luigi start with 'L'?) I wrapped the lovely watch around my skinny wrist and wound the tiny gold wheel. I wound it so tight the wheel snapped off in my fingers.

I almost choked from fear. No matter how hard I tried to stick the tiny wheel back on, it wouldn't fit. I slipped the watch into my pocket and tucked the box back into the drawer. Over the next week I tried fixing it with glue, tape, a bit of wire. Nothing worked. I hid it in my closet and eventually forgot all about it.

Rose never asked me about the watch, despite my obvious status as Suspect Number One. Once, I caught her looking at me thoughtfully, but she said nothing. We all have our secrets.

"Sophie, are you listening?"

I jump. "What?"

"Pay attention, girl. Are we on the same planet?"

"Sorry Dixie. I was just remembering something."

"Remember it on your own time, darling. My time is of the essence, remember. Here's the plan. Stop me if you think of something better. I meet Alex on neutral ground, perhaps a dark alley on a rainy night. I demand to know what's going on. If he can't convince me he's *bona fide*, I bean him with my rock-stuffed Gucci bag and leave him for the street cats to chew on."

"Dixie."

"Joking, I'm joking. Seriously though, Soph, if you want my help we need to get going on this. Call Alex and make a dinner date at the Broadway Café. I'd cut off all my fingernails, well, maybe on one hand, for one of their burgers."

"Dixie, take it easy on Alex, okay? If you rip into him Lou will never speak to me again. Never. He's already never speaking to you."

"I adore Lou," she pouts. "He just doesn't adore me back." Dixie's lips are a wonder of nature. They're bee-stung plump without any artificial bee involved. If there was an award for Best Performance by a Pair of Lips, that mouth of hers would win it. She smiles, stands up, stretches. "I've been up for ages, honeypot, I'm off for a power nap. I promise not to hold anything sharp-edged against Alex. Call me when it's time to do battle with Public Enemy Number One."

I have a bad feeling about this, but in the absence of any better plan I pick up the phone.

Alex sounds wary when I speak to him and who can blame him, after our last café debacle. He looks even warier an hour later when he spots Dixie lazing beside me, filching French fries off my plate. My traitorous mind matches them up again, the cool blond and the fiery Boadicea. What's going on? My subconscious is being mischievous, or else it knows something I don't.

"Alex, meet Dixie. Dixie, Alex." She holds out an elegant hand. A ruby the size of a quail's egg takes up most of her third finger. One of The Sultan's rewards for services rendered, I'm guessing.

Alex blinks. He looks genuinely flummoxed. Dixie has that effect on people. For a moment I think Alex is actually going to kiss her mutinous paw. Then he shakes it briefly and sits down across from us. His eyes are an icy blue today, Ancient Glacier Aqua. "Sophie. I didn't realize you'd have an offsider at this meeting."

"Sophia and I are best friends," purrs Dixie, running her Bambi-brown peepers over Alex. I kick her under the table. "We have no secrets. What's an offsider?"

As Alex opens his mouth, Woody Woodpecker's Heh-heh-heh-HEH-heh ricochets around the café.

"Oops, that's my phone. Jerome's favorite ringtone." Dixie rummages around in her bag, glances at the phone. "Excuse me, I've got to take this." She strides out of the café. She does not look happy.

Alex watches her leave. I watch him watch her leave. When she's gone, and only then, he turns back to me. Before I can say anything he pulls an envelope out of his shirt pocket.

"I thought you should see this." He slides it across the table. "You can have it. It's a copy."

Inside the envelope there's a black and white print of an old newspaper clipping from the *Minneapolis Star*. There are three people in the photo, a woman and two men. One of them is Lou. All of them are young, maybe in their twenties, but there is no mistaking those hairy ears. Lou must have let them grow for months. The woman standing beside him is tall, blonde, sleek as a panther and poutingly beautiful. She is wearing a skin-tight sequinned bodysuit and spangly tights. There is an ostrich plume on her head and a touch of the Baltic around her almond-shaped eyes. The other man is taller than Lou or the woman, muscular and good-looking in a dark Mediterranean way. He is wrapped in thick chains and clad in a loincloth.

The clipping is dated July 29, 1943. The caption reads, "See Tatiana the Amazing Russian Trapeze Queen! Watch Hercules the Strongman carry an Elephant on his back!! See Manfred the Monkey Man and other Fabulous Freaks!! Only at The Greatest Ever American Carnival! Fun for all the family!"

Alex taps the paper. "That's my mother, Olga. Tatiana was her performing name. She was a tightrope and trapeze artist. This is Lou, of course. That's where they met, in the Greatest Ever American Carnival."

My mouth actually drops open. I snap it shut. "What did you say?"

"The carnival. That's where they met. Lou and Tatiana."

Alex might as well have said, "This is where they met, at a costume ball on Planet Zorg." Not once in my entire life has Lou ever mentioned being a carnival act. No-one did, not Rose or the aunts. Not once. Now I know why Alex scrutinized Lou's ears so closely on that first day. It was a confirmation, not a surprise. Alex's father, the Monkey Man. Check.

Of the many questions rampaging around my head the first to pop out is, "This says Tatiana was Russian," as if that disproves the whole outlandish scenario.

"Most acrobats and trapeze artists were Russian. It was easier for my mother to pass herself off as Russian. Nobody knew where Romania was. Most people still don't." I ignore this little patriotic bleat.

"Hercules the Strongman, he doesn't look Russian."

Alex raises an eyebrow. "He's not. He's Italian," he says. "That's Lou's brother. Your uncle. That's Antonio."

Dixie is sitting on my doorstep, smoking. I drop onto the step beside her. "I thought you'd quit."

She huffs a triple O, each smoky ring sliding lazily through the next. Dixie never does anything by halves. "I did. Many times. Quitting is so much fun, darling, I thought I'd light up just to do it all over again." She snorts. "A little stress here, a little stress there. Did I tell you I promised Jerome a pet turtle? What was I thinking? I was thinking, a turtle is better than a rat. That's what he really wanted. A furry little red-eyed rattums. Then there's The Sultan's endlessly inventive demands. And you, my sweet, and your family sagas. At least smoking keeps the damned bugs away."

She blows smoke at a wasp circling her head. "God. How do you put up with this bug invasion? Mosquitoes have bitten me in places no bug should ever go. I've got worms dropping down the back of my neck from your sticky old elm tree. Do you remember that summer we drove up to Pickerel Lake? What a nightmare. Worms were falling all over the car. You turned on the wipers and the windshield was squished all over with worm guts. We didn't even open the doors. I slammed the car in reverse and took off over a river of squashed worms. We were lucky we didn't hit the ditch. Death by vermicide."

When Dixie babbles like this about old times, she's got something on her mind about the here and now.

"Who was on the phone?"

"What happened with Alex?" she counters.

What happened? My life turned upside down and I fell out of it. I know too little. I know too much. A secret kept for half a century must be chipped free. I scrape open a little bit here, a little bit there, but never enough to uncover the whole. It is as frustrating as peering through frosted glass.

"Nothing," I say to Dixie. "Well, everything. I'll tell you later. Are you okay? What was that phone call about? You just got up and disappeared. I was worried." A small lie. After Alex showed me the clipping I didn't think about Dixie until I saw her sitting on my step in a smoky fug.

"That was the residential home on the phone. Jerome's got a bit of a cough, more than a bit actually, doll, he's got pneumonia. The nurse sounds more worried than she's letting on. I'm flying back right away. I have a little boy to nurse and a pet turtle to buy."

She takes one last drag and tosses the butt into the lilac bush. I clamber down to retrieve it. The sun casts her shadow on the sidewalk, elongating her curvy shape into a flatter and darker Dixie.

"Oops, here's the taxi." She grabs her bag. I didn't even notice it sitting by the side of the steps.

"Love you, Soph," she calls over her shoulder.

I sit on the step, slapping mosquitoes and hugging myself. I should be worried about Jerome. He does not need pneumonia on top of everything else. Dixie will take care of him, though. I know she will. She always does.

Chapter 10

Carnival days

I adored the carnival. Summer had truly arrived when the Greatest Ever American Carnival rolled into town in their red and yellow railcars to set up in the dust and noise of the Exhibition grounds. Show people inhabited a world of elephant thunder and lion roar, puke-making rides and, best of all, the flying trapeze.

Every year I begged my parents to take me to the carnival. Every year Rose tut-tutted, pursed her lips, made 'there's scarcely enough money to buy milk' noises. Under a barrage of my nagging, pleading and threats of stowing away on a Greatest Ever American railcar, she eventually relented. But she would not take me to see the sideshow acts. Kind-hearted people like Rose did not pay money to gawk at the grotesque and misshapen.

Lou never came with us to the carnival. I thought he was just being cheap, or didn't want to spend time with me, or was afraid of what he might see. That might have been true, but not for the reasons I imagined. Be careful, he told us. Carnies, very bad peoples.

The year I turned ten, I dressed in my best lime-green pedal pushers and matching polka dot top, hand sewn by Rose, and hopped on the bus with my mother. Fizzing with anticipated thrills I twitched impatiently through the spooky capering clowns, the sword swallowers and fire eaters, who I watched with my hands covering my eyes in case something went horribly awry, like somebody bursting into flames or sticking a sword through their stomach, but with my eyes open a slit just in case something tragic did happen and I missed it.

The lion act filled me with thrills and guilt in equal measure. The roars of the big cats rumbled around inside my chest. I would have given anything to pat their velvet faces. At the same time I knew that lions belonged in a faraway forest or savannah, not being whipped onto chairs in a Canadian prairie town. Rose, indiscriminate lover of all animals and people, never failed to remind me of this.

When the trapeze artists appeared the rest of the world vanished; the scary clowns and other people sitting around us silently faded away. I had eyes only for the beautiful ladies swinging, twirling and flipping, flying through the air without wings in glittery sequinned costumes and pink ballet slippers. Only after the trapezists had swung their last spiraling loops, to much gasping from the crowd, did I draw an ecstatic breath.

Afterward, Rose gave me twenty-five cents and a choice. I could buy my all-time favorite treat, a candy apple, or see the sideshow acts, if I promised not to tell my father. This was out of character for Rose, who would not let me call anyone ugly or stupid, as much as they deserved it. I was so surprised I would have promised anything, even to wash the dishes for a week without complaining.

So freak show it was, I decided, giving up the beloved candy apple and not wondering for a minute why I shouldn't tell my father. Before she could change her mind I dragged her into the nearest tent. 'See the Abominable Snowman, direct from the Himalayan Mountains of Nepal! See the Killer Beast that ate an Entire Village!' In the poster a gigantic hairy white beast, bloody-fanged and huge of claw, pounded through snowdrifts carting a screaming bikini-clad woman over his shoulder. Why the woman was wearing a bikini in some place cold enough to snow didn't cross my mind.

Inside the tent, an ordinary man with feet half the size of a coffee table sat on a chair reading the newspaper. That was it. No hairy monster, no shrieking lady in a bikini, not even any fake snow, just a pair of deformed feet so huge a small child could lie down on one. It was ten times more disappointing than finding out the truth about Santa Claus, although that had been a suspect tale since I was four years old.

On it went. The Fat Lady wore a flowery tent-like dress and was, well, fat. Fatter than any other woman I had ever seen, but not 'So Monstrously Fat she squashes Pianos!'

We trawled through more disappointments. The 'Giant Man-eating Shark with teeth like a Thousand Daggers!' was stuffed and slightly moldy and hung in a glass freezer against an amateurish oceanic scene. The Giant Man restored my battered faith a bit by being so tall I had to look waaay waaay up to see his face, just like the Friendly Giant on TV. Unlike jolly old Friendly, this giant looked mean and had horrible black teeth. In his enclosure there was a table full of interesting goodies for sale, like a silver ring I could put two fingers through and badly wanted.

One look at Rose squashed any plans to beg for a giant ring or a sock wide enough to put two legs in. By the time we had finished with this line of unfortunates, my usually cheerful mother looked as if she'd smelled a dead rat. At the time I thought she was as disappointed as I was. Now I see her imagining Manfred the Monkey Man, sitting in a chair suffering the taunts of strangers.

A man in a shiny black suit standing behind a wheel of fortune grinned at my mother and me crunching our candy apples (she agreed the fake freaks were not worth a candy apple trade-off). The man in the suit ran his eyes over Rose in a way I did not like at all. Rose frowned and pulled me along. Her frown deepened when we walked past a man in a yellow and green striped suit selling knives. A woman pushed through the crowd yelling, "You robbed me you lying thief." She slammed a cheap, broken knife on the table and burst into tears.

Was this what Lou meant by "carnies, very bad?" I recall this so clearly: my mother hurrying after the crying woman, the hem unraveling on the woman's faded brown dress, her scuffed shoes, her faintly sour, cabbagey smell, Rose touching the woman's elbow and slipping a quarter into her hand, which even I could see was rough and red, the nails ragged.

I felt embarrassed and shocked by the woman's shabby clothes and public tears, and I was unaccountably worried for Rose. Would she get into trouble for giving money away to a stranger? Why was my mother always doing these things? Despite feeling sorry for the crying woman with the broken knife and scruffy shoes, I was a bit miffed. If there were quarters to spare I really wanted to see the Wall of Death Daredevil motorcycle riders. If I were a boy, I was sure Lou would have taken me to see them.

Lou is in his garden whispering to the tomato plants when I push through the gate. He smiles when he sees me.

"Sophie! Sit here. The sun, she is warm." He pats a rusting wrought iron chair snaggled in sweet peas.

I can't sit. I pace the courtyard, four steps one way, four steps back, like a caged lion. My rehearsed words stick in my throat. I hand him the newspaper clipping. "Is there something you'd like to tell me, Lou?"

"Oh, Sophia." Lou's spindly legs fold and he drops into the chair. "Oh, *mia cara*." He wipes a hand across his face. "Alex, he give you this? I tell him no. Never."

"Yes, Alex gave it to me. It was a surprise. I feel like I've been walking around with my head in a box for forty years. I don't know you at all. Alex knows more than I do, and you've only known him for ten minutes."

69

Lou runs his finger over the grainy photo. His face is full of an intimate longing that transforms my elderly father into someone younger and less familiar.

"It was long time ago, Sophie. So long ago. Many things I don't know, I don't remember."

"Did Rose know you were Manfred the Monkey Man?"

"Of course. I tell her that, but she agree not to tell you. I tell Rose everything."

"Everything, Lou? Did she know about Tatiana?"

Lou is trembling, with rage or fear, I don't know. I crouch and take his hands in mine. They're rough hands, grimy gardener's hands.

"Please tell me about the carnival, Papa. Please. I won't judge you or anyone else. I just want to know about your life." A heart beat pause. "It might help me to understand about Alex."

Lou shuts his eyes. He is silent for so long I start to worry that he, too, has had a stroke.

"Okay Sophie. I tell you." Lou struggles to his feet. "Come inside, we drink tea and talk. You and me, *mia cara*. Only you and me."

I follow him inside, apprehension thumping my chest. Lou and I are about to sail uncharted waters. Lou and I have never talked one-on-one about anything important. We have had the usual day-to-day conversations: how was your day, what are you doing at school. Ordinary talk I could have had (and did) with the postman or the milkman. All other big-life talk I've had with Rose. How to be a Good Person. (Be nice to people, whether or not they deserve it. Try to help those less fortunate. Be kind to animals.) Without Rose to keep us from cracking up on jagged family rocks and sinking into the dark unknown, I'm not sure where Lou and I will land. Rose is the pole star by which this small family sails.

This reminds me that I still haven't told Lou about Rose's eye flicker and impending MRI. Later, I promise myself. I'll tell him. Later.

70

After Luigi's release from the prisoner of war camp in Ontario, he and Antonio —

"Wait, wait, stop, Lou." My tea spills all over the table. "What prisoner of war camp? What are you talking about? How did you meet up with Antonio again? The last time you told your story, you were an eight-year-old living in an orphanage with your sisters. There's a hole in this story big enough to drive a Greatest Ever American train through."

Lou sighs. "You want to hear about the carnival or no, Sophia?"

On the stubborn-meter, Lou measures eight out of ten today, judging by the thin line of his lips and the crease between his eyebrows. Is this a 'once in a lifetime' offer? I take my chances. "I want to hear everything, Lou. Everything. We need to go back to the orphanage."

"Maybe we wait for Alex. So he can hear, too."

"No."

Lou glares. I glare back. "Just you and me. You promised, Lou."

The cuckoo clock ticks down our standoff. Tick tock tick tock. If that stupid bird sticks its beak out now, I'll jump up and pull it off the wall.

Lou cracks a half-smile. "You a tough cookie, Sophia. So stubborn."

"I'm my father's daughter, Papa."

Chapter 11

Minot, North Dakota, 1928

The air smelled of rain the day Luigi boarded the train. A sharp spring wind blew his neatly combed hair in his eyes. Luigi stood in line on the platform with other boys and girls, all freshly bathed and dressed in clean day clothes, the girls with ribbons in their hair. Each child had a number pinned inside their coat. Number 125 for Luigi. Each child clutched a packed lunch and their night clothes in a small cardboard suitcase. Luigi's ears had been shorn so closely that one earlobe leaked a trickle of blood. He could not see Carmina or Margherita among the girls.

Come along children, come along, ordered a woman in black, herding the children onto the train. Luigi recognized her as the woman who had brought him and his sisters to the orphanage. Frightened by the chuffing black monster the smaller ones, some only two or three years old, howled and wailed. A couple of the tiniest ones wet their pants and were scolded for their inconvenient messiness.

Luigi and the other boys found wooden seats to sit on. The bigger ones elbowed off the weaker ones for a seat by the window. When nearly all the seats were filled with pushing, squirming children the train's whistle blasted. Luigi heard yelling and swearing. "Very bad words," grins Lou. A sour-faced man in black shoved a tall boy down the aisle. Luigi could not believe his eyes. Antonio. He and the rest of his backstreet gang had been nabbed taking bets on a cockfight.

Antonio pushed the boy sitting next to Luigi out of his seat and plunked down close to Luigi, who gaped at the brother he had not seen for half a year.

"Antonio tell me, Luigi, we're gonna escape," remembers Lou. "Escape from what, I say. Don'tcha know nuthin, Antonio say. This is an orphan train. We're gonna be slaves."

Luigi tried to ask Antonio questions, like what was an orphan train and why they were on one when he still had a mother, didn't he? His brother hissed, don't let on you're my brother, they'll take you away. They don't let family stick together. Then he folded his arms tight across his chest and stared out the window. Luigi shut his mouth like Antonio said and tried not to cry. Something bad must have happened to his mother, and nobody had told him.

"So terrible," whispers Lou. "My Mamma, she die and nobody tell me? I feel so bad I want to be sick."

The train chuffed out of New York into the countryside. Sticky soot from the train's chimney blew in through the windows and blackened their clothes. The air, damp and doggish, smelled of excited, frightened boys, wilting ham sandwiches and cigar smoke from the three men in black who puffed away in the train car. Outside, a grove of apple trees shed a soft pink rain of blossoms. A herd of mooing brown cows galloping away from the train made the small ones who were not already weeping shriek with terror. At one stop a lean Red Indian dressed in beaded buckskin trousers with a feather in his braided black hair leaped onto the platform landing. Lou half-rose to take a better look but Antonio hauled him down.

Siddown! he hissed. Don't call attention to yisself.

The Indian rode to the next town, where he disappeared as silently as he had arrived.

"The Red Indians, they ride for free, but no seats for them inside the cars. They get worse treatment than Italians."

Over the next few days the train screeched and roared to a halt many times. At each stop, the orphan train children walked two by two through the dusty towns to a church hall or a school to sit on chairs on a stage or stand in rows. Some of the children dutifully sang little songs the nuns had drilled into them. Others, ordered in advance, were led away by their new foster parents. The farmers and townspeople looked the unclaimed children up and down, opened their mouths to see their teeth, pinched the girls' cheeks to check their color or squeezed the boys' biceps for firmness. Many farmers wanted Antonio, tall, good-looking Antonio, who hit back at the men who squeezed his muscles and bit one fat toad who stuck his dirty finger in the boy's mouth.

Nobody wanted small, skinny Luigi, whose ears began sprouting again without regular razoring. Each day, fewer children re-boarded the train. By the end of the fourth day, the only children left were two not-very-pretty dark-haired girls (all the yellow-haired ones were taken) and a handful of boys blighted by attitude (like Antonio) or by a twiggy build and suspected deformity (like Luigi). The men in black looked increasingly grim. Luigi was a mistake.

"Children's Aid don't know about my ears. They see my name on a list at the orphanage, they think I am a different Luigi. No childrens with bad ears or cough or runny nose get put on orphan trains. I am big problem. They see this when my ears grow hair on the train."

This mistake vexed the men in black, whose mission was to offload all the children, not haul any rejects back to New York. As they got off the train in North Dakota, one of them stared hard at Antonio and Luigi.

Be good boys, he said, don't cause trouble. This is the end of the line. It's your last chance for a new home.

"I don't want a new home." Lou spits out the words. "I want my old home, with Mamma and Antonio and my sisters."

The boys' train ride came to an end in the little farming town of Minot. A silent Swedish farmer and his pinch-mouthed wife put both disappointingly dark-skinned boys in their horse-drawn wagon (after Antonio kicked and shouted that he wasn't goin' anywhere without his 'friend' the Swedes gave up and took the skinny little hairy-eared freak as well). The boys sat among stinky sacks of cow manure and scratchy hay bales for the six-hour ride into their future.

Chapter 12

Rose and Tatiana

"Hi Sophie, it's Andy from PaintMe. Again. Tried texting you but no reply. Loved what you did with the SaskCentennial, GreenSheaves, yeah, perfect, very cool. Got something else for ya, give me a call." Beep.

"*Salve*, Sophia, this is your *zia* Carmina. Margherita and I, we are flying to Saskatoon on Friday, time is ... yes ... 12:25. That is in the afternoon, Sophia. Not midnight. We are bringing the Valpolicella. Sophia, please tell Lou. *Ti voglio molto bene, ciao bella*." Beep.

"Hello Sophie, this is Paula, from Dr Armstrong's office. There's been a cancellation so we can get your mother in for her MRI on Thursday, that's this Thursday, the fifth of July. Please call me back as soon as possible." Beeeeeep.

Thursday, 1pm, Paula tells me. That is when Rose is scheduled for her MRI. Good thing you called, she says, we were about to schedule in someone else. I should call Lou. Little guilt monsters with Dixie faces jump up and down, nipping at my conscience, braying Call Lou call Lou call Lou. Lou has had to deal with the bad old times lately. He does not need this worry, I convince myself.

Thursday afternoon is clear, calm, and hot enough to burn my fingers on the steering wheel. Luckily the drive to the hospital is short and I find a parking space right away. There is more hustle bustle in Rose's hospital room than I've seen since Rose had her first stroke. Dr Armstrong is here and so is a briskly efficient hospital nurse with 'Martha' on her name tag. They confer while Martha makes notes.

As the star player in this bit of theatre, Rose is doing what Rose always does. I sit quietly beside her while Dr Armstrong explains how the MRI works. Anyone having an MRI must lie very still on their back for up to two hours in a large cylinder-thing that, in the information leaflet, looks like a Star Wars hyperspace tunnel. No problem there. Rose has not moved without help in two years. It's doubtful she'll sit up and ask for a cup of tea halfway through the scan.

"Is there any history of metal fabrication or welding or grinding?" Nurse Martha's pen is poised. I blink. "I have to ask," she says, tapping the clipboard. "You'd be surprised how many people take up welding as a hobby. That's a no, then?" I nod. "What about pacemakers, implants, jewelry, dentures?"

Someone, trusty Mel, I hope, has removed Rose's wedding ring. Rose never removed that ring, not even to dig up potatoes or wash the floors. The flesh is narrower where the gold band has squeezed it for forty-nine years. Her thin finger looks obscenely bare.

"She has all her own teeth." It sounds like something I would say about Sass. I try again. "I mean, my mother has good strong teeth. She's never needed dentures." I panic a bit about the other forbidden items. What if Rose has a metal plate in her head or a pin in her hip from some childhood accident I know nothing about? For a moment I regret not telling Lou about this scan.

"Right." Nurse Martha nods. "We'll be taking your mother in soon. If you'd like to wait, there's a coffee shop downstairs. The doctor's office will call you when we have the results."

That's my cue to leave. I squeeze Rose's hand. As usual it's cool, and thin and limp.

It started with a headache, Lou told me, after I raced home from Turkey to find my father near collapse and my mother in a coma. She was washing the dishes, said Lou. She told me her head hurt, there was pain in her eye. How long had she had this pain? She don't say. You know Rosa, she don't complain. She say she take some pain pills and lie down for a little time.

Rose never took drugs for anything, so this worried Lou a lot. When he came into their bedroom later to check on her, she could not move her right arm or leg, could not speak from her twisted mouth. One blue eye looked at him with a terror so contagious Lou could barely dial the phone for the ambulance. He waited by her side. Rosa Rosa Rosa he murmured. *Rosa mia, non mi lasciare.* Stay. Stay. He cried a little. By the time the ambulance arrived, Rose's eyes had closed.

A black BMW sits outside my house. Alex sits inside it talking urgently on his cellphone again. It must be a hefty heist this time. When he sees me he climbs out and waits while I park my humble Toyota.

"I hope you don't mind my coming over without ringing." He spreads his hands wide. "Could we have a proper chat? We haven't got off to a very good start."

I bite back the words Why. Don't. You. Go. Away. Be nice to people, says the voice of Rose in my head. Rose would treat Alex with unfailing courtesy, just as she would mailmen, paper boys and probably burglars.

"Okay." I nod toward the house. "Would you like to come in?"

"Could we go somewhere, ah, neutral? Maybe for a walk? Or if you like I can drive somewhere."

A drive in the AssassinMobile isn't what I had in mind. The trunk in those cars is spacious enough to hide at least one body. A likely scenario flashes through my mind: I get in, we go for a ride down some farmer's road, Alex bonks me on the head with a tire iron or maybe a rock, then stuffs me in the trunk and dumps me in the river. After that, Your Honor, she was never seen again.

"Okay, let's go." I march to the car, yank open the door and slide into the passenger seat. Alex hesitates, as if suspecting a trick, then jumps in and pulls smoothly away from the curb.

Wanuskewin, I decide, is the place to go on this summer's day. We don't say much on the short drive to the park; I give directions, Alex follows them. He is a skillful driver for someone piloting a large car on the wrong side of the road. Wanuskewin is one of my special places. For a moment I wonder if I'm tainting it by dragging this intruder around its quiet prairie trails. Be nice, says my mother's voice, again.

Alex is quietly smitten with the park from the moment he spies the bison statues charging across the plaza. He gives a low whistle. I switch into amateur tour-guide speak.

"Wonderful, isn't it. Wait 'til you see the trails and the First Nations' archeological sites. The museum is fascinating, too. Maybe you can come back and see that sometime. The Cree and the Sioux and other tribes loved this place, and still do." On and on I babble. What am I doing? This was a mistake.

"What does it mean, Wanuskewin?"

"It means 'living in harmony'." We glance at each other, and glance away at the same time. I'm sure I see him smile.

I set out along the Trail of the Buffalo winding over wild rose and wolf willow, through birch groves and bracken. Sage and wild juniper crushed underfoot scents the breeze. Alex follows, stopping to run his fingers across a buffalo rubbing stone crusty with lichen.

Now that I have Alex alone, without Lou running interference or Dixie to prompt me, I can't think of a thing to say.

"How's Tony?" I manage.

"Good. He and Olivia are busy planning their wedding. It's a big job these days, apparently."

My own wedding took six months to plan and all of my savings. Derek and I said our vows in the handsome stone church on the river where my parents had taken their own vows. Elvira showed up staggering, lipstick-smeared and breathing whiskey. The aunts were in attendance in their finest plumage, also my cousins, and our high school friends, and Lou's card-playing friends, and Rose's parents and her friends from the bakery.

In front of everyone I promised, I do, Derek promised, I do. When we kissed, his mother screeched you'll be sorry, he comes from bad seed. Carmina swiftly silenced her with a gloved hand. I did not like her before that prescient outburst. I hated her afterward. But we ignored the old witch, danced so close our hearts beat in time, ate Italian food made by the aunts, fell into bed in the city's fanciest hotel (the one now home to Alex), and made soul-searing love in a mess of crushed satin sheets I'd stuffed into my suitcase for our honeymoon.

I'm suddenly aware I haven't said a word for a while.

"Is everything all right, Sophie?"

"Sure. Oh look, chokecherries. Rose makes the best jelly from these berries." I pinch a fat berry, squirting out the purple juice.

"How is your mother?"

I stop. Alex bumps into me. "Sorry."

"She's the same." I realize I can't ring-fence every single family detail from this man, who's obviously not an assassin. There are plenty of head-bashing rocks around, no witnesses, and I'm still standing here gabbling nonsense under a birch tree.

"She had an MRI today, to see if there's been any change." I scuff my shoe in the prairie dust. "Please don't tell Lou yet. I'm trying to protect him from more disappointment."

Alex shoots me a look. It is annoyingly similar to the one Dixie gave me. "I know, I know. Lou's old enough, he has a right to know blah blah.

80

I'll tell him when I get the results. How did your mother die?" I ask abruptly.

Alex blinks rapidly and looks away. For a moment I think he is not going to tell me.

"She fell off the trapeze," he says quietly. "There was no safety net that night. The punters paid bigger ticket money that way. It was the last act of the night."

"Oh my god. That's so terrible, Alex. Your beautiful mother."

He rubs his forehead. "It's worse than that. I saw her fall."

I suck in my breath. "You saw your own mother fall to her death?" I can see it all: the dazzling Tatiana flashing through the air, grasping at the trapeze bar and missing, a blue shooting star falling from the sky, falling falling—

"She let go," he says flatly. "She'd been depressed for a long time. Everything was a struggle for her after Lou left the carnival. She really loved him, you know. She told me that. I love your father Luigi very much, that's what she said. He wasn't just some carnie fling for her."

We have climbed high on the trail. He looks away toward the valley, to the silvery slash of the creek running through it.

"I'm so sorry about your mother, Alex." My mind is racing, processing crazy thoughts. Was it possible that the gorgeous Tatiana loved Lou? "That must have been an awful thing to see."

"It was a nightmare. I was six. She died instantly. She broke her neck." He looks me full in the face. "That was a long time ago. I try not to remember. It's almost as if it happened to someone else."

"Have you told Lou? About how Tatiana died, I mean."

"Yes. He was very upset. He blames himself."

"That's silly." Silly? Maybe not. What do I know?

We walk on in silence. If Alex blames Lou for his mother's death, he's not saying. Of the many mysteries piling up around my father, the biggest is how hairy-eared little Lou managed to woo Tatiana who, I'm guessing, could have had the pick of the carnies. But if Rose loves him, why not Tatiana? Still, nags the doubter voice. Consider the odds. What about that tall, good-looking Antonio? The thought flicks me like a cracked whip. Maybe Alex should be tracking down a different Sanzari brother.

★

Carmina and Margherita flit into town as cheerful and chattery as parakeets. Carmina is swaddled in blue and green silk from her neck rolls to her dimpled knees, while slender Margherita is elegant in a flowery pink and peachy frock. They are coiffed and rouged and bejeweled and utterly magnificent. My aunts fill my house with a twittery concern for my welfare, specifically what I've been eating and how much. It is not enough, they fret, pinching my cheeks, you want to die of skinniness, like a barn cat? Carmina kisses me, pats my hair, and hugs me to her rhinestoned bosom before passing me on to Margherita for repeat treatment. Even Sass, prowling out to sniff the Parma ham, endures a vigorous pat-down.

I stash Toronto's finest deli prosciutto, the Parma ham, and a mountain of provolone and other fine cheeses in the fridge, but concede defeat and abandon the bale of freshly baked olive focaccia bread on the kitchen table. This culinary largesse is typical of my aunts.

Carmina and Margherita. These widowed aunts and their daughters, my cousins, are my only extended family. Like me, Rose is an only child. My late grandparents, though kindly in a faltering English way, faded to invisibility when held up against my aunts' fire and light. I have been under their collective Italian fairy godmother spell for my entire life. This makes the questions I ask, after their customary post-lunch *sonnellino* with eyeshades in darkened rooms, all the more distressing for them.

"Oh, Sophia," cries Margherita, wringing her hands.

"Oh Sophia," sighs Carmina.

This gentle reproach does not stop me badgering my aged aunts. "I'm sorry. I don't mean to upset you, but I need to know about Lou's life. Your lives, too. Besides, you promised, Carmina. Remember, in your email."

"Ask Lou," suggests Carmina.

"Yes, ask your Papa," chimes in Margherita.

"He leaves things out. I think he makes things up." I brandish the tape recorder. "He tells me about rats in your house and that your father was killed by thugs. He tells me that all of you were living in an orphanage." I pour myself another glass of Valpolicella, that's how desperate I am to win them over. "Don't you think I have a right to know my own father's history? Asking Lou is like squeezing blood from a turnip. He tells me things, maybe they're true and maybe they're not. I want to hear what you know about Lou's life. I need to know the truth. Please, Carmina."

Carmina and Margherita exchange glances. "The truth can hurt," warns Carmina, pursing her generously lipsticked lips. "Like a stab with a knife, and poison poured in after. Remember that, Sophia."

Chapter 13

New York, 1928-1932

One summer day, Mamma came to see Carmina and Margherita. Mamma looked very pretty. She wore a sky-blue silky dress with a low waist, and her eyes were bright as stars.

I am taking you home, darlings. Isn't that wonderful! We'll be together again. Get your things, we're leaving.

Both girls stared at this smiling lady dressed in fancy clothes who flicked a cigarette in a holder and blew smoke past their ears. Was this the mother they had not seen for nearly a year?

Dov'è Luigi? asked Carmina. Isn't he coming with us?

Mamma's face sucked in as if someone had punched her in the stomach.

Don't speak Italian to me, Carmina, She tapped ash on the floor. We speak English now. Only English.

Carmina looked down at the grey flakes at her feet that one of the other girls would have to sweep up.

Dov'è Luigi?

Mamma ignored her. Gripping their hands she pulled them along. Come girls, the car is waiting and someone at home wants to meet you. Your new Papa.

"Imagine this," says Carmina. "No-one tells us what happened to our missing brother Luigi. We do not dare even to think our lost brother

84

Antonio's name. No-one tells us Mamma found a new Papa somewhere, a new Papa who has so much money he owns a car."

The car was big and black and shiny. The girls had never ridden in a car in their lives. Margherita, who had not spoken a word since their Mamma told them about their new Papa, promptly did what she always did under stress and threw up her breakfast porridge all over herself and the shiny leather seat. Mamma slapped her, hard; Mamma, who had never struck any of her children in her life. Then she hugged both shocked little girls tight.

Sorry my darlings my sweet babies I'm so sorry *merda!* Johnny will be so mad about the car don't worry don't worry. Wiping down the seat with a lacy handkerchief, then with the hem of her pretty blue dress, in a kind of terror. By the time they reached their new home all three of them were crying and Carmina was mightily worried.

The house was as huge, dark and gloomy as a morgue. The girls had their own bedrooms, maids, a nanny and a manicured garden with an apple tree they were forbidden to climb. There was imported Italian marble in the bathrooms and Turkey rugs on the floors. It was a world away from an orphanage or a rat-infested walk-up one-room flat. It should have been paradise.

"It was …" Carmina begins.

"Hell," genteel Margherita finishes tartly.

Papa Johnny owned speakeasies on the Lower East side. "That's where Mamma met Johnny," Carmina explains. "She was a waitress in one of Johnny's speakeasies. She never told us that. Too shameful! It was a sin for a nice girl to work in a place like that. She told us she had worked as Johnny's secretary in a shipping business. Our *zia* Constanza, Mamma's younger sister, told us the truth many years later, after Mamma died."

Johnny had fallen hard for Mamma's chocolate-black eyes and narrow waist, still trim despite the trials of having four children and a murdered husband. Two months later they were married.

85

"Not long enough for one to know the other," Carmina shrugs. "But that was how it was, then. Mamma thought that to marry Johnny was her only chance for better things. Ours also."

Johnny and his cronies were indeed in the business of shipping. They ran bootlegged rum across the Canadian border during Prohibition. It was a license to print fat stacks of money. Despite all this loot, Papa Johnny was as bad-tempered as their old Papa. No, worse. He slapped Mamma and he beat Carmina, too. Carmina who had never been beaten before, could not, would not, keep her mouth shut, as Papa Johnny ordered. Mamma begged her to do what he said.

Please, please Carmina, don't talk back to your Papa.

Margherita was too young to know any better. She called their mother's new husband 'Papa Johnny' and stayed well out of striking reach. Carmina refused. He's not my Papa, I won't call him that. She called him nothing at all. There would be more beatings with a leather belt, or sometimes a heavy hand on bare skin, Johnny's blunt-fingers lingering a little too long on the flesh of her buttocks. After the tears and Mamma's pleadings came the bribes. Clothes and toys and bicycles and hot lazy days of ice cream and hot dogs on Coney Island. Carmina wasn't fooled.

As the second summer in the big house poached them all into a sweaty stupor, Mamma stayed in bed most of the time. When she did get up, her hair was stiff and greasy, and her breath smelled of something bitter. Margherita started to wet the bed.

"Shh! You don't tell our niece such private things, Carmina."

"She pulled out her eyelashes one by one. All of them. She blinked like a little blind mouse," says Carmina fondly.

Carmina would not give in and would not give up. "Every day I asked Mamma where is Luigi," muses Carmina. "Every single day. Mamma would never tell me. She stayed in her room more and more. After the baby died, she was so sad."

"What baby?"

Carmina pauses and crosses herself. "Little Johnny. Our half-brother. He was born so small, with bad lungs and a hole in his heart. He died only a few months old."

After the baby died, Papa Johnny stayed away from the house, sometimes for days. The girls learned to make themselves invisible when he did come home, raging drunk and roaring at Mamma to get the hell out of that bed and behave like a proper wife. When no more babies were forthcoming, Mamma took to her room and stayed there. The house grew dingier and darker and dirtier after Johnny let the cleaners and other servants go. There were no more toys. The girls made do with their old clothes. Carmina picked apart dresses and blouses and re-stitched them to make them fit, as she had done in the orphanage.

"And again, rats!" laughs Carmina. "In this big fancy house we had our furry friends the rats. They ran over us in the night with their scratchy feet."

One day Johnny arrived with half a dozen rough-looking men. They hammered planks over doorways. After they left, the family lived in three rooms among the relics of their privileged life. In this way, five years passed.

Chapter 14

Alex and the aunts

My aunts, as I have mentioned, have been known to embellish their stories, dabbing a little plot pizzazz here and a tantalizing character twist there. This history is almost too dreary to believe. Carmina is still as a stone. Margherita dabs her eyes with a matching pink and peach hankie. I hug them both.

"That's a hideous story. I'm so sorry for all of you. I had no idea. You've never breathed a word of this," I say, eyeing them both. "In fact, you've spun some pretty fanciful tales of your childhood."

Carmina peers at me over her rhinestone spectacles. "These were bad times, times of the devil sent to steal our souls, Sophia. We try not to think about it. So we make up new stories, happier stories. Is it so wrong, to be happy?"

This is a lot to mull over. The happiness question I set aside to ponder later. Perhaps Carmina is right. Substituting bad times with good has worked for her. She is happier than three normal people put together. There are a lot of parts missing in Lou's story, though. As if reading my mind, Carmina squeezes my hand.

"We will tell you the rest of it, what Lou told to us," she says, "but not now. Later. Margherita and I, we are sad from remembering these bad times. Now, we like to play canasta. Oh and Sophie," says my card-shark aunt, dealing the hands, "I want you to tell us about Alex."

I nearly choke on my wine. "How do you know about Alex?"

Carmina looks up over her cards. "Lou telephoned me, I don't know, maybe two weeks ago? Such a surprise! I was so worried, I thought something bad has happened, maybe to Rose or to you, *mia bella nipote*. But it was good news. He was so excited, Sophia! I don't remember the last time I heard Lou so excited."

Not at my own coming. That was a different kind of excitement altogether.

"Well," I stall. What can I tell the aunts about Alex? I stick to the bare facts: height, weight, coloring, place of residence, type of work, name of dog, leaving out the whole fantastic carnival angle, trying my best to keep a neutral line on things. I fail. "I'm still not convinced this Alex is who he says he is. How do we know he's not some downunder con artist looking for an easy mark?"

"We will know," smiles Carmina. "If this man Alex has the Italian blood, the Sanzari blood, we will know." Then, like Dixie, they chorus in unison, "When can we meet him?" as if he is some bestselling writer or better yet, a visiting celebrity chef.

Tonight, is the short answer to that question. We are all dining at Lou's tonight. Alex will be there. The aunts slap down their cards and spring up from the table.

"We will cook!" cries Carmina, rummaging in the fridge.

"Oh, what a feast we will cook!" Margherita's eyes shine. *Pomodori ripieni* and *insalata verde*, from Lou's garden. *Pasta napoletana, minestrone di cavolo verza, calamari fritti, braciole di manzo.* All of Lou's favorite foods (mine, too), from fried squid to stuffed rolled steak, with *zabaglione* for dessert. No matter what happens tonight, we will all be as fat as pigs by the end of it. While the aunts are ransacking my scanty kitchen contents and compiling shopping lists, I call Dixie. I regret it immediately. She sounds tired and on edge.

"Jerome is still very ill with pneumonia, Soph. He's got some kind of vicious superbug. He's been in hospital for a week now, one entire, hideous, lonely week."

Her message is loud and clear. Why haven't I called to see how he's doing? Or how she's doing? There is no excuse except cowardice. I mutter about the aunts, stutter out an apology, and promise to call tomorrow before hanging up and fleeing to my bedroom. I sit on my bed, staring out the window at Sass stalking a robin. When I tap on the glass she ignores me, twitches her tail, and pounces. The robin flaps off in a tweeting fright. Sass glares at me through the glass. Of course it's my fault. So much is.

Tumultuous is the only way to describe our arrival at Lou's house. Mrs Woloschuk's door cracks open and a poofy red head pops out. I nod and she nods back, conspiratorially, reminding me that I have not checked in with her as promised. She flings open her door and starts puffing toward our happy group, but I shake my head slightly and briefly touch my finger to my lips. Her face falls. I watch from the corner of my eye to make sure she goes back inside. I can't risk her spilling the beans about our anti-Alex conspiracy.

Alex stands quietly amid the aunts' shrieking and hugging and Lou's excited jabbering. Lou pulls him forward. "This is Alex." He struts a little. "My son." I look away.

"Oh, so tall!" Carmina grips Alex by the elbows. That is almost as high as she can reach. "Come, Alex, let me look at you."

The aunts examine Alex from every angle. They run their fingers through his hair — so blond! — and peer into his eyes — so green! Alex calmly endures this cattle-buyer behavior from my aunts. I almost expect them to check his hooves for foot rot. If they believe he is the fruit of Lou's loins they're not saying. Like Mrs Woloschuk, my aunts clearly think he is a fine specimen of a man.

The aunts set about unpacking the shopping and stowing their overnight bags, chattering at us over their shoulders all the while. They've decided to stay with Lou for a couple of days, to visit their brother but also to whip Lou's house into shape after I let slip that things were getting out of hand in the mouse-dropping and dust-bunny department. It is typical of my elderly aunts to roll up their silky sleeves, despite my protests that I can deal with things (although I haven't).

My father and my aunts have made some kind of Sanzari pact to put aside any further talk of the past tonight. Try as I might I cannot drag another syllable out of any of them about what happened to the family.

"Later," whispers Carmina after my third attempt. "We'll talk another time. Now is the time for fun." 'Later' could mean anything from 'in an hour' to 'beyond the grave'. There is nothing I can do about it. At no point during our evening does the question of Alex's paternity arise, nor am I allowed to mention Lou's past. Carmina shakes her head gently when she sees me gathering up enough steam to delve deeper into the story.

I concede defeat and become as merry as any forty-something divorcée can be when drinking too much terrible wine with an unwanted half-brother and three elderly relatives in their eighties. It's the most fun I've had for a long time. If I could bottle my aunts' special brand of bonhomie I'd be rich and the world would be a better place. Lou, Alex and I have made a tacit truce which Carmina and Margherita seize upon and shape into something similar to an ordinary family gathering.

Salute! cries Lou at regular intervals.

Lou and my aunts all talk at once, mostly in such thunderous rapids of Italian I struggle to catch one word in ten. The aunts tell story after story about their children and Benson the labradoodle, and tut over the price of cheese. Carmina shrieks, Margherita giggles. Under an unusually heavy load of wine, Lou clowns around with whatever vegetable comes to hand.

91

Cabbage leaf hats, green bean mustaches. I crack up. Alex leans back and smiles.

Lou looks exactly like the little man made of fruit and vegetables on the sign for his now-defunct shop, Sanzari's Fruit and Vegetables Best Quality. Signor Patata was the little man, named for his potato head. Signor Patata had zucchini legs and carrot arms, peas for eyes, a cherry tomato nose, and a cucumber slice for a mouth. He even had celery tops for ears. Lou once made a Signor Patata just for me. I devoured him bit by bit. It was a fiendish way to coax me to eat my vegetables. Later, Lou cut out Signor Patata from a piece of wood and painted him to match the vegetables. He hung him up to amuse the urchins who would otherwise steal his oranges.

The three Sanzari siblings settle into parts from a long-running play: Carmina the bossy but benevolent eldest sister, Lou the bothersome but adored brother and Margherita the baby, beloved and sweet. As an only child I played all of those parts during my childhood, choosing them to suit my wants at the time. I demand a pony! If you don't give me a pony I'm going to run away. Please Mamma please Papa may I have a pony? None of them worked. I never did get a pony.

After several hours of high hilarity Lou starts drooping. The aunts insist "you young ones" run off and leave them to clean up. This is a generous if orchestrated gesture, but it's late and I'm tired. We say goodbye, *arrivederci* and even the Romanian *pe curând*, which the aunts coax out of a grinning Alex. Carmina and Margherita look like they could crank on all night. I have no idea how they do it.

When we are nearly at our cars, Alex turns to me.

"Your aunts are wonderful."

"They are," I agree, noting the 'your'. "They're very special. I love them both to pieces."

Alex jiggles his keys. "Sophie, I want to ask you something."

"Ask away."

"Tony's wedding is in December," he says in a rush. "In New Zealand. I would like to take Lou to the wedding. Can you think about it carefully before you object? No, please let me finish. I know it's a long journey for someone as old as Lou, but he's very keen to come on the trip. Tony really wants him to be there. I'll fly here and travel back with him every step of the way." He pauses. "You're invited too, of course, if you'd like to come."

I barely register this offhand invitation over the thousand protests clamoring inside my head. Lou is too old, it's too far, I won't allow it. As if I'm Lou's guardian and could stop him from doing anything he sets his stubborn old Sanzari mind to.

"Why didn't he tell me about this himself?"

Alex hesitates. "He wanted to avoid any more confrontations."

My face burns. Whatever I say won't matter. My Papa will hop on a plane to the bottom of the world with his supposed son Alex to meet his supposed grandson Tony, whether I agree or not. The look in Alex's eye stops me from spitting out my catalog of arguments. He is silently pleading and the closest he has come to humble since he arrived. I almost give in on the spot.

But I can't. Not without absolute, one hundred per cent proof that Alex deserves this much of Lou's life, and mine, too. Lou is not a separate package. He is still my father and Rose's husband. No matter what Alex says or does to win me over (and I admit, his steady-as-she-goes charm is chipping away at my resolve), if he is to stake out a place in our lives I demand to be convinced unconditionally.

"Okay. I'll say yes. Under one condition."

"What's that then?"

I look him straight in the eye. "That you take a DNA test to prove you're my father's son."

Alex's face shuts down, becomes somehow still and more inscrutably Eastern European.

93

"You really don't trust me, do you. After all the evidence, the things I've told you. The clipping I showed you."

"That's all very interesting, but it proves nothing. You seem like a pretty smart guy. You could have got that information somewhere else. And if you recall," I add, "you did say you'd do whatever it takes. Remember? In the café?"

Alex's mouth tightens. "I've been very careful with my investigations and research. I have waited a long time. I didn't want to cause problems for you or your mother. But if that's what it takes," he fairly spits, "that's what I'll do. I'd hoped Lou wouldn't need to be involved in this. He has to take the test too, as I'm sure you know. But I'll take the test. No problem. Does that satisfy you?"

I nod. Relief (the truth will now be known) and fear (the truth will now be known) wash over me. It occurs to me that since Alex actually agreed to the test, the truth might not be what I want to hear. Worse, Lou will be none too happy to be forced into this game. But it's the only way, I tell myself, to end this once and for all.

"I have one condition of my own," says Alex. "When the results come back positive, Sophie, you stop behaving like a spoilt brat and let me get to know Lou without any more of your interference. Time is running out. Lou is not getting any younger. I've missed out on knowing my father for an entire lifetime." Alex turns on his heel and strides off.

My cheeks sting as if I've been slapped. Alex takes out his cellphone and barks into it as he drives off. I have enough wits left to think that maybe, just maybe, the jig is up. Maybe Alex will find he's been called back to New Zealand on 'urgent business' before he's forced to cough up some telltale DNA proving he's not, and never was, my father's son.

The 'spoilt brat' jibe hit a nerve. That part lies too near the truth. A story springs into my head, the old fable about a frog and a snake and a pond. The snake asks for a ride across the pond on the frog's back. The frog sensibly declines, telling the snake he knows he'll bite him. No I won't, swears the snake. So the frog agrees. Of course the snake bites the frog and they both start sinking. Why did you do that, asks the dying frog? Now we'll both drown. I can't help it, says the snake. I'm a snake.

I'm not proud that our happy family evening with the aunts ended up this way. I should call Alex and apologize. When Lou hears about my latest demand from Alex, he might pitch me into the same no-speaking zone as Dixie. The thought makes me almost physically sick to my stomach.

Lou will forgive his only daughter. I guzzle some Alka Seltzer, flip open my laptop and start searching for DNA testing companies.

Chapter 15

Alex flees the scene

Carmina phones me at some brutal hour of awakening acceptable only to octogenarians. They are taking Lou out for a pancake breakfast, would I to like to meet them? Alex is coming to pick them up. I beg off, pleading work commitments, and promise to see them later. I do not want to see Alex, and I can't imagine he wants to see me.

With Alex and Dixie and Lou and Rose and the aunts filling up every space in my life I have ignored the PaintMeKidz range for too long. Burying my black thoughts I knock off all those cheeky colors with my perkiest kiddie-tempting labels. Pixie's Picnic (a pretty blue-green). The Fairy Queen's Birthday (pink, of course). Pirate's Treasure (a bold bronze). By the end of the morning I have finished the list and emailed it to Andy.

All this work is making me hungry. My stomach is threatening to start digesting itself unless I toss it a morsel, so I build a Parma ham and provolone on focaccia sandwich from the aunts' stock of goodies. The doorbell rings as I'm stuffing it down my throat. Alex is standing on the porch. He is not looking as cool and calm as he did a couple of weeks ago, or even last night. He looks frankly terrible: thin-faced, almost gaunt, and so pale he's nearly white. Persecution Pallid.

"Alex." I crack the door halfway open. "What's up? Is something wrong with Lou?"

"Sophie, sorry to come here unannounced. I have to fly back to New Zealand. It's urgent. I just came to tell you."

So. The jig is up. The thought of taking a DNA test has put the wind up him. He is fleeing the scene. As if reading my mind, Alex holds up a hand.

"I'll take the test, Sophie. It's not what you think. Tony is very ill. He has contracted meningitis. There's an epidemic of it in New Zealand this winter. I'm flying out today. Lou knows. I told him this morning."

"That's awful news, Alex. I'm really sorry." Despite my conflicted feelings, I mean it. I am not a snake. "How's Lou taking it?"

"He said, 'Tell Tony *guarisci presto*'," says Alex, doing a serviceable job with the Italian. There is no way Alex is lying about his son. It is all the man can do not to burst into tears.

"How bad is Tony?"

"He's in hospital," Alex wipes a hand across his eyes. "People have already died from this infection. Some babies and children have had their legs and arms amputated. It's the worst thing a father can hear."

"Oh my god, Alex. Is someone with him? Where's his fiancée?"

"Olivia is in London at a medical conference. She's flying back tonight. His mother is in Auckland." Alex stops short of a snort. "As if that's any help. She's not much of a mother. She walked out on Tony and me when he was a baby. I've been speaking to her on the phone but it's like talking to a brick wall. Anyway," he finishes abruptly, "it's not your problem. I'll be back soon, Sophie, and we'll sort this out once and for all. Take care of Lou." Alex gives me a nod and practically runs to his car.

The focaccia sandwich sits uneaten on the table. I've lost my appetite. Alex's words grind round and round inside my head, not about about Tony's fight with meningitis, although that is bad enough news for anyone to hear from halfway around the world. Something else Alex said churns in my mind.

She walked out when he was a baby. Tony is very sick. The worst thing a father can hear. She's not much of a mother. She walked out when he was a baby. She walked out.

I rush for the toilet and barely manage to flip up the lid before I am messily, violently ill.

All of us do things we are not proud of at some time in our lives. All of us do this, even the best people, among whom I do not count myself. Some people steal. Others tell lies that start out small but get knottier the more they try to cover their tracks. Soon they are so snarled up they choke in their own elaborate web. It is a relief when the truth comes out.

The thing I'm not proud of will never go away. It will never be resolved. The truth is already known. It is the kind of failing that makes you question the most secret part of who you are, makes you ask yourself what kind of person would do this thing.

Derek and I had a baby. There, I've said it. The baby was born sick and screaming and life-threateningly small. I was so tired, so very, very tired from a tearing birth that dragged on so long and so bloodily I wished I could die and get it over with. It was not the euphoric experience I had expected. I had a baby, but there was nothing to be happy about. I felt nothing for this child except a loathing so terrifying I could tell no-one about it, not even Derek. He coped better than I did with this frail, imperfect scrap we had produced.

I began to despise him too, my own darling husband who I loved more than anyone else on earth. I hated his gentle shushings and "just try to hold the baby, just try" and "it'll be all right, Sophie," when plainly nothing would ever be all right again. What kind of mother despises her own husband and newborn child? Especially a child so helpless and damaged that many operations would be needed and some vital parts would never function properly.

When the baby was six months old, I walked out. I abandoned them both. It was better for everyone that way. That's what I told myself then. It's what I tell myself now. After half a dozen years, it still sounds like a lie.

★

Lou's eyes are rimmed red. His voice quivers. Carmina and Margherita sit on either side of him patting his hands.

"So terrible, Sophie, Tony, he is in *ospedale*, Alex is so worry he fly away to New Zealand." He spits out that small, benign country's name as if it were a radioactive waste dump. "Why these things happen to good people, Sophia?"

My father is really asking, why is there always a price good people pay for being happy? It is a fair question. My attempts to untangle that one have failed. There are prices to be paid just for being alive.

"I'm sure Tony will be fine, Lou. He's Alex's son. He's probably a survivor like his father. Alex will make sure he gets the best care." I don't intend to tell Lou what I read this morning online. Four people have died of meningococcal disease in New Zealand this year and the epidemic is not over yet. The disease can kill within days. It's as if a medieval plague has erupted from some foul subterranean miasma. Still, Alex has enough steel in him to move mountains. Tony will get through if he has inherited one iota of Alex's willpower.

Lou hands me a photo of a smiling young couple taken on a golden arc of a beach on a clear blue day. "This is Tony. Also, his *fidanzata*, Olivia. Alex give me this photo before he leave."

Olivia is cute and brown-eyed and curly-haired. Beside her Tony shines like a silver sun. He is predictably blond and chisel-cheeked like his father, with that almond slant to his eyes and a wide, curving smile I immediately recognize as Tatiana's. His arm draws the girl in close.

"He's a very good-looking young man." I hand the photo back. "They're a lovely couple. He'll be fine, Lou. Try not to worry."

"Yes, try not to worry, Luigi," says Margherita.

"Let's play canasta," says Carmina.

I slope off to the sitting room while Carmina deals the cards. Lou's house is cleaner than it was on my last visit. The mouse poop has been furiously eliminated, the furniture gleams in an oily lemon-polish way and a vase of tiger lilies and white carnations brightens an end table. This is the way the house would look if Rose still lived here.

When I wander back to the kitchen Lou is looking perkier and there is a bit of color in his cheeks. Carmina pulls out a chair. "Sit, Sophie."

I sit. We smile at each other. "I'm so glad you're here. Lou is lucky to have sisters like you."

"It is good to have sisters and brothers in times of trouble." Carmina gives me a meaningful look.

I let it slide. "Tell me more about what happened, Lou, after the orphanage. Please?"

Lou, Carmina and Margherita glance at each other and grip Lou's hands tighter. Lou shrugs. "Why not. I am already sad."

Chapter 16

Minot, North Dakota 1928-32

After Mamma and Johnny moved to the big house and retrieved the girls from the orphanage, Mamma tried to get the boys back. For years she begged the Society to tell her where her boys were, just to tell her the name of the state they lived in, so she could look for them.

It was too late. She had signed the papers. She had given them up for good. The men in black assured her the boys would be better off with the fresh country air and wholesome food in the west, far away from the drugs and drink and gangs of New York. They would grow big and strong on milk and beef and butter in their new families. They would go to school. They might even learn a trade, like blacksmithing, or become farmers themselves.

Instead of a bright new life of fattened cows, Antonio's prediction came true. The boys were treated if not like slaves, then like unpaid farm hands. Life was tolerable at first. The Swedish farmer and his silent wife were neither the best nor the worst of foster parents. The couple had no children of their own. They had no idea what to do with one permanently bewildered and one permanently scowling Italian boy. They had hoped for Northern European children, Scandinavian or even German, some laughing little blond boys, not these dark, fey creatures.

On their first day in their new home, burrowed into straw in the barn, Antonio told Luigi the news he had been saving until no ears could overhear. Their Mamma was not dead. She was alive and living with the girls and a new man with a lot of money in a big house. Luigi cried and cried. Why didn't Mamma come for me? Why don't we live with Mamma?

"We are not orphans. Why we go on the orphan train? Antonio don't know. I don't know. We don't belong in that place." He thought about little Betty from the orphanage whose mother gave her away because the new Papa didn't want her. Luigi could not believe Mamma would do that, but maybe the new Papa was not very nice. Luigi didn't like the new Papa already.

For a few months Luigi attended the little country school (Antonio flatout refused to go — school was for sissies), walking an hour through the rough prairie grasses and biting ants. He shouldn't have bothered. The other children teased him relentlessly about his clothes, his dark wop ways and poor English, but especially about his ears, which were a delightful bonus to the bully boys. Nothing had changed. Children were as casually cruel in the country as they had been in the city.

Lou's sprouting hairy ears shocked the Swedes. What sort of creature was he? The kind best left in the barn, along with that tough dago kid who wore danger all over him.

"The farmer and his wife, they never know Antonio and me are brothers. They never know. We stick together but we don't tell them, so they don't take one of us away and give us to some other farmer."

From sun-up to sun-down the boys hauled water, cleaned the house, collected eggs, tossed hay bales onto wagons, dug holes, mended fences with barbed wire that ripped the hands, fed and milked the cows, shoveled snow from the road. At night they stumbled bone-weary to their beds of straw, to sleep with the farting pig. In summer, sun-up arrived only a few hours after darkness fell. Sometimes there was no point trying to sleep; the coyote howl and barn owl hoot kept the city boys awake until dawn. The summer sun scorched the skin off their backs as they bent in the fields. In the winter, the cold seeped so deeply into them Luigi thought his bones would break. He had never been so cold that spit froze on the ground and the skin of his hands cracked and bled.

The boys were fed just enough to fuel them for the next day's chores. The farmer's wife set their tin bowls on the doorstep. There was bread and some milk with the cream skimmed off and at Christmas, when Christian charity overcame her, a turkey wing with a bit of meat to share. The boys ate huddled together on the back step. The smell of roast beef or turkey and vegetables tormented them from the kitchen where the farmer and his wife bent over their full plates.

The farmer paid them attention only when the cow kicked over the milk bucket or the pig broke out of the pen. If Antonio was not around, he beat Luigi with whatever came to hand, a belt, a broom handle, the horse's reins, greasy and stinging with horse sweat. Once or twice a week Luigi heard the crack of a fist on bone and heard the farmer's wife quietly crying.

"Life was hard." Luigi gazes at his hands. "I cry every night, for Mamma. Antonio want to fight the farmer, but I say don't Antonio, you make things worse for me."

"So many children, snatched up and put on those trains," Carmina interrupts. "All those boys and girls, thousands and thousands, taken from their parents and sisters and sent to other people, even to Canada and Mexico. They were children! The Children's Aid people told Mamma they are part of the family, they would go to school in the week and church on Sunday. Not Antonio, not Luigi. In the big house, we did not know our brothers lived in the barn like animals."

English or Scottish children found better luck than the Italian and Irish children with their suspicious accents, heathenish Catholicism and tricksy foreign ways. On one of the rare days the farmer took the boys to town with him to help load the wagon with seed and bales, Luigi saw a boy, a plump-cheeked boy younger than himself, riding a pert little chestnut pony. Luigi recognized the boy as one of the kids wailing for their mothers on the train.

103

He was one of the lucky ones. The Swedish farmer kept a skinny black and white dog to hunt down rats, but after the dog chased the chickens he shot it and forced Luigi to bury the bloody bundle of fur.

The first time Antonio and Luigi ran away, they made it only to the next farm before the farmer came after them on horseback. The second time the boys ran away (this time walking all the way to the next town), the farmer took away their shoes until the first snow fell in September. He locked them in the barn at night with the cows and the pig and the lone bony horse. There was no more school for Luigi.

"Ten years old and no more school for me. What job can I do as a man, with that small learning? So many times we run away," says Lou. "Many many times. Summer, winter. We always get caught. Some other farmer tie us up and drag us back like cows. A few summers after we come to that place we run away, and he don't drag us back like cows. Maybe that farmer, he don't want us anymore. He already have too much trouble. The farm was bare dirt, nothing growing. The cow give no milk and the chickens die. Even the farmer get thin from no food."

On the day the well dried up, the farmer's wife hanged herself in the barn.

The boys joined the lines of ragged men who walked, hitched rides on wagons and hopped freight trains across America looking for the jobs blown away in the Great Depression dust. There were so many people stuffed into the boxcars that the boys climbed up and clung to the roof. The lucky ones stuck there; the unlucky fell off silently under the wheels. Sometimes families clambered aboard clad in burlap sacks, the thin women suckling infants no bigger than month-old kittens. The trains chugged past boarded-up towns and hobos huddled around stinking, smoky fires lit from tires.

Once, as the boys walked down another nameless road in another blasted state, a man in a sharp black suit gave the boys a ride in his car. The boys were excited. They had never ridden in a car. When the man in the black suit laid an exploring hand on Antonio's knee, Antonio punched him in the face and pulled Luigi out of the moving car with him.

"Antonio, he fight many times. Men try to steal our food, even our clothes. My shirt have more hole than cloth but still they try to steal it. These are very bad times for people, no work for anyone, and dust — so much dust! Everywhere, blowing, everything turns black. Nothing grow. If something grow, grasshoppers come and eat it all up. Men walk anywhere to find some little work, maybe on the railroad or digging a ditch. So many men, in dirty clothes like us. Sometimes they give us some bread or water and we give them a cigarette. Antonio, he know how to find things."

Antonio fought, blustered and thieved his way across the country, dragging Luigi along light as air, light as a bundle of sticks, the meat thinned from his bones. They fell off the train in New York one late autumn afternoon, two bundles of shoeless rags with eyes burned red from the dust and sun.

"They were standing on the step," says Carmina. "Luigi and Antonio, our lost brothers. They were so tall, well, not Luigi, but Antonio, and dirty and smelly. Luigi, he looked like a starving animal. We were scared to death of them." She pats Luigi's cheek.

"When we dragged Mamma to the door," adds Margherita, "she fainted dead away on the imported Turkey rug."

Chapter 17

Who knows about Rose

Tony is still in hospital. He is not doing well. The doctors worry about gangrene. They fear they may have to amputate an arm, or worse, more than one limb. On the phone Alex's tone is clipped, clinical. He makes me promise not to tell Lou how bad things are.

"Can you tell Lou I rang, Sophie? I'll ring him again soon when the news is better."

I picture the handsome young man with his arm around his fiancée. I mentally delete the arm. It is not an image worth conjuring.

"Of course, Alex. I'll talk to Lou. I'm so sorry."

"Tony's a fighter," he says abruptly. "He's going to win this one."

I have barely put the phone down when it rings again. It's Paula, from Dr Armstrong's office. They have the MRI results for Rose. Can Lou and I come in to see Dr Armstrong, please?

My heart plummets so far I can almost feel it hit my feet. "Can't you tell me the results on the phone?"

"Dr Armstrong would like to speak with you, and your father. Is he able to come also?"

"Ah, no, he's — he's unwell. He's very elderly and he's already had bad news this week."

There is a pause on Paula's end. "Well. Alright. I have a two o'clock slot available today. Does that suit you?"

"Okay," I breathe. "I'll be there." I phone Lou with the censored news that Tony is still in hospital. I talk to Carmina and ask her to keep Lou busy today. "Take him for a drive to the Berry Barn for some pie. He loves saskatoon berry pie."

Carmina agrees that saskatoon berry pie at the Berry Barn is a fine idea, although not quite as fine as whipping up a saskatoon berry tiramisu at home. I hang up before she can quiz me about why Lou needs babysitting today. Then I phone Dixie. There is no answer at home or on her cell. I leave a message, telling her about Tony and Rose's MRI. I ask her to call. She does not call back. I text her. She does not text back. It is not like Dixie to ignore a text. She is such a compulsive texter she even texts herself shopping lists. I have a horrible feeling that today will bring a hat trick of bad news.

The doctor's office is quiet and peaceful. It does not feel like a place where life and death play out in so many brutish ways. Dr Armstrong's gaze, when I am eventually admitted into the inner sanctum, is contemplative. When he explains the MRI results, I am so deaf with dread I have to ask him to explain it all over again.

Against all odds, Rose's stroke-damaged brain is fixing itself. That is not what Dr Armstrong says, exactly, but it's the message I grab hold of. A few tiny vessels in one part of her brain have knitted themselves back together, or maybe other ones have sprouted up to replace them. Whatever has happened, the MRI shows some activity that didn't appear on her last scan. He points out the different-colored parts on the scan. It is quite pretty in a Peppermint and Raspberry Swirl way. I picture little brain cells waking up like Sleeping Beauty and busily scooting around making up for lost time.

"The MRI shows some improvement in blood flow. We don't really know what this means in terms of her prognosis," says Dr Armstrong. "There is a slight, and I must stress slight, chance she might regain some function, but it also may mean we don't see any meaningful improvement at all. We'll continue to monitor her."

The boulder that has been sitting on my chest since Paula called rolls away an inch. I gabble my thanks at the doctor and fly out the door. Mel looks up when I burst into Rose's room. "Sophie! It's not Tuesday is it?" She glances at the calendar of cute kittens above Rose's end table. This one is the second calendar of kittens I've bought for Rose since she's been lying here in this small room. I explain to Mel what the doctor said, or at least my understanding of it.

"Well. That's some good news, isn't it?" She smiles and adjusts a gadget on the drip that feeds and sustains my mother. Mel is not as celebratory as I had expected, but she probably hears 'maybe good news' all the time. We both gaze at Rose. Her hair is starting to thin from lying on the pillow. Although Mel and the nurses' aides do their best with what's left, it still ends up in more of a fluffy white halo than the thick sleek coif she's worn since I can remember. My mother looks as she always does, peaceful but entirely absent. I don't know what I expected. Some outward stirring, a finger twitch, a sign to show us that those awakened brain cells are working full time to bring her back to us.

It is time to tell Lou. I've put it off so long I'm beginning to ask myself uncomfortable questions about my motives for not telling him. The purest motive is that I want to keep him from falling deeper into the pit of despond if it all comes to nothing. The most devious is that I want to keep Rose's awakening to myself.

Oh, Sophie.

Lou listens carefully to my explanation about Rose, and then he asks me to tell him again. I explain as best I can, trying to be positive but not too positive.

"Sophia. You say the doctor, he say Rose maybe get better? She wake up?"

"That's a lot to ask. It's hard to know, Lou, but this is the best news we've had since the stroke. Mel — you remember Mel? She saw Rose's eye twitch."

"When?" demands Lou. "When this happen? Do you see? Why you not tell me this?"

"Um, no, I didn't see it." I conveniently ignore the last question. Maybe he'll forget he asked it. "The tests show something's going on. This might be some good news after everything bad that's happened."

"Maybe *buona fortuna* for my Rosa." Lou looks thoughtful.

"We can hope for the best, can't we?"

"We always hope," says Lou. "But hope, she is never enough."

This is an unLou-like thing to say. He has often been unjustifiably cheerful in the years since Rose's stroke. He pats my arm absently. "I go to see my Rosa now. I see for myself this thing."

I dig around in my purse for my car keys. "I'll take you, Lou."

"No Sophia, *grazie* but I go by myself. Is best."

Best for whom, I'm not sure. Lou is not as much of a menace as Mrs Woloschuk on the roads, but he is slow on the reaction times these days. Still, if Dr Hodges says he is okay to drive, it's not my place to hobble him.

"There might not be anything to see," I warn him. "It all takes time."

"Time is no friend to old men, *cara mia*."

Lou has never cast himself in the 'old man' role, at least not in my hearing. It is a measure of how much Rose's stroke, the last few weeks of Alex and me squabbling, and now Tony's illness have sucked out of him. Running deep beneath everything he says and does, he misses Rose every day of his life. Forever is getting shorter all the time.

After Lou leaves I join the aunts, who are spluttering in uncomplimentary Italian over a Masterchef re-run cranked up to maximum volume on TV.

109

"Ah, Sophia. Here you are." Carmina points a knitting needle at the TV. "This silly man is making pasta so terrible not even a starving dog would eat it. Turnip and parsley in pasta? Pah. Here, come sit with us."

I sit, make small talk about Sass, exclaim over the disgusting excuse for pasta. I should tell the aunts about Rose, but that is best left up to Lou. Now that Lou is not around, it's my chance to winkle out their verdict on Alex.

"Carmina, now that you've met Alex do you think he's Luigi's son? He doesn't look like Lou."

"That means nothing," Carmina retorts. "Neither do you. You look like your beautiful Mamma. Maybe Alex does too."

"What do you think, Margherita?"

"He has very nice ears," muses my junior aunt, who is so averse to confrontation she's been known to walk around with her fingers stuck in her own ears. "Smooth and neat like seashells. Not hairy. But Alex looks like Luigi around the nose, I think."

This is ludicrous. The nose of Alex could be described as noble. The nose of Lou could, in a generous moment, be likened to a parsnip.

"But —"

"But what?" Carmina holds up a be-ringed hand. "My mind is sometimes tricked by slippery tongues telling me I should do this thing or say that thing or believe another thing. My heart never lies. My heart speaks the truth. This is what my heart tells me." Carmina folds her hands and sits back. Margherita and I wait for Carmina's heart to speak. After a torturous pause, it does, at length.

"When we were children I tried to protect my younger brother Luigi, but I was only a girl. Other children, mostly boys but girls too, they threw stones at him, called him names, beat him up all the time. Just for looking different."

We wait, and wait some more. "Carmina?"

"No interrupting, Sophie. This is a hard story to tell. Our Papa ignore Luigi on good days and beat him on bad days. He did not think Luigi was his own son. Papa did not want to know that such a deformed thing could come from his own seed, so he punished him. Papa was sure Mamma must have done something very bad to give birth to this creature, so he beat her too, until Antonio stop him.

"Antonio was Papa's favorite. He was so big and good-looking, like Papa. Luigi loved Antonio as much as any brother can love another. Antonio, he was embarrassed to have a brother like Luigi, but Mamma she tell him, you look out for Luigi. You are the oldest son. Take care of your little brother. Luigi has a big heart.

It is Luigi, not Antonio, who help Mamma and try to rescue little injured things, like birds and kittens. His big heart has room for everything and everyone in it. Everyone. Do you understand what I tell you, Sophie?"

It takes a moment to sink in. "You're telling me," I say slowly, "that you're not going to tell me whether you think Alex is Lou's son."

"Such a smart girl." Carmina pats my hand. "Let's have something to eat. All this *brutta* pasta on TV make me hungry for real food."

I cast a pleading look at Margherita. She smiles and nods. I will get nothing more from the aunts. Carmina's heart has spoken. If Alex makes Lou happy — and it pains me to admit, he does — then the truth does not matter. The path to happiness is paved with lumps of truth-fiddle.

Chapter 18

Dixie and Jerome's big surprise

Dixie is huddling in my leopard chair nursing a cup of coffee. She's been crying. Her mascara is smeared and her eyelids are so swollen her eyes have shrunk to dark holes. The skin around her left eye is a suspicious Violent Violet.

"Dixie! What's wrong? What's happened to your eye? Why didn't you tell me you were coming?" I drop my bag of leftover pasta and pull up a chair.

"I didn't know I was coming," Dixie blows into a tissue, "until I came. It's too hard, Sophie. I can't do this alone. Jerome is still so sick and I'm so tired, so very tired, darling. And The Sultan — he's so selfish. He doesn't understand. We had a fight. A biff bam socko fight."

"He hit you?"

"I threw a can of lobster bisque at him. I missed. He didn't. Whack! Right in the eye. I picked him up and tossed him out of the apartment. There was banshee-decibel yelling. A neighbor called the police." She sniffs, blows again, hard. "That's the end of The Sultan, the traitorous swine, the absolute, positive end of ends."

Good riddance. The Sultan, who hails from some tiny Middle Eastern emirate, isn't really a sultan, just the obscenely wealthy thirteenth son of one who got into some messy trouble involving an underage Filipino housemaid and was sent abroad to pester women elsewhere. Dixie did not

112

love him, the nasty weasel, but she was fond of his money. I wrap my arms around her, rocking her gently. It's an unsettling feeling to be the one doing the consoling. That's Dixie's job. I'm not sure I'm any good at it. I pat her hair, murmur there there, there there.

Jerome, she tells me, between sniffs, is still in the hospital. "He's already been incarcerated for two weeks, the poor little tyke." He's a tiny boy lying in a great big bed in a ward full of highly infectious children with deadly coughs and chokes and sneezes, which Jerome lives in daily danger of contracting, the longer he's kept prisoner among them. So she is bringing him home in a couple of days with a private nurse and intravenous antibiotics and a warning from the doctors that she is endangering her child's wellbeing, if not his life.

"He's not getting any better, Soph. He's not getting worse but he's not getting better. I can't leave him in there. He keeps asking me, Home, Mommy? It's breaking my heart."

"What can I do, Dixie? What would you like me to do?"

If she asks me to fly to Vancouver to help with Jerome, what will I say? If she asks to bring him here I don't know what I'll do. The last time Jerome visited was a five-star disaster.

It was a year ago, nearly to the day, I realize with a little shock, a stifling Saturday in July. One of those days that heats you up inside and out. Things had started as well as could be expected with a visit from Jerome and Dixie. Jerome played hide and seek under the kitchen chairs while Dixie and I chatted carefully about nothing important. I was sweaty and on edge and we both drank too much wine. When I stepped into the kitchen to open another bottle, something long and snaky waving outside the kitchen window caught my eye. I stuck my head out the window. What I saw turned my bowels to water.

Jerome was up on the roof capering along the edge like a mad dwarf. He had looped a piece of rope around one small foot and he was flapping his arms, squealing, "Bungeee! Bungeee!" The other end of the rope was attached to nothing at all. The rope swung back and forth in lazy reptilian loops.

It was my fault. Not the rope, the roofers must have left it behind. But I knew Jerome was coming. I should have put the ladder away. I pulled my head in and yelled for Dixie.

She strode into the kitchen, took one look at Jerome and swung both legs out the window. Her voice slowed, deepened. "Jerome, sweetie. Come down, darling." Jerome teetered on the edge of the roof, waving and shrieking, "Bungee Bungeeee!" His spindly legs pumped up and down. He lurched, caught himself, pranced some more. In my mind's eye I saw him spiraling off the roof.

Dixie murmured in her slow drawl, "Jerome, please come down, lovey. Please come down. Sophie has a surprise for you. Don't you, Sophie."

Jerome stopped his dance. "SophieSophie Suh Prize Sophie."

I croaked something that Jerome interpreted as a 'yes'. He started scooting backward down the ladder with the rope still swinging from one foot. Down below, Dixie stretched out her arms and murmured encouragement. I couldn't watch. I rummaged frantically in the kitchen drawers. A cork? No, Jerome had seen plenty of those. A piece of crumpled wrapping paper … aha, an ancient Christmas cracker. When I rushed into the room waving the cracker Dixie was slumped in my leopard chair with Jerome on her lap, rocking and rocking, her mascara smeared down her cheeks and her lips pressed into his fine quiff of hair.

"Sophie, sweetie, what an excellent Suh Prize. Jerome, you and Sophie pull, harder, yes! Wheee!"

The cracker popped open. Dixie retrieved the green and yellow paper hat and stuck it on Jerome's head. It sagged over his ears. She handed me the trinket from inside, a plastic bracelet with 'Love' spelled out in beads. I snorted but rolled it onto my wrist. "What about you, Dix?"

"I've got the fortune." She unwrapped it. "Happiness will be yours."

She crumpled up the paper and barked a laugh. "Oh god. Oh god. I hope so. I very very much hope so."

So much for fortunes in last year's Christmas crackers. A year later, Dixie is again sitting in my leopard chair looking the far side of happy. I bleat a bit more about Jerome, how can I help, what can I do. I sound unconvincing even to myself. Dixie pulls away, eyes me, wipes her face with a tissue, scrubbing off the mascara. Her eyes water. I'm ready with another tissue but she shakes her head. I have been tried and found wanting yet again.

"I'll sort it out Sophie, don't you worry. I've been in the wars and look, no scars. No obvious ones, anyway. I just had one of those moments and needed a friendly shoulder to blubber on. I feel better already, except some sadistic troll is pounding nails into my head. I'll take some painkillers, if you've got some."

I hunt up a couple of generic-brand tablets and a glass of water.

"Really, Sophie. And the antidote is where? Don't you have anything more sophisticated than those Victorian-era horse pills?"

"Sorry Dixie, It's either these or a frozen fish stick."

"Pitiless cow." Dixie swallows the pills and closes her eyes. She is asleep in minutes. Without those Dark Guinean Chocolate eyes drilling into me she looks beaten, vulnerable, and older. Her skin sags away from the slanting planes of those cheek bones I have always envied. I smooth a strand of hair from her face. She doesn't stir when I drape one of Carmina's crocheted afghans of many colors over her. My aunts are enthusiastic knitters of synthetic yarn in hues seen mostly in National Geographic photos. Acid Rain Rouge. Bruised Boxer Purple. Migraine Chartreuse. Beneath the afghan, Dixie is an exotic, wounded bird.

A real bird is singing in the lilac bush, a trilling, lilting song of summer. I stand outside in the sun listening, until the little tweeter spies Sass lurking behind my knees and flaps away. When I come back inside, Dixie has poured another giant mug of coffee and is tucking into a piece of Carmina's leftover *zabaglione*.

"This is divine, Sophie. Carmina is a top notch aunt. I'm claiming her for mine once you've finished with her. You can leave her to me in your will. So tell me sweetie, what's the latest in the Sanzari saga?"

"Don't you want to talk about Jerome?" There is something too bright and brittle about Dixie. I wonder if she has stashed some other little pills in her purse.

She shakes her head. "Don't worry, Soph. Truly, the dark shadow has lifted and a sapphire sky beckons. I'll get through it. Now, tell me everything."

"If you're sure —"

"I'm fine. Truly. Tell all. Don't skimp on the details. Give me the full story, with violins and drum rolls."

I bring her up to date on Rose's MRI, Tony's illness, Alex's sudden departure, Lou's despair, the aunts gamely holding us all together with canasta and pasta, and the abridged version of the Astonishing Life of Lou. Dixie listens and smiles, yahoos over Rose, frowns, and frowns some more when I mention the Swedish farmer.

"That's terrible. Truly awful, Soph. Beast! He should be shot."

"Dix, that's a bit extreme, don't you think? Besides, that happened decades ago. I'm sure he's already dead."

"Then dig him up and shoot him." She paces around the room. "There's no excuse for treating children like that." Dixie is such a good mother. All her friends know this.

Except she's not Jerome's mother.

No, Dixie is not Jerome's mother, which comes as quite a big Suh Prize to people.

Dixie is Jerome's father.

Chapter 19

Dixie, then and now

When Dixie was a man, she played football, drove a mail truck, fixed plumbing, built things out of wood. In her female form she curates a small art gallery in Gastown, dresses like a streetwalking rock star and mothers Jerome as fiercely as any lioness protecting the runt-cub of the litter. Her man-heart beat to steadying rhythms. Her woman-heart is an infinitely elastic organ.

Would Dixie have shape-shifted so completely if she had known the price she would pay? Her longest-running male companion, the horrible Sultan, is a miserable cad with suspect proclivities. Dixie's mother has disowned her, although that is a disputable loss.

The loss of Lou is greater. Lou regards Dixie as a person of evil, Satan's Number One Commandant. He will not speak a civil word in her company, nor does he allow me to speak about her.

For me, the world tilted on its axis once her shape-shift was complete. If I couldn't trust someone I'd known forever to stay true to the world I knew, whose world could I trust? It would have been easier to fall off (and I tried, many times, to let go) than to keep climbing, hand over hand, finger and claw, toward the unreachable. Still I cling on, my mind in mayhem and my heart burned to ashes.

Chapter 20

Lou and the aunts

The aunts burst into my house chirping and rustling their grocery bags. Lou follows them. His smile flips upside down when he spots Dixie.

"Hello, Lou. You're looking as dashingly Italian as ever."

Lou stands stone-faced by the door. Dixie shrugs and flings herself upon my aunts.

"Carmina, what an elegant frock! So stylish, I just adore pleats. You could teach that dowdy Eternal Monarch a thing or two about fashion. You look positively dewy, Margherita, how do you keep that baby-smooth complexion? That color is perfect with your skin." Dixie chatters with the aunts, spreading cheerful lies. "I walked into a low-flying elm branch, I'm thinking of suing the tree." She behaves as if there is nothing unusual about her bruised, swollen face and sudden appearance in my kitchen. Under the aunts' tut-tuts and coos, Dixie uncoils like a sleek black cat offering herself for a tummy rub.

Lou hasn't moved. "Sophia, I leave now."

"Come on, Lou. Dixie is my friend and my guest. Come in, sit down."

"I cannot stay in the room with this person." The screen door bangs hard enough to rattle the tea cups.

"I should find a hotel." Dixie gathers up her purse and jacket. "I don't want to start a Hatfields and McCoy-style family feud."

"You're not going anywhere. Where would you go? Lou will get over it."

The aunts whisper among themselves.

"Luigi, he's having the troubles," says Carmina. "Give him time, Miss Dixie, he will love you like we do."

"How much time, Carmina?" I smack the table. "I'm sick of him treating Dixie like she has some kind of disease. It's been five years. Where is this big heart with room for everyone you keep telling me about? How long do I have to put up with my father treating my best friend like some kind of freak? He of all people should know better."

"Oh Sophia," Carmina sighs. "Don't you *capisci*? That is why it is so hard for Lou to see Dixie. She's a beautiful girl, but, forgive me, *mia cara*, she is not a girl. She is something else. Like he is something else. That is why."

Dixie listens to all of this in silence. "That's a fascinating theory, Carmina," she says tartly. "But it's not true. I am a real female now. I've had the snip and clip, nip and tuck. Virtually all womanly parts are present and accounted for and available for doubters to view." To my horror she starts unbuttoning her blouse. She has definitely taken something else to numb the pain. Carmina stares. Margherita shuts her eyes.

"Dixie." I hold up my hand. "Stop. That's enough."

Dixie stops. She looks exhausted and so sad it nearly breaks my heart. "I'm sorry, Carmina, Margherita, I apologize. I'm dying for some sleep. Is it okay if I have a wee nap?"

"I didn't know," whispers Carmina, after Dixie is out of earshot. "About Miss Dixie. I thought she is a man in women's clothes. Like Mister Palutti in our building, number 618. Sometimes he wear dresses and makeup, and a blonde wig. He look terrible, he has a hairy chin and no style. Not like Dixie. Other people in the apartment are not nice to him. They call him Fruity Palutti." She sighs and starts unpacking the shopping bags. Margherita sits round-eyed and silent, plucking at the hem of her dress.

"Dixie is still the same person. It doesn't matter what's happened on the outside." I can say that now, and I mean it. In the beginning it mattered more than anything else in my life. If I can take Dixie as she is, anyone else surely can.

After her nap Dixie vanishes as abruptly as she appeared. I drive my aunts to Lou's house, intending to have it out with him over Dixie, but he's so depressed and weary and near-tears that I abandon the attack. Nothing happened during his visit to Rose. He sat beside her for an hour, maybe two, and nothing happened. I try to explain it is not as if she can open her eyes at will. Lou won't accept this. If she wants to return to him, she will do these things. It's that simple. If it were him, Luigi, trapped in that brain, he would summon the energy from every cell in his body to return to life with his loved ones. It sounds like a criticism of Rose, a failure of will. I try, and fail, to control my irritation.

"Give it time, Lou. These are early days. I'm sure Rose is trying her very best. What else would you like to talk about?

Tony and Alex. Alex and Tony. Tony is improving by the day. He is still very ill in hospital, but at least he's in one piece. His arms and legs are no longer in danger of rotting from too many bad germs and being chopped off like a tree branch. This is what Lou had come to tell me, before That Person forced him to leave his own daughter's house. Alex phoned him today to tell him the good news about Tony, and also the bad news that he'll be staying in New Zealand until Tony is out of danger and out of the hospital. I'm surprised to find I've got used to having Alex around, like an old sofa or a potted plant.

Lou's despond could fill buckets. Alex is gone. Tony is still ill, still *un po' 'morto*, as Lou puts it. A little bit dead. Carmina and Margherita, who have already stayed longer than they planned, are flying back tomorrow to their labradoodle and canasta tournaments.

"I'm still here," I point out. Here am I, your daughter, Sophie, the consolation prize. "It's your sisters' last day, Lou. What would you like to do before they leave?"

Lou mumbles something vaguely self-pitying, sighs, flops back in his chair. The urge to muffle him with a pillow is so strong I rush out the door before I do something else to add to my list of eternal regrets.

A robin pecking in the grass cocks a bright eye at me. No, he is just tilting his head, the better to pull an earthworm the size of my little finger out of the dirt. Lou's garden seethes with super-size earthworms going about their dim dirt-eating business. He could start a worm-farm to give himself something to do. I am mulling over the vision of Lou setting up an earthworm-selling stand on 8th St and Broadway (Sanzari's Vermi Superior Quality!) when Mrs Woloschuk huffs into view. She is pushing a supermarket cart stuffed to the brim with plastic grocery bags. The shopping cart rattles like a cattle truck over the cracks in the driveway. I hasten down the steps.

"What are you doing with that cart, Mrs Woloschuk? Where's your car? Here, let me help."

Mrs Woloschuk stops for breath. Her brow is slick with sweat despite the cool day and there are dark patches under her arms.

"No more car, Sophie. I heff anudder liddle crash, I hit a men's car, only a liddle bump but my car scrape some paint and make a dent, not too big, maybe like something I make if I kick it with my shoe, the man he say nasty things about my mudder, I call him idyot in Ukrainian, he call the policemens. On Monday, Lena take me to see the judge — so scary, Sophie, I nearly have the heart attack. The judge say, no more drive car. So I sell car. Not for much money. Lena say I can take tecksi to supermarket with money from car."

"Yes you can," I agree, although I wonder why Lena, that lazy perogy-puffed doughball of a daughter, couldn't give her elderly mother a lift now and then. "Why are you pushing a supermarket cart when you can pay for a taxi?"

Mrs Woloschuk puts a hand to her heaving bosom. "Why I should pay a tecksi when I am strong for walking home? Tecksi waste money. Pshaw. I save for senior siddizen bus trip to Florida dis winter. To geddaway from snow and see da beeyoodeeful flowers."

I refrain from pointing out that a) walking off with a shopping cart is theft, and b) she looks like she might keel over any second and never see the beeyoodeeful flowers of Florida.

"That sounds like a lot of fun, Mrs Woloschuk. I hope it all works out."

"How is your fadder? How is Lou?" Mrs Woloschuk eyes me keenly. "And dat man? You find out who is he?" she croaks in such a booming stage whisper that Lou could hear her behind closed doors with cotton balls stuffed in his ears. "So good looking, dat man," she sighs, irksome as ever.

"Lou's fine, thanks. I'm still investigating that man so I'd better go in. Nice to see you, Mrs Woloschuk."

"If you vant my help some more, you say, Sophia." She winks like a vaudevillian. Mrs Woloschuk is a survivor. I could learn something from her, apart from shopping cart theft and criminally scary driving.

Inside Lou is sitting up perky as you please chattering to Carmina, who is knitting another afghan, and Margherita, who is crocheting a tea cozy, or perhaps a sweater for a penguin.

Carmina glances up from her knitting. "There you are Sophie. We talk together, all of us, and we don't want to do something today. We stay here, with you, with all our family. Have a nice dinner. What do you think?"

"What a perfect chance to hear the next instalment of Sanzari family history before you two go home. All of you stay right where you are. I'll pour the wine."

123

Chapter 21

Hamilton, Ontario, Canada 1932-1940

After Johnny recovered from the shock of having two more of Maria's brats turn up, he tallied Antonio's assets. Luigi he dismissed as an irritation, just as he ignored the house falling down around him and the holes in the girls' shoes. Antonio was another matter. Road-tough and street-savvy, Antonio was 16 going on 26. Johnny correctly sized up this muscular teenage threat to his own manhood and made a phone call to a friend called Lucky. A week later Antonio again found himself on a train, this time to Canada, to start a job with a businessman named Perri in the city of Hamilton, Ontario.

"Are you talking about Lucky Luciano? *The* Lucky Luciano, head of the Five Points Gang in Manhattan's Lower East Side? And Perri is Rocco Perri, the Canadian bootlegger?" Nice Italian family turns mafioso. It is such a stereotype. "I can't believe it."

"You don't have to believe," snorts Lou. "If you don't want to hear this story I like to watch the TV."

"Sorry. I'm listening." I already knew a bit about Perri from writing a high school English essay about him, one that earned me an A+ and more scorn and abuse from those classmates with 'wog' primed on the tip of their tongue. If I remember my own words, Perri headed the Canadian arm of a Calabrian mob called 'Ndrangheta. 'Courageous man'. He fattened his wallet by gambling and running booze from his own breweries over the border, the better to relieve the suffering of the thirsty citizens in New York, Philadelphia and Chicago. With his handlebar moustache and silver-handled ebony cane, Perri was the picture of dandified prosperity. But Antonio had arrived at a bad time. Prohibition was running out of steam and Perri was running out of respect.

"Antonio, he send money to Mamma, not much but some. He never tell Mamma what job Perri make him do, and Mamma never ask. Mamma hid the money from Johnny. All he do is drink it away."

Luigi and the girls kept their heads down and out of Johnny's clouting range. As soon as she could, Carmina found a job in a laundry. Luigi ran errands, helped Mamma with the housework and kept an eye on Johnny when the girls wandered into view. Then one Sunday after church, Johnny vanished.

"Mamma she wait for him to come home for Sunday dinner, but no Johnny. She wait and wait, two days, three days. We never see him again."

A week later a man in a tight black suit and a black hat yanked open the door without knocking. He ordered the family to pack up and get out. The house was no longer theirs. Johnny had debts. With Johnny 'vanished' and the family turfed out of the house, the debts were paid. But don't try anything funny, he said, eyeing the girls. There might be consequences.

"Mamma was so scared. These are not nice men. She dig up Antonio's money from under the apple tree and she buy tickets for us all to go to Canada. We all go on the train. Mamma say to the Canadian people we have family in Canada who will pay for us to live there. Her son has good job working on the railroad." An inventive lie, but it worked.

Antonio found a small, run-down two-room apartment in Hamilton's Little Italy for the family to live in. After much wheedling and arguing he persuaded Perri to let Luigi 'work' with him. Perri wasn't keen on bringing the hairy-eared little freak into the game. The bootlegging business had collapsed with the end of American Prohibition. Perri's gambling and betting empire hadn't yet borne fruit. Things were tight in the criminal world, too. Still, the King of Bootleggers had to keep up appearances.

Luigi had no skills except a quick brain, a tight lip and an endless capacity to do what he was told. As personal servant to Perri and his live-in lady, Signora Annie, Luigi started every day the same. He sluiced water from the outside pump over his face, pulled on his only pair of trousers, a wash-worn white shirt and a black serge suit jacket rubbed shiny along the lapels and pockets. The clothes were too warm for the muggy spring days but Signor Perri insisted his 'boys' dress the part. When Perri's driver showed up one morning wearing a navy tie instead of a black one, Perri's henchman shot him in the hand. *Quello è un bastardo!*

So Luigi followed orders. Load crates onto trucks. Carry Signora Annie's shopping baskets. Polish the doorknobs of Perri's big fancy house on Bay Street.

"Nineteen rooms, that house have. Nineteen! Who needs so many rooms? Signor Perri and Signora Annie, they have no children. He have no children with his first wife either, that Bessie. She die in gangland murder, in her own garage."

The King of Bootleggers was a decent sort of criminal, a dapper gentleman who spent his bootlegger loot on fuel and food for hundreds of Italians left desperate in the Depression. His thugs for hire were another matter. After an all-day drinking binge, Perri's right-hand man forced Luigi to kneel at his feet and lick his wingtips clean.

"I do what he say. I don't make trouble. Antonio, he look away. He is embarrassed to know me, his own brother."

Antonio could charm the skirts off women, convince any man to open his wallet, and throw his fists when the wallets didn't open quickly enough. One day Luigi saw Antonio whip out a knife and slice off a rival gang member's ear.

126

"I am so shocked. I tell Antonio, what you doing? This is bad trouble. Antonio, he have so much money from Perri. He do what he want. I am afraid for him, and a little bit afraid of him, too."

When Antonio beat one of Perri's debtors unconscious for not giving him the answer he wanted, it was too much for Luigi. He quietly left Perri's gang. He left the flat he shared with Mamma and the girls and rented a room in a men's boarding house. He cooked an egg or a bit of bread over a candle for his dinner, chased away the cockroaches, gazed thoughtfully at the fat mice scampering along the baseboard. Every day, he looked for work. Every day, there was nothing.

One Saturday morning in August, Luigi plucked up enough courage to ask the vegetable seller, Manolo, for a job. Manolo, who had creaky joints and one lazy eye and no sons to help push his barrow, laughed in his face. Then he said, *Sì, sì* okay but I cannot pay you. At night Manolo taught Luigi all there was to know about the ripeness of peaches and the fleshiness of melons. During the day Luigi pushed the barrow for Manolo, calling out in the streets. *Pomodori*, fresh tomatoes.

Every week he visited Mamma and the girls. Luigi brought them wilted lettuce and spotty apples, sometimes a few dollars, but Antonio was rolling around in so much loot Mamma took nothing from Luigi. Save your money, she said. Luigi scrimped and saved every penny until he had almost enough money to buy the elderly Italian's barrow.

"For my own cart for to sell-a the vegetables." Lou's eyes are moist. "My big dream is to be my own boss. Not take orders from anyone. Not-a lick anyone's shoes."

Then war broke out in faraway Europe, trapping the Sanzari family in a world beyond imagining.

Chapter 22

Lou blows his top

I drove Carmina and Margherita to the airport this morning, said my farewells, and cried like a ten-year-old on the drive back. The aunts were both unmercifully cheerful.

Arrivederci, mie amate zie, ciao belle. Sii felice, take care of Lou.

If even a tenth of what Lou has told me is true, Lou is in line for some pampering in his declining years. Rose performed this job with love and dedication and a simple kindness that I have not inherited. I wonder how much she knew of Lou's history. It's a struggle to link this brutal, surreal tale to my skinny, ordinary-looking (apart from the ears) Papa, who sits at the kitchen table dipping his biscotti in his milky coffee and sighing.

With his sisters vanished to Toronto, Alex disappeared to New Zealand and Rose refusing to surface on command, Lou is difficult to entertain. I suggest outings to the Berry Barn, an Italian movie festival, a visit to his friend Nico's hothouse rose gardens. None of these appeal to my morose Papa. Weeds launch an assault on his vegetable garden, which he fails to defend. His moods yo-yo so alarmingly I'm on the verge of making an appointment for him with Podgy Hodges for some stress-relieving substance.

In a ridiculous bid to take Lou's mind off things I invite Mrs Woloschuk over for coffee. This does not go well. Lou is in no mood for her endless chatter or her wild bush of hennaed hair or her lumpish offerings of fresh potato perogies. He is barely civil and Mrs Woloschuk, who is usually impervious to insult, is visibly hurt. I see her to the door, whispering my apologies for Lou's grumpiness, which I shamelessly blame on 'dat man,' and promise to bring her up to date on developments. Soon.

'Dat man' phones daily. This is the highlight of Lou's routine. Today's bulletin: Tony is out of hospital and resting at home under the professional and caring eye of Olivia. Tony walked today. Tony is eating his favorite dish, lamb shanks. According to Lou, now that Tony is out of the woods Alex sounds like his usual self again. It's bedeviling that Lou even knows what Alex's usual self is, given their short acquaintance.

"Alex say Tony, he get stronger every day. He even laugh sometimes, and have the little walk. Alex, he say he come back for visit soon. When Tony is okay, then he come."

Tony either has superhuman recuperative powers or else Olivia has a miracle worker's touch. Within a week Tony is deemed fit to return to his world and Alex has beamed himself back into ours. I tot up the number of trips he has made across the planet in the last few weeks. Peddling pesticides must be profitable. This latest is a short visit only, to make sure Lou is as healthy and happy as he can be, given the recent worrying circumstances.

It's a stretch to say I'm pleased to see Alex again, but it's a relief to share the load. With the second (or is it third) coming of Alex, Lou perks up. He even plucks a dandelion or two while we sit outside in the searing July sunshine. Listening to the two of them make pleasant chit chat about Tony and the wedding is infuriating. I can't help myself. If I'm ever going to talk to Lou about the DNA test, the time is now.

"Lou." I jump into a rare lull in their conversation. "Alex and I have something to discuss with you." Alex shakes his head slightly. I pretend not to see.

"Alex has offered — well, he's agreed to take a test."

"What kinda test?" demands Lou. "For the driving? Alex is-a good driver. On the wrong side of the road, even. Not even one-a accident he have. Not like Mrs Woloschuk. She crazy, that woman."

"No, no, not that kind of test." I could stop now. It's not too late. Alex watches me carefully.

"To be the Canadian, that test?" Lou's face lights up.

"No, Lou. It's a, a DNA test," I rush on. "To make sure he's really your — um, to make sure he has Sanzari blood. Just, you know, a formality. It's an easy test, you give a little bit of spit and so does Alex. It's not painful. Then we send the samples away. We'll have the results in a few weeks and then we'll know."

"No! No test!" Lou bolts from his chair so fast it tips over and slams onto the floor. "Why you do this, Sophia? Why you make so much trouble? Alex is my son. Why you not believe this? Why you not believe things I say?"

I could reel off a long list of reasons why we need this test: Alex's story is shaky, there's no real proof, Alex looks nothing like him, he could be anyone's son, and on and on, but Lou's fury radiates off him in waves. He actually shakes his fist at me. Alex lays a hand on Lou's shoulder.

"It's okay, Lou," he says quietly. "Take it easy. I've already agreed to this test. There's nothing to worry about."

"Sophia — she the one with the bad blood. Always she make trouble, always. She make trouble between me and Rosa and now with you, Alex. I want to be happy, and every time she ruin things. *Basta! Vattene!*"

Lou's rudeness sprays over me as if I've been spat on. I gather up my purse and keys and walk out, dashing away tears. I'm weary down to my bones from parrying with Lou. He's right. *Basta.* Enough. I am leaving, as ordered. I may never come back.

The river is still running high this summer. There are floods to the south and torrential rain is forecast, says the voice of doom on the car radio. Black clouds drag their dark underbellies across the western sky. I can almost smell the electricity in the air. I park my car near the weir, where pelicans dive for fish in the roiling waves, where once a young nurse was found murdered and buried.

I shiver and start to walk. I walk and walk, faster and faster. I burst into a run. My purse flaps off my shoulder and my feet hurt in my three-inch heels. Joggers and cyclists give me a wide berth. I run and run until I skid on fresh dog turds, twist my ankle and tumble in the dirt and leaves. A jogger stops. I bark something rude and wildly wave him on. He takes off as if he's escaping a lunatic, which he is. The heel of one shoe is broken. The knee of my favorite jeans is torn. There is dog turd on my sleeve. I drag myself up a birch tree and limp back along the path in my broken shoes. The car is only an arm's length away when the gathering clouds burst in an ear-banging clap of thunder. The summer rain drenches me to the skin.

When I was six, Lou drove me to a birthday party. I wanted Rose to take me, but she was in bed and feverish with a snotty cold I'd brought home from school. The party was for my friend Sandra, who I didn't really like and wasn't really my friend. Sandra had rolls of fat on her neck. She wore prissy white ankle socks with ruffs. Most of the time her finger was stuck so far up her nose she could have poked out her eyeball from the inside.

Sandra had been forced to invite all the little girls in our class to her birthday party, on orders from her mother. I was forced to put on my too-tight black patent leather shoes and my green gingham dress trimmed with white rickrack, on orders from my own mother. It'll be fun, Rose said, laughably uninformed. How do you know it will be fun? I whined. You don't know Sandra, I added darkly. She picks her nose and flicks the boogers.

You're an only child. It's good for you to be with other children, said Rose, ignoring the booger remark.

That, too, was an argument of dubious merit, like saying cooked liver is good for you. When I wasn't wishing for a brother, I liked being an only child. Other children were loud, obnoxious aliens who deserved to be eaten by bears. It would be rude to refuse this invitation, Rose admonished. That was the end of the discussion. Rose would not tolerate rudeness.

Rose had given me two dollars to buy a gift for whiny, booger-picking Sandra. I resisted the temptation to stock up on a year's supply of candy necklaces and skip the party altogether. Instead I drifted through the aisles of the local hardware store, my two dollars clutched tight. After deliberating over a goldfish bowl (without goldfish) and a set of two plastic ice cubes in the shape of pink elephants, I chose a small china poodle. The poodle was blue with gold glitter on its knobby china ears and pom-pom tail. The man at the store wrapped the china dog in a square of pink tissue with a blue bow.

Lou drove me to the party in silence. In my child-eyes Lou was worse than hostile to me in those early years; he was indifferent. Hostility took effort, indifference did not. He and Rose chattered to each other all day long, but when my father and I were alone Lou could never think of a thing to say to me, except 'How was-a school,' which didn't apply in this case. His ears, I noticed with alarm, were hairier than usual since Rose had taken to her bed. I stared out the window at the leafy elms and big stone houses in Sandra's street, feeling the black hand of doom squeeze my chest.

Things would have been fine if Lou hadn't insisted on walking me to the door. I can go by myself Papa, I said, almost begging. You can go home now. Mamma might need you.

Lou rang the doorbell. The door opened. A dozen little girl faces stared up at Lou. Then one of them started to giggle, and another, and soon the whole bunch were laughing and some were pointing. By the time Sandra's apologetic mother arrived to shush them back inside, I'd thrown the china poodle onto the steps, smashing it to bits, and ran down the street in my pinchy-toed shoes. After ten minutes of frantic searching Lou found me hiding beneath a cotoneaster hedge, blubbering into my rick-racked sleeve. We drove home in a shamed, despairing silence throbbing with words unsaid. Lou told Rose I felt sick in the car and had asked to be taken home. My red eyes and blotchy face backed up the lie. Lou never drove me to a party, or anything else, again.

In that cruel and one-eyed way of children I blamed Lou, not the laughing little brats, for the party debacle, for the relentless teasing at school afterwards, for the brother I never had to protect me from the laughing little brats. Children just want to fit in. With a hairy-eared father like Lou, I never could fit in. I never said I was ashamed of him, but I knew, and he knew.

I was convinced that Lou would talk to me if I were a boy. I imagined our companionable chats: let's go down to the river and catch-a the fish, let's go camping in-a the tent in the back yard. Let's do something together, just you and me, Papa and Sophie. Later I realized, with an ache, that gender wasn't the only reason we didn't talk. Lou and I just didn't get along. The distance between us stretched into an ever-thinning filament that snapped us closer only when I married Derek and upped the chances of a grandson.

Lou wants to be alone. Alone with Alex, that is. Lou hasn't called me, nor have I picked up the phone to call him. I do know that Tony is recovering well enough for Alex to stay in town a little longer, so he's checked out of the hotel by the river to move into Lou's spare room. This subtle territory-grab bothers me less than it should. Sharing the parental-care burden isn't such a bad thing. Alex plays reluctant go-between between

Lou and me, phoning daily to report Lou's state of mind. My estranged father is happy, eats well and laughs a lot, when he's not crying. If Alex is having second thoughts about claiming a place in our nutty family, he's not saying.

I understand my father's reaction to the idea of the DNA test. Lou must be worried that Alex is the product of another one of Tatiana's dalliances and not his spawn at all. He doesn't want to know. After all these years of having a daughter, he is still desperate for a son. Losing Alex is as unthinkable as losing Rose.

It is tempting to wave the white flag of surrender, to believe Alex's story without any further shots fired from the cannon. No. As exhausting as this battle is, I can't let it go. After a last bit of soul-searching, I've ordered the DNA test kits for Lou and Alex.

I've also ordered a test kit for myself, without telling Alex or Lou. It's an extravagant expense. The dishwasher still isn't fixed, Sass is due for her annual vet check-up and one of my fillings is threatening to fall out the next time anything sticky comes near it. I've been thinking it over for days. The pros outweigh the expensive cons. Coughing up the several hundred dollars for the test will be worth it, I tell myself, when I present my results to Lou and Alex as a magnanimous show of solidarity (if, heaven forbid, Alex's results are positive) or a triumphant aha! if they're not. There's no harm in using solid science to remind Lou that I am his only daughter, and not to be disowned.

Alex has agreed to stay until the kit arrives and the samples are sent away. We haven't discussed how to persuade Lou to supply his part of the test, if Alex can't coax him into it.

Dixie calls to say Jerome is mending like a trooper. We're all rainbows and star-shine over here, she trills. I choose to believe her, despite the worrying wobble in her voice. What about The Sultan, I ask. Have you given him the boot? Oh, The Sultan, she laughs. He's next on the 'to-do' list. Truly, darling. I'll break it off. Tomorrow.

On my visits to Rose I tell my mother only pleasant, boring things. I tell her I'm thinking of painting my kitchen in one of PaintMe's new season's colors. I named it Eye of Sprite, a pale but nippy green. I don't tell her about the bad things: a suicide bombing in London, planes crashing, my fight with Lou, which throws all world disasters into meaningless shadow. Instead I hold her hand and talk about the weather. I watch her face. Something is happening, I'm sure of it. Something I can't see is building up from deep inside. One day Rose will move. She will open her eyes and smile. I will be there to see it.

Summer has ramped up. I burn my bare feet on the concrete walking to the mailbox. Sass forsakes the forbidden pleasures of the outdoors to lie inside on the cool tile floor in the bathroom, rousing herself occasionally to check for heat-doped prey that may have blundered in through the cat door. During the day I take my laptop outside on the deck. PaintMe has branched out into wallpaper; my latest assignment is to name the new retro range. Tangerine Twister. LottaDotta. Hey Hey Paisley.

In the evening I slather myself with bug repellent, stoke up a smoky fire against the mosquitoes, and gaze at the stars. Last night I woke up on my lounger, cold and mozzie-poxed, as the aurora borealis danced its electric green and pink fandango above my head.

Without Lou to worry about, life is surprisingly peaceful, even fun. Never underestimate the healing power of a good long break away from those you love, I tell Dixie on the phone, before hastily explaining that I don't mean her. Now that I don't have to feed Lou, visit Lou or do Lou's shopping I have lashings of time on my hands. This morning I have a mad craving for a cinnamon bun and an even madder desire to make some myself. Baking was Rose's forte. She has a knack with yeasty dough which I have not inherited, along with the kindness. Our baking sessions together usually ended in cookies I could break a tooth on (and did once) and pie crust so flabby not even the birds would eat it.

I rummage around for my one apron, a frilly orange and green Christmas gift from Dixie that arrived with explicit instructions to wear it strictly with high heels atop my sexiest underwear. I sling it over my T-shirt and jeans and set to work.

The yeast rises like yeast normally does, puffy and pungent, but when I shake the flour out of the bag it explodes all over me like a stomped-on puffball. The teeny heart-shaped bib on my apron is not up to protecting me from flour bombs. I brush flour off my face and chest and ponder the baking bowl. Did I put in the sugar? I taste the dough. No sugar. I toss in another cup. When I crack an egg I manage to drop it on the floor, where it stares at me with an accusing gloopy eye before bursting its pale yellow yolk and seeping into the cracks.

I'm trying to mop up this mess with a paper towel when the doorbell rings. I ignore it. No-one comes to my door at this hour — or any hour — except Jehovah's Witnesses brandishing *Watchtower* magazines or big-eyed Brownies offloading cardboard-flavored cookies. The doorbell shrills again. I yank open the door. Alex is standing on my doorstep. He eyes my floury face and slimy hands.

"Is this a bad time, Sophie?"

"Of course not, Alex. I always look like this. No, everything's fine, I'm just in the midst of a little baking disaster."

He waits. I wait. He shuffles from foot to foot.

"Oh, sorry. Would you like to come in?"

I push open the screen door. Alex is casually jaunty in an open-necked robin's egg blue button-up shirt. He has shed the white gangster shoes for those brown leather slip-ons worn by boatie types who live near large bodies of water. His legs are brown and long beneath park ranger-type khaki shorts with pockets. He looks as relaxed as if he were on a summer holiday instead of being incarcerated at the Sanzari Elder nuthouse.

"Shorts, Alex?" I raise an eyebrow. "You're in boots and jeans country, you know."

"I don't understand that. It's much hotter here than in Auckland. Everyone wears shorts in the summer down there."

"Guys here have such skinny white legs they'd rather drink antifreeze than wear shorts. So. Why are you here?"

Alex shifts against the door jamb. "You're nothing if not direct, Sophie. I admire that. I'm here because Lou sent me. He misses you."

I snort like a piglet. So undignified, but I can't help myself. "Right. He misses me so much he sends a messenger to tell me he misses me. He hasn't called me for a week. And you know what? I haven't missed him either. It's nice and peaceful here by myself." I scrub some dried dough off my apron as I lead Alex into the kitchen.

"Sophie, all families have problems, trust me. Lou is headstrong but that looks like a family trait from what I can see."

"Flattery will get you nowhere, Alex."

"Can you give it a try, Sophie? Lou won't be around forever."

I refuse to think about that. It's bad enough having one mostly dead parent. The dough gives a yeasty wheeze and collapses.

"That does it. I'm done with baking."

"Not a success, then."

I toss the dishtowel in the sink. "Rose is the baker. I'm just the daughter of the baker."

"Look, Sophie. Come over for afternoon tea and a piece of Ukrainian bread. That chatty lady next door, what's her name, Ox- something, brought it over."

"Oksana to her friends. Mrs Woloschuk to the world at large."

137

Either Mrs W is trying to woo Lou with loaves of love, or she's wangling her way into the house to spy on Alex.

"She's quite the lady," he says. "She reminds me a bit of my Romanian grandmother. She also loved to talk. My grandmother brought me up after my mother died."

I look up from scraping the dough into the garbage can. "Really? That must have been tough. Did she live in New Zealand with you?"

Alex closes his eyes. For a moment I think he's not going to answer.

"No, she didn't. After my mother died I was sent back to Romania. The carnival didn't want me around. Romania in the '60s, The Ceauşescu years — it's something I don't talk about much."

"Why? Was it that bad?"

"Worse than bad. My grandmother had a small farm but the communists took it all. She worked like a slave in the fields. We both did. She died when I was sixteen. The doctor said it was a heart attack, but it was starvation. We had practically nothing to eat."

Am I the only one in this Shakespearean tragedy with a relatively normal upbringing? I'm beginning to understand what drives Alex to plant his flag in our family patch. The difference between our childhoods presses on me. While I pranced around reading books and complaining about being forced to eat Lou's fresh vegetables Alex and his grandmother labored like slaves, scratching in the dirt eating what, I don't know. Snow? Insects? The little bit of Romanian history I've read is steeped in blood and brutality.

"That sounds diabolical. You've had quite the tough life."

"We all have our troubles, Sophie. Enough about that. I really came to tell you that Lou has agreed to take the DNA test. It's taken all week to convince him, but this morning he said yes."

I stop scraping the dough. "Why didn't you tell me that before? He's agreed to this willingly?"

"Grudgingly."

"Well. Good for you. Alex." I search his face for a clue. "You must be extra confident about this test."

He twists a ring on his finger — not his wedding finger — around and around. "I am confident. I believe my mother. Why would she lie? This is a good thing, Sophie. I'm happy to do this, if it settles things once and for all between us."

"We'll see." I can't help myself.

"I know you're reluctant to accept what's happened, for your own reasons. Maybe someday you'll explain them to me. I want to know Lou better. I'm not here to cause trouble or get between you and your father."

"Too late," I blurt. Oh crap. The gate between my brain and my mouth has malfunctioned too often lately. "Alex, I didn't mean —"

Alex heads for the door. "You're always welcome at Lou's whenever you want to visit. And Sophie," he calls over his shoulder, "he's ready to talk about the next part of his life story, about his time in the internment camp. He'll tell me whether you're there to listen, or not. Suit yourself." The screen door whacks shut.

Damn the man. He has turned out to be a real conniver. I pull on a clean T-shirt, grab the package that arrived from Pennsylvania yesterday and set off in hot, cranky pursuit.

Lou and I have laid down our cudgels, sheathed our swords, holstered our pistols, thanks to Sheriff Alex's measured justice. Lou greets me formally, not quite shaking my hand but not kissing me either. Someone, Alex I imagine, has laid out Mrs Woloschuk's bread with some butter and saskatoon berry jam along with, optimistically, three plates and three cups. We talk about the weather. Lou and I are exquisitely polite. I don't dare bring up the topic of the wretched test.

After we've finished our coffee and chewed through Mrs Woloschuk's fruity loaf, Alex nods. I set the two tests on the table. Alex and Lou carefully swab their cheeks and pop the swab in the container. I keep my

139

eyes on Alex's swab, on the alert for some tricky sleight of hand. I spot nothing amiss.

"That's all done. I can mail these on my way home. We'll have the results in a few weeks."

Alex and Lou both give me a look.

"I'm not going to switch samples," I huff. "That only happens in the movies." It is tempting, I admit. There is a spare swab in the kit. I could bribe some stranger, or even swab Sass.

Lou waves away my attempts at cheer. "Sophia. You take-a these test, send them away. Then we know the truth."

Alex clears his throat. "That's a done deal, then. Remember what I said, Lou, there's nothing to worry about."

Lou is not convinced. He shuffles around the kitchen, picking up dirty dishes, wiping imaginary stains from the counter. Alex guides him to his chair at the head of the table and sets another cup of coffee in front of him.

"Lou, please try not to think about it. Let's talk about something else. What about your life in Ontario? We're keen to hear about that, if you're up to it."

Lou glares at each of us in turn.

"This-a life, she is like a bad movie, only bad people are in it. You want to know, I tell you. Don't say I no warn you."

Chapter 23

Petawawa, Ontario, 1940-1943

Drifting in a deep and dreamless sleep, Luigi did not hear the heavy steps in the hallway or the knock on the door. He had woken, as usual, at dawn. He'd pushed Manolo's barrow, piled higher than his head with new lettuce, carrots and potatoes from the Chinese market gardens, pushed it up and down the streets of Little Italy until twilight fell inky and close around him. It was another day like all the other days. Wake up at dawn. Push the barrow. Sleep.

At the end of this day, the tenth day of June 1940, at a few minutes past midnight, Luigi slept through the knocking on his door until the door flew open and slammed against the wall. Luigi jumped out of bed, wide awake and scrabbling for the thick pine plank he kept under his bed for emergencies.

"I think it is Perri's men, they find me and make me pay for leaving the gang." Lou's hands tremble on his coffee cup. "I am fear for my life so I try to escape."

Clad only in his undershorts, he wriggled halfway through the bedroom window before rough hands dragged him back.

Yer not goin' anywhere ya filthy wop. Where's that wop brother of yers?

Luigi didn't know where Antonio was. Antonio lived his own life now; Tony Sanzari was one of Perri's favorites. Luigi hadn't seen him for more than a year. When he tried to tell the men this, one of them punched his face so hard his ears rang like Christmas bells. Before his eye swelled shut Luigi spotted the badge and blue serge uniform of a police officer. Not Perri's men, then. What had he done wrong?

If Luigi had not been sleeping the sleep of the innocently exhausted, if he'd been awake at ten o'clock that evening, he might have been listening to the radio he'd found in a rubbish dump and laboriously fixed with bits of scavenged wire and a couple of valves. He might have heard the Canadian Prime Minister, the Right Honorable W. L. Mackenzie King, announce to all of Canada and the world that the War Measures Act gave the Royal Canadian Mounted Police the power to drag 'residents of Italian origin' out of bed, away from their families, their homes, their jobs, and off to jail. The police searched every street, every house, every business, club and restaurant. Any Italian man, from teenagers to the aged, could legally be hauled off like a sack of spuds for the crime of being an Italian male and therefore a fascist until proven otherwise.

The police manhandled Luigi into a car idling at the curb. The car was black, with no markings, no police insignia, no lights, no sirens. Four other men were already in the car, all of them handcuffed and silent, some of them blooming purple and black around the eye. Luigi recognized their faces: Paolo the shoemaker, Giuseppe the bricklayer, Doctori Falconi, who had treated Mamma for her cough and refused to take a cent in payment, but who was fond of a truss of fresh Roma tomatoes.

Most shocking of all was the fourth man. Dom Ignazio Borrelli, the elderly priest who gave Luigi communion each Sunday at the Church of the Holy Souls on Barton Street. Bare-kneed and bewildered, Dom Borelli looked like someone's impoverished grandfather. If a venerable priest of the Roman Catholic Church could be snatched away in his nightshirt like a common criminal, ordinary barrow-men were in for a tough time.

Luigi knew one other man in the car: the driver, Bart Thomas. Bart lived in the wooden house next door to Lou's boarding house. Bart's wife Sally sometimes bought Luigi's fruit for her four small children, if she had a penny to spare after Bart spent his wages at the pub. Luigi, who knew the sting of a drunken backhand from his own childhood, often slipped an extra apple or an orange into Sally's bag. Now Luigi understood. This night-time raid was the price he paid for daring to feed an Englishman's family.

A cluster of neighbors, men, women and children, loitered in the street watching them drive away. Luigi knew them all. He'd said hello to them, they smiled back, they'd often say a few words, send their children to beg a carrot or two for a cake. One of them, Marco Urbani, was a carpenter from Napoli. Once or twice they had gone down to the pub for a beer. Luigi wondered what kind of deal Marco had done with the police to escape the round-up. Luigi couldn't hear the shouts of the crowd, but the rock that struck the window by his head told unbearable truths.

"I bow my head and weep," says Luigi. "If my neighbors, my friends, even other Italians betray me there is no hope, *nessuna speranza*. That is the worst thing of all."

"Do you want to stop, Papa? You don't have to go on."

Lou waves a hand. "I tell everything now." There are tears in his eyes. "And I never tell again. *Capisci*? Never."

Internment Camp Number 33 had held prisoners in another time. Luigi and truckloads of men found themselves staring out from behind the same barbed wire-topped fence that had imprisoned Germans and Austrians during the First World War. This time there were Italians and Ukrainians, Poles, dozens of different nationalities, but mostly Germans again, and Italians. Luigi shared his barracks with Italians from places he'd never heard of, from Quebec, other parts of Ontario, even as far away as that damp eastern coast, Nova Scotia. Some ill-starred Italian sailors were roasted off foreign ships unlucky enough to be sailing through Canadian waters.

For the second time in his life, Luigi wore a number pinned to his jacket. Prisoner number 212. The men were issued denim pants with shiny stripes down the sides and stiff denim jackets.

"I ask why the red circle on the back. Another Italian man, he tell me, it make it easy for the guards in the tower to shoot someone if they try to escape."

Later that day there was a hubbub outside the camp. Someone famous was in the car parked outside. All the men rushed to the gate. Out of a sleek black sedan stepped men Luigi knew all too well: Rocco Perri, who had been nabbed by an RCMP secret agent and some other chill-eyed men in black, Perri's worst henchmen. Last of out of car was Antonio, a little fatter around the stomach, a little crueler around the mouth, but still as handsome as the devil's own son. Luigi spotted his brother straight away. When the guards led their very important prisoners through the gates some of the inmates jeered, others cheered, and all were soundly thumped by the guards for their foolish enthusiasm.

"Me, I don't look at these men," says Luigi. "I don't want more trouble." When the brother he hadn't seen for over a year passed by close enough to touch, Luigi pulled down his cap and turned his head.

Deep among the dark and silent pines, Camp Number 33 was neither the best nor the worst internment center. The men rose early for breakfast. There were gardens to weed and three meals a day, a doctor to tend you if your guts cramped or you nicked yourself with gardening shears or sliced a finger sawing wood. A man and his teenage son delivered bread from a bakery in the nearby town of Petawawa. Sometimes the boy came alone and lingered for a while to watch the men through the barbed wire fence.

Lou's ears provided a fine source of amusement for trapped and angry inmates. He endured the usual monkey jokes and even the occasional pounding. When he didn't fight back, most of the men soon went off in search of other sport.

After lunch one day, Luigi offered a small chunk of bread to a thin-faced Italian with a hungry mouth who didn't seem bothered by his dining companion's ears. The man was a railway worker from the west, from a place called Saskatchewan. Lots of land there, he said, people grow wheat and potatoes and vegetables. But there are not many people. The winters are so terrible many people leave after their first year in the place. So cold, so cold, you never felt such a cold. It crack your bones and freeze your marrow.

Luigi heard only 'there is land'. He began to dream of a flat land furrowed and sown with his own tomatoes and cucumbers. In his dreams the vegetables grew as high as his waist and the sun always shone. It was a pleasant way to pass the days and nights.

Luigi kept out of Antonio's sight. "Is it better to say he is my brother? I don't know. He come there with Perri and other bad men. Some of them, they are fascists. I don't want to know about Antonio. Then one day Antonio find me digging weeds in the garden."

There was a reunion of sorts, some hugging and back-slapping. Antonio tipped back his cap, promising to look out for Luigi, promising he would provide for Mamma and their sisters. He boasted of connections on the outside, even from behind barbed wire. Their womenfolk would be fine. They would have protection and plenty to eat. Luigi didn't ask his brother if he was a member of the Fascist Party. "I don't talk about the war. I am *codardo*, not like Antonio. He stand up to other men, even if he is wrong."

Antonio's promise came true, at least for Luigi. From within Barracks 8 Perri, inmate number 298, dispensed largesse from his food parcels: fresh chicken and salami, even chocolate, appeared like a conjurer's trick. Luigi traded his modest share of this loot for a sharp razor to keep his ears neat.

145

Antonio spent more time with Luigi digging in the garden or sweeping leaves and fewer days with Perri and his gang. The two brothers cobbled together a tolerable present and patched up their past. For two years Luigi was as happy as any prisoner detained without charge or trial could be. In all that time, he never stopped thinking about Mamma and his sisters.

Four months after Luigi was hauled into the camp, he received his first letter from Carmina. The girls and Mamma had looked everywhere, asked everyone, where is Luigi? Antonio, too had vanished, poof, like smoke. They refused to think the worst. It was as if the boys had got on another orphan train to who knows where. It was a relief to find them in prison, not dead. Carmina wrote to Luigi: we are fine, Mamma, Margherita and me. Can we visit? What can we send to you? When will you come home? Why are you in a prison camp?

"I am so happy to read her letter, I cry. I am so worried bad things happen to my sisters and Mamma. I write to Carmina. Other men, they ask their family for some food, some vegetables, maybe a little meat. I need money for shaving and haircut and ear-trimming but I never ask Carmina. I am so ashamed, I am the man of the family, is my duty to make the money for my Mamma and sisters. But I am here, in this prison camp, for how long nobody say. Why, nobody say."

Carmina was not allowed to visit Luigi, so she sent what she could: some carrots, an apple. Next time, she promised, a little salami. What she did not tell Luigi: the three women lived on thin soup and bread, so they could send money and food to Luigi.

Other things Carmina didn't tell Luigi: neighbors and shopkeepers now looked sideways at the Sanzari women. People said ugly things; those Sanzari boys were no good, they had been taken away like the criminals they were, they must have done something wicked and anti-Canadian to disappear just like that. Italians were dirty, lazy, tricksters, they stank of garlic and deserved what they got. Italian shops were stoned, Italian jobs vanished, Italian families were refused relief. The wives pulled their mouths into a sneer and turned their backs on these Italian women, who must be fascist collaborators.

11 Dec 1941. Across the Atlantic, Benito Mussolini stands on a balcony overlooking the Piazza Venezia in Rome and, with fatal insolence, declares war on Allied Forces. *Il Duce's* leap onto the Nazi bandwagon turned a tolerable life for the imprisoned Italians into hell. In Camp No. 33, the guards were quicker with the baton, the kitchen stingier with the rations. Other men, the Poles, the Ukrainians, darted filthy looks at the Italians, called them 'dago fascists' and worse. Fights broke out between fascists and antifascists, between Italians and everyone else. Noses were broken; tentative new friendships lay in pieces all over the camp. A gang of burly thugs with nothing better to do set upon Luigi, this hairy symbol of freaky Italian-ness, smashing fist against jaw so efficiently Luigi could not eat anything but broth for a week. He told none of this to Carmina, who sent him a letter every month. Back and forth they wrote, inventing cheerful lies.

Lou leans forward. "Antonio, he not tell me the truth. I find out many years later. Carmina, Margherita, they had the terrible time, worse than us. Antonio, he a big man in camp, like he say, but not outside. My Mamma and sisters have no-one to protect them. People spit on them in the street, they call them names. They put the night soil on their doorstep, *scusa* Sophia but this is true. All the time they worry about Antonio and me. When someone throw rocks and bottles at the window, they are so *impauriti* they leave their house. They move away to the big city. I hear nothing for a long time."

Italians changed their names and histories, the better to fade quietly into the shadows. Smokey-voiced Carmina reinvented herself as the French chanteuse Camille Sarazin. She sewed a pretty red dress from an old curtain and took to crooning love songs in the types of clubs and bars Mamma had always warned her about. Mamma found a little work scrubbing floors and taking in laundry. Dimpled Margherita — now Marguerite — measured out ribbons and lengths of dressmaking fabric in a small haberdashery. It was as if time had collapsed and folded them back to their New York poorhouse days. Mamma's cough got worse and worse, until she could no longer work. She lay in bed whispering prayers for her sons.

When Carmina's next letter eventually found its way north to Luigi, it spelled out terrible news. Mamma had died not long after their move to Toronto. Her slum-rotted lungs smothered her in the end. Neither Luigi nor Antonio were at liberty to watch as their gaunt mother, barely four decades old, was laid to rest in a pauper's grave on a snowy November morning.

Time ground on in the camp, day by day, week after week. Some men were permitted to leave after only a few months. Others, like prisoner number 298 and his associates, were among the last to be set free.

17 October 1943. The King of Bootleggers and his men, Luigi and Antonio among them, walked out of Camp Number 33, and into a hostile world.

Lou clenches his fists. "My sisters, they tell people in Toronto they are not Italian, they are the French people. For twenty years, they say they are the French people. This is what happen to Italian people in that war. We lose ourselves, we become something else. I never see my Mamma again. That is a terrible thing. She have no sons to bury her. The Prime Minister, that Maloney —"

"His name was Mulroney, Lou."

"Maloney, baloney. Fifty years after we are free, he say sorry to Italians who is locked up in that place. Fifty years! All that time other people in Canada, they think we are all fascists, they think we are criminals, prisoners of war. They don't know we are people like them. We are taken away from our families, there is no trial. We are not guilty of any bad thing. We are treated this way only for being Italian."

Lou wipes away a tear with his sleeve. I let mine fall.

Chapter 24

Oh, Dixie

Dixie has been in a car crash. Three of her left ribs are cracked and her nose aligns less perfectly than it did before The Sultan hurtled his brand new Hummer off a curve straight into a giant spruce tree in Stanley Park.

Why did some efficient hospital person from Vancouver phone me with this bad news? Dixie has listed me as her next of kin, that's why. What a cutting sense of humor she has. The nurse at Vancouver General puts me through to Dixie's room. Her voice is unrecognizable; she sounds like someone with a clothes peg on their nose honking into a ship's funnel.

"Do not speak one admonitory syllable, Sophie. I know I screwed up. I said I would leave him. I didn't. But it's my denial, not your denial. Let the punishment fit the crime."

"That was a big time screw-up, Dixie. Do you know how lucky you are? Unbelievably lucky. I could be organizing your funeral. You should buy a Lotto ticket."

"I'm well overdue for some luck, Soph. He's really gone this time, I swear upon Jerome's little blond head."

According to Dixie The Sultan, who escaped without a scratch, fled the scene, leaving her trapped in her seat spouting blood. The police dogs sniffed out his quivering carcass from under a nearby goat's beard bush. He pleaded diplomatic immunity quicker than you can say 'filthy rich'. His tattletale breathalyzer results will never see the light of day in court.

"That pathetic excuse for a man left the country *tout de suite, ma cherie*, after plumping up my empty bank account with a monster-ish lump of hush money. The überSultan would not be amused if he knew that his teetotal son got pissed as a pickled pig's trotter and smashed up Daddy's very expensive birthday gift. I'm not proud of that little piece of blackmail, but pride goeth before a new pair of Italian boots and a luxury holiday in Cuba sometime soon."

"Blackmail, Dix, for shame. That's a grubby little sin. The nasty little beast had it coming, though. He could have killed you."

"I'm hard to get rid of, Sophie, as you well know. How about it? Fancy an all-expenses-paid holiday in Rhumbaland? Hot times in Havana?"

I nearly drop the phone. "Do you, or do you not, have three cracked ribs and a smashed nose, Dixie?"

"Oh my, so I do. Don't make me laugh, sweetie, it feels like a train shunting back and forth over my ribs. You're right, no rhumba-ing for me anytime soon. Sophie my love, it's been fun, but here comes a nurse with a long pointy object full of pain. Bye darling, call again soon. We need to talk."

Whatever Dixie wants to talk about, I'm sure I do not. There is an undercurrent of Jerome in her tone.

A peaceful visit to Rose is what I need. Alex has taken Lou to buy some new trousers. Lou could use a little wardrobe advice from Alex. His old pair of hobo-wear pants bag around his knees and sag away from his skinny bottom.

With the two men out of the way, I have a lot to report to my mother. I tell her about Dixie's latest drama, omitting the blackmail part. Whatever Rose might think about this escapade, she's not saying. Then, for a long time, I talk about Lou. I ask if she knew about the internment camp and

Perri's mob, a story I had no inkling of and could not invent if I tried. Rose receives all of this in disappointing silence. At times like this I feel more alone with Rose than I do when I'm by myself.

There are so many things I want to ask her. Why did Rose fling the English Rose dinner plate at Lou? Perhaps she was heat-crazed. Like this summer, it had been relentlessly hot for days. Rose shocked us all when she threw that plate. This was my gentle, non-violent mother, who had never once lifted a hand to me, no matter how often I sassed her back or pilfered coins from her purse or dribbled cherry Kool-Aid stains on her best white tablecloth. She had never spoken a sharp word to Lou in my hearing. Suddenly, she was hurling crockery at him. I remember sitting stiff as a board in my chair, crying. Rose dropped her dishtowel and cried too. Lou walked out, slamming the screen door. He had not come home by the time Rose put me sobbing to bed.

That night I lay on my bed tallying everything I loved in my room. My stuffed bear, a pink china piglet, the curtains Rose had sewn to match my bedspread, pink with tiny violets and daffodils, a shelf of favorite books and my most treasured possession, a pink and white music box. When the lid was opened, a tiny ballerina in a stiff pink tutu flipped up and twirled to the music. Carmina had sent it, wrapped in pink and silver paper, for my sixth birthday. I loved it beyond all other things.

What would happen to my things if my parents split up? Where would I live? I stayed in my room for two days, refusing to come out, hoping to blackmail my parents into reconciling. On day two Rose dragged me out of bed, wrapped me in a blanket, and rocked me on her lap, there there, my darling, there there.

What were they fighting about? I didn't think it was money. Rose, like Lou, appreciated the value of a hard-earned dollar. She still worked part-time at the bakery, so she did not have to ask Lou for housekeeping money. She told her friends this when she didn't know I was listening. If it wasn't money, what was it? Fear chewed right through me. Money problems could be fixed. Other things, I knew, could not. This fight felt like something had been as irreparably broken as the English Rose-patterned plate smashed to pieces on the linoleum.

For a week Rose and Lou barely spoke to each other. Lou had never talked to me much; now we sat wordless and wound tight at mealtimes. I became mute with the fear that my parents had fallen into some irreconcilable spiral leading straight down to the dark pit of divorce. It made me breathless and weak to imagine that awful thing happening to my own family. My biggest fear was becoming one of the 'divorced couples' kids' who hit other kids in school and stole money and cigarettes from the corner store. The kids who had done something unknown and unforgivable to cause such family rupture.

On day eight of this war of silence, I broke down at the breakfast table. I couldn't stop crying. Mamma, Papa, please don't please don't. Bawling so hard I hiccupped and my chest was sore for days. My mother, at first soothing, then impatient, became so alarmed at my nonstop sobbing she called the doctor. *Andrà tutto bene*, whispered my father, as my mother stroked my hair and rocked me. They never fought again, at least not in my hearing.

Rose would not tell me what the fight was about. Not then, not ever. I was a child. It was adults' business. Now, without one speck of evidence, I can't help wondering whether Tatiana was somehow the cause of it.

I'm leaning over Rose to kiss her cheek when I see it. Her lips move. I swear it. The corners of her mouth quirk into a little smile and unquirk just as quickly. I scream for Mel.

"Her lips moved, Mel. I saw it. I saw it."

Rose moved her lips. Rose has something to say. What could it be? Be nice Sophie. Take care of your Papa. Remember to wind the cuckoo clock.

I love you, Sophie.

I don't care what she says. I want to hear my mother speak to me again.

When I tell Lou the news about Rose, he demands to see her. Now. Back we go to sit beside Rose, Lou in his new slim-fit grey cotton Wal-Mart trousers. Lou has snipped the last of the burnt-orange tiger lilies from their stems and wrapped them up with day-glo pink lilies, bachelor's buttons in blue and wispy white baby's breath. We arrange them at the foot of Rose's bed, where she cannot fail to see them should her eyes creep open for even a microsecond. We wait, and wait. Lou's head droops, his eyes flutter.

After hours of waiting, there is not even a toe twitch from Rose. I prod Lou gently. "Lou, should we go? You look tired."

Lou shakes his head. He wants to stay a little longer. Lou bends over the bed, stroking Rose's forehead with a shaky hand while murmuring something I can't hear, in words not meant for me.

I walk out into the bright summer day, down to the river, down to the grassy park near the hospital where Rose and Lou and I picnicked many times, where I rode the little children's train and my favorite white horse on the merry-go-round, where we ate Italian salami sandwiches on sourdough while everyone around us had spam and mustard on spongy white bread, and my parents held hands and laughed, and it felt like summer would never, ever end.

Chapter 25

A family dinner

lex, Lou and I are going out for dinner together. Out, as in to a place of dining not owned by a member of the family. Together, as in just the three of us. This is a first. The importance of this event is not lost on me. Lou is primed to show off Alex to the wider world.

Guido's Pizza Ristorante on 22nd St is Lou's choice. He never goes anywhere else, spurning my suggestions of steak and lobster elsewhere. This is a pity, since Alex insists on footing the bill for this landmark outing, and my own impecunious finances do not stretch to lobster tails and escargot on any day of the week. Alex will get off cheaply on this dinner. Still, I can always ping him on the wine.

Lou is dressed up in his best (his only) suit and a pressed blue shirt. Alex drips casual elegance in a pair of dark moleskin trousers and a silky white shirt that shows off his tan without tipping him into the realm of disco daddy. From the back of my closet I've hauled out a green satin sheath with a tiny empire-waist belt buckled with rhinestones. It's too dressy for 22nd St, but I'm not about to be outdone by Mister Sartorial Southern Hemisphere.

Lou's friend Guido greets him like a long lost brother, kissing each cheek and hugging him close. Ditto for me. I have always liked Guido. He and Lou used to play cards every Wednesday night in the back of Guido's restaurant among the cases of tomato sauce and cartons of dried pasta. On

154

the rare special occasion they still gather back there, slapping down cards, drinking wine and cackling genial Italian abuse at each other.

In my early teen years, Guido Pacelli (who had yet to marry his wife Tina, sire six rowdy, good-looking boys and blow up like a blimp) was the closest thing the city's Italian community had to a movie star. He was a Dean Martin look-alike with swoopier hair and a less photogenic nose. Rumor had it he'd played a small part as a gangster's get-away driver in a no-budget movie never seen in Saskatoon.

Fame didn't matter. Guido was the bee's knees. Guido wore black chinos and tight white T-shirts with a cigarette pack tucked in the sleeve. He drove a ruby red '59 Cadillac convertible fitted out with a stitched white leather interior. It was a monster of a thing, as chromed and finned as a rocket ship gone to ground. Sometimes on hot summer days Guido picked up Rose and me for a drive downtown to meet Lou for lunch. Guido always took the long way with the Caddie's top flipped down, rumbling up and down 8th St a few times just for show. Rose wore big white sunglasses and the wind whipped the scarf tied over her hair. Cruising, Guido called all this driving up and down. People on the street stared and whistled at my slim blonde mother in her polka dot sleeveless frock and matching scarf. Years later, I wondered if Guido was in love with Rose and I was just a convenient excuse, brought along to stop any neighborhood tongues from wagging over these afternoon rides.

Rose. There are signs that my mother is surfacing from whatever dark pool she's been submersed in for the last two years. Parts of Rose immobilized for two years are twitching back to life. A tic in her left foot. The flick of an index finger. Once, an eyelid flutter and, most exciting of all, a few rounds of lip-moving. The doctors are guardedly pleased at the way Rose's brain is slowly knitting itself back together, however minutely. These things sometimes happen, they say. There is no medical explanation. People have a greater will to live if they have something to live for.

155

What could that be? Nothing has changed in Rose's life, or our lives, except the coming of Alex. I know he has visited Rose with Lou. I prefer to think Rose is fighting her way back to be with Lou and me, not out of curiosity to meet her husband's unverified son, whom at this moment Lou is introducing to Guido.

Lou does not say, this is Alex, my son. He says, this is Alex, from New Zealand. Lou offers nothing more. Guido asks no questions. Alex's diplomatic touch is all over this little act.

Gripping Alex and me by the elbows, Guido propels us to his 'best table' by the window near a potted ficus plant. It is the table Guido always reserved for Lou and Rose (and later, for Derek and me) on the rare nights my parents dined out. Guido's décor has not changed in four decades; candle stubs drip wax down Chianti bottles, red and white checked tablecloths match the frilled curtains sagging off bent rods, duct tape patches up the red vinyl chair seats. The ficus tree periodically sheds a leaf in our plates. It's cheerful, cheap and chock full of childhood memories. I love this place almost as much as I loved Guido's Cadillac.

Lou and I order our usual — lasagne for him, with extra meat sauce, and chicken ricotta cannelloni for me. Alex scans the entire menu before deciding on veal scallopini.

"*Buona scelta!*" Lou claps his hands. "Best choice, Alex. Guido, he make-a the best *scaloppine di vitello* in Saskatoon."

Guido bows deeply, as if his *scaloppine di vitello* has bested all the chefs of Italy, not just our little prairie city, and withdraws to uncap a bottle of wine. Lou chooses Chianti for a change, not the malign Valpolicella. Over a dish of warm olives we chat about Lou's garden (best *pomodori* ever, basil she not so good, too many worms), the sunny verging on murderously hot weather, the muskrat Alex spotted on one of his daily walks by the river, Tony and Olivia's imminent wedding.

156

Despite Alex's stinginess with details, the wedding sounds like something out of a fairy tale. There will be a ceremony on a beach beneath a spreading crimson tree with some unpronounceable name that Alex calls the New Zealand Christmas tree. This tree will be covered in red blooms, guaranteed. The red tree, the golden beach, the blue sea, fresh crayfish and scallops for the reception fetched up from the deep by Tony's diving mates, it sounds perfect. Lou can't stop smiling. Both he and Alex seem to have conveniently forgotten our deal: no positive DNA test, no trip for Lou.

Guido zooms in to check on our meals, refill our glasses and whoop it up with Lou, who's in a whoop it up mood. "Howza your son, Guido?"

"Which-a one you mean, Luigi? They all good boys, nice families, married nice girls, maybe not that Sandra, she too bossy. I think maybe one son he marry that beautiful girl Sophia Sanzari, so we join together our families, but no such-a luck."

Thirty-some years later he can still make me blush. I had a hopeless puppy-dog crush on Guido's oldest boy when I was twelve and he was sixteen. I would ride my bike to the restaurant just to moon over the curve of Nicky's lips and the flex of his bicep as he set my cherry cola on the table. Six months later Nicky got a girl in his class pregnant with twins. I told my broken heart I was sick of cherry cola anyway.

"You Alex, you have-a wife, a son?"

"Divorced. I have a son, Tony. He's getting married in December."

Guido bellows for more wine, on the house, to celebrate weddings, friendships and sons.

"Lou," says Alex later, after Guido has cleared our plates. "Do you think you could talk about the carnival now? Can you tell me how you met my mother?"

I'm surprised and grateful. Alex had every right to ask Lou about his mother in private. It is his story, after all. Without any prompting or bribing, Lou starts to talk. It's as if he's speeding up as he nears the end of these mysteries. He talks and talks, long after Guido's other customers have paid their bills and left, long after Guido turns down the lights with a quiet *ciao* and locks the door.

Chapter 26

St Paul-Minneapolis, Minnesota 1943

Antonio sauntered through the open gates of Camp Number 33 with Rocco Perri and the gang. Come with us, Antonio said to Luigi, Rocco thinks you're okay. There's always a job for someone like you. Someone who does what they're told and keeps their mouth shut.

Luigi weighed up this offer as a compliment and a job prospect and found it wanting on both counts. Having wriggled out of the gang, Luigi was in no hurry to sink back into that pit. He set off to find his sisters and to see the place where Mamma was buried.

Carmina and Margherita — Carmen and Marguerite, when not at home — welcomed him with thin arms and swollen hearts. The two women had found a room in a ladies' boarding house that smelled of fusty rugs and fried onions. No gentlemen callers were allowed after five o'clock in the evening. Carmen still sang her break-your-heart songs at weddings and funerals and sometimes in bars. Marguerite now served customers tins of beans and sacks of flour at a dry goods store.

One particular gentleman had his eye on Margherita, said Carmina, nudging her pretty younger sister. He is a soldier, an English veteran wounded in Europe. He is very handsome. You don't notice his missing arm so much. He gives Margherita gifts of stockings and chocolate. He is smitten. Expect wedding bells soon. I will sing for them a special song, said Carmina. Margherita squirmed and blushed.

The sisters took Luigi to a small Catholic cemetery ringed with oak trees bare of leaves. There was no headstone on Mamma's grave, just a simple white cross.

Maria-Therese Sanzari b. January 15th 1899 d. August 23rd 1943.

Andanta con Dio.

Luigi laid his small bouquet of white daisies on the grave, and wept.

There was no work in the town for the men who drifted in, especially men as odd-looking, scrawny and Italian as Luigi. He found a little work ditch-digging, then shined rich men's shoes on a downtown sidewalk as winter's early snowflakes skirled around him. The worst job was cleaning out latrines for a railway work unit, although the freezing cold tamped down the smell and the Italians among the workers shared their bread with him. The sisters earned enough to keep them clothed and fed, but Luigi's pride took as much of a pounding as his feet as he walked the streets of Toronto searching for work.

"I feel so useless. Pah! What kind of man cannot find work? Carmina and Margherita, they bring home the money. If not for my sisters, I die like a starving dog in the ditch."

In his many idle hours Luigi dreamed and schemed; he would go west to Saskatchewan, to claim a little plot of black, loamy earth to call his own. He would grow and sell vegetables. He would buy his own vegetable cart and never work for another man again. When he had enough money he would send for his sisters and they would all live on that flat, fertile land.

Antonio never came to visit or sent a letter. One of Perri's rivals and some of his cronies had moved into Perri's territory during his spell at Petawawa. These were very bad men, with hearts of clay and no honor. Rocco Perri disappeared like a ghost, maybe to Mexico, nobody knew for sure.

One summer evening Antonio appeared at the door. He was thinner and bruised around the mouth, and his eyes were narrow and sharp from darting into every dark corner.

I have a plan, Antonio told Luigi. You and me, we leave this place, there's nothing for us here anymore. We hop freight trains across the border to America and join up with the Greatest Ever American Carnival.

What is that? asked Luigi. What is the Greatest Ever American Carnival? I have my own plan.

"I try to tell Antonio, I want to move west, I want to grow the tomatoes and sell them, but Antonio, he laugh."

We Italians are workers, not farmers, said Antonio. It'll be fun. We will make so much money you can buy all the land you want in that frozen prairie hell.

Saskatchewan, Luigi corrected him. It's called Saskatchewan. A big place with land to grow food, no mob, no Italian gangs. Fresh air.

Antonio shrugged. We're brothers. We stick together, he said, ignoring his own frequent absences. Where's your sense of adventure? The carnival is the best place for me and you. They need good men like us. Look. Antonio shoved a newspaper in front of Luigi. *The Billboard*, it said at the top. It was a paper for circus people.

Luigi carefully read the ad, dated April 15. The Greatest Ever American Carnival wanted working men, canvas men, all sorts of men doing things Luigi had never heard of.

It says to write to them. Luigi pointed at the paper. Here.

Forget about writing, said Antonio. They see us, they'll hire us.

What Antonio didn't say was, When they see a hairy-eared freak like you, Luigi, we'll be raking in the dough.

Luigi weighed up Antonio's broken promises and lawless habits against his own lack of prospects and the immutable bond of blood. He again found the offer wanting. But what could he do? He and Antonio were brothers.

And so on a late summer afternoon, with the hot smell of asphalt and dread in the air, the two brothers walked away from their sisters again. Each of them had a clean shirt and some bread in a small canvas pack slung over their shoulders. Luigi carried a stone where his heart should be.

Hopping freights was harder than in their younger days of hitching rides back to Mamma and the girls in New York. The first time Luigi tried to leap onto a train outside Toronto, his fingers slipped from Antonio's outstretched hand and he fell. Antonio cursed blue murder and incompetent brothers but jumped down from the boxcar after him. They rolled around into the weedy ditch like bags of dirt. On his next attempt Luigi managed to crawl into the slow-moving boxcar, only to be kicked back down by the car's resident hobos. Third time lucky: Antonio and Luigi heaved themselves into an empty car and hunkered down in the dark for a long ride to somewhere else.

They rattled through monotonous pines and rocks, rocks and pines. Days later the train chugged across flatter land, even more monotonous. In the town of Winnipeg they changed boxcars, sneaking across the tracks under the cover of a dusk thickened by prairie dust. Later that day, the two brothers crossed the border into the United States of America, their birthplace and home of the world's most wondrous show, the Greatest Ever American Carnival.

At its most famous, the carnival hauled almost one hundred trains stuffed with performers, animals, and tents across North America. It was a marvel, a menagerie, a swinging shouting bash and splash of color and cruelty. There were lion acts, the big cats on chairs or stuffed into sidecars, the tamer cracking his whip, sticking his head in a tiger's mouth, elephants who stood on their hind legs or balanced on a ball on all four or lightly rested their drum-sized foot on their tamer's head, the tamers beating them with bull hooks and electric prods when they moved too fast or not fast enough or when they attempted some simple animal revenge, tatty-furred tigers, snakes with evil glints in their eyes, mournful dancing bears, monkeys drinking tea. The carnival dragged all manner of sorry creatures around the continent, from town to dusty town, from state fairs to Canadian exhibitions.

Unlike the miserable beasts, the human sideshow freaks were treated like small gods from another planet. Even a decent-sized fat lady could double the carnival takings. But it was the world's true human oddities who spun genetic weirdness into gold: Myrtle Corbin the Four-Legged Lady, Mademoiselle Gabrielle the Half Lady, the Human Owl, Lobster Boy, Wang the Human Unicorn and the Human Blockhead, who later died at the age of 94, none the worse for pounding nails into his head for decades.

What Antonio knew, and Luigi did not, was that hairy humans brought top dollar. Lionel the Lion-faced Man, JoJo the Dog-faced Boy and Percilla the Monkey Girl; all of these human marvels suffered from a total-body case of Lou's hairy-ear condition.

The two brothers trudged the dusty midwest streets of St Paul, scrounging food and sleeping rough, waiting for the day the Greatest Ever American Carnival rolled into the Minnesota town. Antonio hung around the midway offering bribes to the carnies and chatting up the ladies with black-rimmed eyes who were clad in smaller frocks than the trained monkeys. When Antonio at last charmed his way into an interview with the maestro, Marcello the Marvelous, Luigi's bit of ear fluff didn't impress him.

We have had the most maaarvelous, the hairiest, the most hideous freaks in any carnival on the continent, boomed Marcello the Marvelous (real name Frankie Rankin, ex card-sharp, of Saratoga, Florida). Short, stout as a beer barrel, dressed in a red suit with a Panama hat and polka-dot red and white hat band, Marcello didn't suffer fools. This is nothing, he scoffed, flicking a fat finger at Luigi's ear.

But, see here gents, this is yer lucky day. Our main freak is, shall we say, indisposed (Marcello-speak for Henri the the Human Pincushion being drop-dead drunk for three days on bad hooch and going blind in both eyes

163

afterwards). I'll take on this little freak, as a side act y'unnerstand, not a top bill You, what's yer name, waddya do? A good lookin' fella like you, we can use, if ya got yerself an act.

Antonio Sanzari, fire-eater, said Antonio, grinning a confident fire-eater's grin.

"I try to stop him," says Luigi. "This is bad idea. What he know about eating the fire?"

Fire-eater, said Antonio, shrugging Luigi's hand off his shoulder. You give me a torch. I'll show you.

So Marcello did, and Antonio did, and Antonio blistered his tongue and mouth so badly he couldn't eat anything for a week. Marcello hired him anyway.

You start with the rousties. This hairy freak really your brother? Okay, he comes too. Looks nuthin' like you. Must be a monkey swingin' in yer family tree, Marcello roared, flashing teeth made of gold. Luigi stared at the sky, thinking about a patch of damp black earth, green things growing; thinking about a land so vast you can never see the end of it.

Marcello the Marvelous put Antonio's flame-throwing career on hold while his mouth healed. He sent Antonio off to fight for his life among the other rousties, who eyed up the tall, well-muscled Italian and grinned at him through broken black teeth and fingered the sharp, secret knives they kept strapped to their calves. Antonio's years with Rocco Perri had taught him a trick or two about how to knock a man out cold with his left hand while slashing another one across the face with the right. Soon Antonio was one of the bare-chested men swinging a wooden mallet against tent stakes, shoveling elephant dung, spreading sawdust inside the tents where the lions and tigers performed. Every day he asked, Mister Marcello, when do I get my fire-eating act?

I'll tell ya when, kid. Keep shovelin'.

164

While Antonio slept in a rail car with ten other rousties (plus someone's pet parrot, who dropped a stinking white slurry on everyone's kit), Luigi found himself quartered in a 'living top' with the India Rubber Man, a lamenting Armenian from Pittsburgh. Lou wandered astonished among the other acts: the sword swallower, the snake charmer with his toothless cobras, a man tattooed from head to foot with flags from many nations, a pistol-spinning cowboy who could shoot a cigarette out of a girl's mouth from twenty paces. There were magicians and mind-readers, Huzzein the Hypnotist and the Human Ostrich who swallowed live rats and hoicked them back up squeaking. There was Daisy the Fat Lady who weighed in at 816 pounds 12 ounces (measured after breakfast, weightier after dinner) and who kept a nippy pet poodle under her petticoats. Inside the Tent of Marvels was a five-legged horse and jars full of unimaginable pickled things, such as a monstrosity that looked like a two-headed pig but was some poor mother's stillborn twins joined from the neck down, floating with their arms forever wrapped around each other.

The Fat Lady and the Human Ostrich commanded a hefty 25 cents per person for the privilege of watching Daisy eat frosted cupcakes or seeing the Human Ostrich torment a rodent. They performed three shows daily. Luigi — reinvented as Manfred the Monkey Man — performed for 10 cents a ticket, staring out at the crowds who stared back at him. The men stood at the front, arms folded, the women half-hidden behind them, holding back the cheerfully fearful children who would not be held back, not the boys anyway, who grabbed at Luigi's ears (he soon learned to keep a safe distance) while tossing peanuts into his enclosure.

Play up for the audience, Marcello ordered him. Don't just sit on yer butt, or yer fired.

So Luigi made up a little dance with a cane and top hat. He drank tea from a china cup while hooting ooga-ooga-ooga. The crowds loved it. After eight months of this demeaning but profitable nonsense, Marcello upped the charge to 15 cents for Manfred the Monkey Man's show and gave Luigi a raise.

Antonio demanded his cut. I got you the job. Fair is fair, Luigi. Cough up. Okay?

Okay. *Sì*, Antonio. Luigi didn't mind. Rousties didn't make as much as freaks. Antonio was his brother. Brothers stick together.

Marcello never did give Antonio a fire-eater's job — ya don't learn quick enough, ya'll kill yerself. Instead he stood by smoking a Havana cigar while two rousties wound yards of chain around Antonio's well-toned arms and body. Months of hammering and shoveling had swelled his biceps to the size of cannonballs. He flexed his muscles. The chains broke like spaghetti.

Our new act, grinned Marcello, slapping Antonio on the back. Hercules the Strongman.

Antonio demanded, and got, 15 cents a show like Luigi, plus his cut of Luigi's earnings. Luigi didn't think this was entirely fair, but he didn't want to make trouble.

For a while there was peace between them. Then came Tatiana, beautiful Tatiana with her eyes of tiger-green, grinding brotherly love to dust.

Chapter 27

Tatiana and Rose

In my left hand I hold the grainy newspaper photo of Tatiana. In my right hand I have a photo of a young Rose smiling from behind a stack of loaves in the bakery. Apart from their fair hair, the two young women share not one thing in common. Tatiana is a smoldering volcanic sun. Rose is a silver moon casting a pale light. They are orbits apart.

I hold the clipping of Tatiana, Luigi and Antonio close to Rose's face. Do you see this woman? Do you know anything about her, this Tatiana? If something hadn't happened to this woman we might not be here, you and I. Luigi and Tatiana would have been married on the back of an elephant draped in red and silver and gold, dancing their wedding fandango with clowns and dwarves and fat ladies while lions and tigers roared a wedding toast. You would have married someone else, perhaps someone your parents approved of more than Lou, a postman or an accountant. Someone with prospects. You might have had more children, maybe boys. I would not be here watching your face, your hands, for any little twitch. I would not be here listening to my father unfold an extraordinary life without you in it.

None of that matters. You know Papa loves you best.

I pull up the clean white sheet, smoothing it beneath Rose's thin face. I tuck my mother in, as she did for me every night until I was twelve and proclaimed myself too old for the slip of the sheet drawing up (white cotton in summer, pink flannelette in winter), the tuck beneath my chin, the cocooned warmth sending me to sleep. I remember the flash of something lost across my mother's face when I put an end to the tucking-in.

I was wrong to stop her. We are never too old for tucking-in. We are never too brave for that cocooned warmth and the kiss on the cheek, a last touch of skin before morning.

Chapter 28

Luigi and Rose

Rose and Luigi, Luigi and Rose. It's as unlikely a pairing as a wombat and a swan. In their wedding photo she is a shy, pale sylph in a high-necked white gown with a wide skirt and lacy sleeves. She clutches a cascade of blood-red roses. Lou, in a dark blue suit with a white carnation on the lapel is grinning so wide his eyes nearly disappear.

This is the story of Lou and Rose, as told to me by my mother, with embellishments, of course, by the aunts, who weren't even there.

Once there was a pale young woman with a quiet heart. Rose lived with her buttoned-up English parents in a small post-war house on the west side. On her eighteenth birthday Rose fell in love with a young policeman, who interrupted his beat duties on 2nd Avenue to carry Rose's birthday parcel (a new dress, blue with white polka dots) to her bicycle for her. The young policeman possessed not only manners but prospects: a car, enough money for a down payment on a small house on the up and-coming east side, and the promise of a full government pension after he retired. This bounty so impressed Rose's parents they all but threw their daughter at him.

After a few months of taking Rose to Joe's Diner for burgers and the Roxy Theatre for a movie or two, the young policeman placed a small but sparkly diamond ring on her hand and asked her to marry him. Rose blushingly accepted, urged on by her parents but especially by Rose's mother, who thought their daughter and her tow-haired suitor would make beautiful babies. Descended as they were from landless serfs in England, Rose's parents also foresaw a rapid climb up the social ladder by welcoming an up-and-coming lawman into the family.

Unfortunately the handsome young policeman liked a drink, or two, or six, after a hard day of chasing pickpockets. One sultry summer evening, Rose's fiancé roared up in his 1956 Chevrolet Bel Air smelling like he'd fallen into a barrel of whiskey. When she refused to get into the car with him, he slapped her so hard she fell to the pavement.

Rose plucked the small but sparkly diamond ring off her finger and handed it back. No amount of the young man's pleadings and groveling and promises to never do it again budged her. That single drunken slap killed his chance to wed the girl of his dreams. Toppled off the social ladder in one fell swoop, Rose's desperate mother tried to make Rose see sense. He promises not to do it again. Give him another chance, Rose, he's a good man, he has a good job. It's a woman's lot in life.

Rose, who had always been an obedient and model daughter, refused to listen. She said, No. I will not. Rose listened to her head, not her shattered heart. She refused to speak to the young man again. The young policeman phoned and knocked and begged and pleaded. When he threatened to steal her away by force, that was truly the end for Rose.

With her mother's remonstrations clanging in her ears, Rose moved out of the little post-war house into a sunless basement suite on the west side, far enough away from her parents to breathe but not too far, in case they needed her. The one-room suite on Avenue C took up the bottom half of a small house owned by a roly-poly Italian widow, Apollonia, who had stiff black bristles on her chin and a keen and knowing eye. Rose found a job in a 33rd St bakery also run by Italians, who laughed and cried and wept and hugged everyone, including their shy new girl. In the early morning she hauled pans of hot loaves from the oven and slid in more loaves. Sometimes she came home with leftover crusty bread to share with Apollonia, who knew the value of a free loaf.

Apollonia also knew the best place to ferret out bargains on wrinkly cucumbers and bruised tomatoes. One momentous Friday, Rose accompanied Apollonia to 20th Street on her weekly vegetable-buying foray to Signor Patata's Fruit and Vegetables Finest Quality, proudly owned by one Luigi Sanzari.

For Luigi, it was like seeing the sun rise for the first time.

For Rose, it was like being stalked all over again.

Once slapped, Rosie was twice shy of men, especially a funny little hairy-eared Italian shopkeeper whose adoring gaze draped itself around her like a too-snug velvet cloak. When Luigi tried to press the plumpest tomatoes and the sweetest oranges into her hands, she fled. Not one to let opportunity's knock go unanswered, Apollonia nipped the fruit from Luigi's outstretched paws and made off at a fast waddle.

Luigi did not see Rose again for the whole of that summer, but he thought about her every day. Attempts to pry information out of the Italian widow Apollonia failed, unless of course Luigi slipped a little something into her shopping basket.

Sì, I know this *bella ragazza*. (One lemon, grudgingly given and received.)

No, she is not *mia figlia*. (A bunch of beets, slightly wilted.) Not *mia nipote*. (Two tomatoes.). Not from my family.

No, she is not married. (A bunch of shining green grapes and a too-ripe watermelon for this promising news.)

Engaged? Hmm. (Two green peppers.) Maybe. (Peppers snatched back.) No, not engaged, not now, I'm having a little fun with you, Luigi. A little joke. She have no boyfriend. (One peck of sweet peppers, mixed colors. Apollonia's favorite vegetable.)

These clues-for-produce scenes played out tortuously for Luigi over these long, lonely summer months. Luigi plundered his patch in an attempt to winkle more information from Apollonia. During the day he dreamed of the beautiful girl with peach-soft skin. At night he slept alone above his shop, and despaired.

On an autumn afternoon, when the maple leaves had turned their most flagrant crimson and a pewter sky threatened snow, Apollonia took pity (also, the pantry looked particularly bare at this waning edge of summer).

This girl you love (Luigi blushed) she live in my downstairs suite. Her name is Rosa.

Rosa, said Luigi, breathless. Rosa.

Apollonia borrowed Luigi's wheelbarrow to haul her ill-gotten loot: bags of sweet corn, tomatoes by the bushel, pecks of peppers, long firm cucumbers, Pumpkins. Potatoes. Parsnips. The last of those sweet, sweet peaches.

Oh, Luigi.

The following Friday, having plucked up courage (plus a fragrant bouquet of white carnations, periwinkle blue bachelor buttons and velvet-faced red roses from his garden), Luigi appeared on Rose's doorstep (actually Apollonia's doorstep, Rose not having a doorstep of her own).

Buona sera, signorina.

Still wounded from her failed engagement, Rose did not feel inclined to make small talk with Luigi or any other man. But there was something about his bright, pleading eyes, and the shiny nap to his dark blue suit, perfectly pressed, and the romantic sound of Italian words, that pulled thrillingly at something near her heart. Apollonia snatched the flowers from Luigi and shoved Rose not-so-gently out the door.

Go. Have a little fun. Stop moping around *casa mia.*

Luigi walked Rose to a little Italian restaurant near his vegetable stall where he knew the owners, and the owners knew him. Everyone, including

Rose, after a while, laughed and chattered and teased each other and ate good southern Italian food: *orecchiette con cime di rapa, 'nduja bruschetta.*

Ignoring her horrified parents' strongest warnings, Rose fell slowly, gently in love with Luigi. He was sweet, kind, funny and as generous as he could be on a vegetable seller's income. Also, he drank very little. As months passed, his hairy ears mattered not a mote when weighed against such attributes. In winter, Rose took Luigi skating on an outdoor rink at a nearby school. Luigi fell over more times than he stood up. In spring, they walked along the river, watching the water grind and seethe with spring thaw. In summer, oh, summer, the best time of all, the time of ripe fruit and clear blue days, the smell of mown grass and shivering wheat.

Exactly one year to the day after their first date, Rosa and Luigi announced their engagement at an intimate party for fifty in their favorite Italian restaurant. Rose's mother wept into her handkerchief for many reasons: Luigi's Italian-ness, his much-older age, his lack of prospects, and, most terribly, his strange furry ears, lurking in his genes to damn the next generation.

On a steamy day in June, a Catholic priest married Luigi and Rosa in Saskatoon's finest church on the river, amid further lamenting from Rose's Anglican mother. Luigi's florist friend Nico (and Son) personally delivered the truckloads of roses that bedecked every pew. Rose chose Apollonia as her matron of honor. Tightly wrapped and rigged in blue chiffon, the victorious Italian matchmaker sailed down the aisle ahead of Rose under a blue silk hat the size of a Cadillac hubcap.

Rose stepped to Lou's side, her face hidden beneath a lace veil. To honor her new husband, the bride carried a red jalapeno pepper among the elegant red roses of her wedding bouquet.

Chapter 29

Rose

I am walking down a country road. Everything is a sullen ash-grey: the road, the trees, the sky. There is an ominous hum in the wind, and no birds sing. An elderly lady drives by in a little black car. I wave and yell, Pick me up please. Stop, take me with you. She turns and smiles gently. She doesn't stop.

The ringing phone drills into my ear. It's 3:22am, that time of the morning when a ringing phone can only mean bad news. I grope for the phone, willing it to be a telemarketer in another country who hasn't mastered the difference in time zones.

It's not. It's Mel.

Sophie? she says quietly. I'm so sorry. I'm so sorry.

Something inside me falls away and shatters. Mel is murmuring, it was another stroke, a big one, we tried …

I do not hear anything more. I drop the phone and cry so hard I retch.

Then I dress myself and drive across town to sit beside Rose in the dark. I hold my mother's cold hand until the dawn light hardens to a bright, pitiless morning.

Chapter 30

Sophie's big mistake

Lou takes one look at my face, and he knows. *"Rosa mia, non mi lasciare!"* He crumples to the floor. I kneel beside him. My face is wet. We're both shaking.

"Please Lou, get up. Please, Papa."

Lou is sobbing so hard I'm afraid he's going to break a rib. I wrap an arm around him, kneeling until my legs ache. Then I get up and make some fresh coffee for Lou, some mint tea for me. Boil the kettle. Spoon the coffee into the pot. Add milk, not too much. Pour the water. Dip the tea bag. Stir. Slow, methodical. It's something to do.

Lou drags himself to the table. He shudders and gasps. When I set the coffee in front of him he takes a small sip. I don't like the way he's looking at me.

"What's the matter, Lou?"

"What-a time you know, Sophia?" he asks abruptly. "When you know Rosa die?"

I twirl my cup. "It was — it was early this morning, Lou. At 3:22 am. I looked at the clock. Mel called me."

"She call you, Sophia? She call you, not Luigi, Rosa's husband. Why she not call me?"

"I — she thought, we thought it was best —"

"Why you stand between us, Sophia? You not tell me about the test she-a take on her head, and now this? You not tell me she die when she die?'"

Lou hurls the words at me. I reel back in my chair so far I nearly topple to the floor.

"I'm sorry. I'm here now, Lou, telling you this."

Lou stiffly levers himself to his feet. Even standing up, he is not much taller than I am sitting down.

"Forty-nine years I am Rosa's husband. Forty-nine years! We are man and wife many years before you are born, Sophia. I am head of the Sanzari *famiglia*. Not you!"

His words break against me. I am strung out too thinly, whittled down to bare emotional bones.

"You don't act like it, Lou! I do everything I can for you, and you treat me like a second-rate slave!"

"Why you do this, Sophia?" Lou is so angry he's spitting. "You want my Rosa for you only. You always so greedy, Sophia. You no want Alex for my son. You think only of you."

"I loved my Mamma!"

"What you know about love?" Lou shouts, clenching his fists.

There it is at last. My father's unvarnished opinion, thrown in my face. Something venomous inside me uncoils.

"That's right, Lou! What do I know about love? You never wanted me anyway! I wasn't a boy! You were the one who wanted Rose for yourself! I wish you were dead, not Mamma!"

The words hiss out. I clap my hands over my mouth. I cannot believe I've said them, cannot believe I've even thought them.

Lou's fists unclench. "Me, too," he whispers. "I do terrible things. I kill Antonio, *mio fratello*. I kill Tatiana. And now my angel, my Rosa, she die. I wish I die, too." Lou's legs give way and his head hits the floor with a crack. His eyes roll back.

"Lou! Papa! Papa!"

I scramble over to Lou feel for a pulse nothing my brain is shrieking I frantically press on his chest someone is screaming and screaming Help Help I press and press and the door flings open and there is Alex he pushes me aside and takes over pressing on Lou's chest and here is Mrs Woloschuk she folds me weeping and flailing into her soft arms and the shriek of sirens sweeps everything else away —

When people ambush you with news you don't want to hear, there's nothing you can do. Unwanted words fall in and take root. There are so many words I'd give anything to un-hear, if only I could. There are many more words I'd give anything to un-say.

Alex and I wait in the hospital corridor. He sits straight-backed and motionless on the hard plastic chair. I pace, and pace, chew what's left of my fingernails, and pace.

"Sit, Sophie," says Alex. "You'll exhaust yourself."

I pace some more, up down back forth. Then I drop into a plastic chair beside him.

"Can you tell me what happened?" Alex looks calm but his face is closer to Gruel Grey than Perfect Porcelain. It can't be much fun sitting in a hospital so soon after Tony's illness.

"I — we had a fight, Alex. It was awful. We both said terrible things."

"What sort of things?"

I'm too numb to put a more flattering spin on it. "I told him I wished he — I wished he had died, not Rose." There. It's out. A crackling terror floods over me, then something that feels like relief. I burst into tears.

Alex turns to face me. I brace myself for scorn and loathing. Instead he murmurs, "Your mother has ——passed away?"

Alex doesn't know about Rose. How could he? The only two people who might have told him were too busy ripping each other to shreds. I nod. Tears drip off my chin. Alex reaches for my hand and closes it in his cool fingers. We sit like that for a long, long time.

When the doctor pokes her head into the waiting room, we both stand.

"Which of you is Mr Sanzari's next of kin?"

Neither of us speaks. The doctor looks from me to Alex. Then Alex nods at me.

"Sophie is his daughter," he says. "She's his next of kin."

I exhale sharply. Alex gazes steadily at the doctor.

Lou has had a heart attack, she says. Not quite enough to kill him, but serious enough to punch him around and knock him down. He is doing as well as can be expected, but he's weak and needs to rest. Yes, I can see him, for a moment.

Alex touches my shoulder. "Go on, Sophie. I'll see him later." I nod my thanks.

Lou has a tube down his throat and needles in his arms and electrodes taped to his chest. His eyes are closed. He seems more shrunken than usual, and less peaceful. Rose looked more alive than this in her last days.

"Lou." I stroke the hand without the needles in it. "Papa, I'm so sorry." I lay my head on the bed and drip tears onto the crisp white sheet. I stay like that until the nurse comes in to steer me away.

After a death there are many things to be done, ordinary things that gnaw away the days bite by painful bite. Lou is too ill to help with these ordinary things. Call the aunts. Write an obituary. Send out a funeral notice. Plan the memorial service. Where to have it? When? Who to invite? What will I say? Should we supply a light lunch for the mourners or an afternoon tea and cakes?

"Who the fuck cares?" I hear myself snarl at the undertaker. I apologize immediately. He seems to understand. I desperately want to climb into bed, pull the covers over my head, and never come out.

When I call Dixie she says, simply, "Hang on Sophie, I'm on my way," which turns into "not for a few days" while she sorts out a plan for Jerome. In the meantime, Alex helps with decisions about a funeral for a mother who is not his. He is clear-headed and efficient to the point of robotic. I am dizzy and sick and often speechless. I cannot remember saying yes or no to anything. Alex comes to my house. He brings soup, some kind of stew, a sandwich. I try to be grateful but I can't eat or sleep. Dr Hodges prescribes sleeping pills. I sleep a dreamless sleep and wake up in a kind of shaky terror that does not fade with the coming of the light.

I miss my mother. I miss my mother so much, every minute of the day. Every part of me aches, my head, heart, bones; it's as if my own flesh grieves the loss of the living flesh that made it.

Lou's physical self improves daily, despite yo-yoing blood pressure and a worrying rattle in his bony chest. His emotional self is another matter. On good days he takes a few steps down the corridor. He even smiles a little when Alex presents him with a framed photo of a healthy-looking Tony and his girl. (This time they are standing on top of a snowy mountain peak against blue skies.) But most of the time he sits in a chair, looking at nothing. His eyes are bruised with grief and a despair I can't bear to see.

The doctors cannot guarantee Lou will be well enough to attend Rose's funeral, which has been postponed for as long as is seemly. But if I know one thing only about my father it is this: Lou will not miss saying goodbye to Rose. He will be there if he has to be wheeled in on his hospital bed sucking oxygen from a mask.

Alex and I visit Lou as often as we're allowed, now that's he's been moved out of the coronary care unit. Sometimes we visit together, more often apart. Lou and I never talk about our heart attack-making fight on the day Rose died. When I try to tell him how sorry I am, he lays his fingers on my lips and shakes his head.

"Nothing to forgive," he says. "*Colpa mia*. My fault. I am sorry, too, *figlia mia*. Forgive and try to forget. What other thing is to do? If not forgive, it eat up your heart. If not forget, it eat up your mind."

I've decided not to tell Alex about Lou's confessions on the morning of our big fight. Lou was in shock, he was confused, he didn't know what he was saying. As usual, I have underestimated my father. The next time I visit, Lou is sitting bolt upright in his bed talking rapidly to Alex. There's a firm set to his jaw.

"Sophia, Alex, some important things I must tell you," he says without even a hello. "About Antonio. Tatiana, too."

I bite my lip. "Lou — Papa, is that a good idea? You shouldn't get too excited. You don't want another heart attack."

Lou fixes me with a thoughtful eye. "That is why I tell you now. What if I die, and nobody know? The truth, she need to be told."

Chapter 31

Calgary, Alberta, 1947

The Greatest Ever American Carnival trains rumbled from Minnesota, through Oklahoma, Kansas, Arkansas, Mississippi, Louisiana, south, north, east and west. Hercules the Strongman cranked up the charm and jostled along with every other red-blooded male in the carnival for a smile or a smoldering look from Tatiana. Over days, months, years the Queen of the Trapeze laid fiery waste to carnies' hearts, one by one. Antonio blew his chance for love, or at least a quick romp, with Tatiana by showing up at her living top uninvited, clad only in his Hercules loincloth and boozed to the gills. Tatiana shrieked obscenities in four languages and hammered his chest with her small fists until he stumbled out, lathered in shame and rage.

"Tatiana, she is brave but Antonio, he don't take no for the answer."

Antonio bragged, bleated, begged, all to no avail. After months of his thuggish attentions Tatiana asked Marcello to keep Antonio away from her. She was frightened and he was making her crazy. Marcello, who too had less than pure designs on Tatiana, was only too happy to oblige. He ordered two of the toughest rousties to keep Tatiana out of Antonio's grasp. Antonio cast weighty looks at Tatiana that held diminishing amounts of love and rising tides of something blacker.

Manfred the Monkey Man worshiped the Queen of the Trapeze from afar. He watched her trapeze act when he could. A hairy-eared freak couldn't compete with the tsunami of testosterone surging off the carnie pack. He kept his head down, kept out of the way, and got on with the daily grind. Then one rainy morning Tatiana slid in beside him in the kitchen tent as he was eating his pork and beans. She started to talk.

"She tell me so many things about her life. I am excited and scared to sit next to her. She is so beautiful, she have the white skin and green eyes like you Alex, and hair like a mane of a lion in the sun. I don't say anything. She talk and talk. Then she leave. I am happy she talk to me, but I think she don't know who I am. She just want to talk to someone."

Luigi thought that was the last time he would ever find himself anywhere near Tatiana. He was wrong. Each time Tatiana came into the kitchen tent and saw Luigi sitting by himself, which was always, she sat beside him and told him things about her trapeze act, how smelly and grumpy her trapeze partner was; things about her mother who was still living a hard life in Romania. Eventually, shyly, Luigi told her things, too. He told her everything, from the slums of New York to the Petawawa prison camp. She laughed abruptly when she found out Antonio was his brother. At the ragged end of spring Tatiana invited Luigi to her spacious living top, stroked his furry ears, and made love like a lioness to the astonished Monkey Man.

"So much *passione!*"

"I think we get the picture, Lou." My face is warm, and Alex is pink around the edges. Lou is so transported he has probably forgotten we're even there.

"I am so surprised, so happy I don't care anymore if I am Monkey Man. Tatiana, sometimes she is happy, sometimes she is sad, but we talk and make things right. She say she want to leave the carnival and do some other job. Maybe type letters in an office. You can type? I ask her. She say no, she can learn. I am afraid for her. Marcello, he don't like any carnival acts

182

to leave, not good act like Tatiana. But we talk like this, and we make the plan."

The pair planned to desert the show somewhere in western Canada, wherever they could sneak off and hide until the Greatest Ever American Carnival pulled out of town. Luigi knew their plan was doomed. Manfred the Monkey Man and Tatiana the Trapeze Queen didn't look like ordinary prairie folk. But he could not say no to Tatiana. In Calgary, Cowtown, Home of the Stampede, it all came unstuck.

"I don't see Antonio so much. At first he treat me pretty good, then more and more he is jealous for Tatiana. He start acting like our Papa, like Johnny. He drink so much, every night, he drink. I don't want him to know about me and Tatiana. This is bad trouble."

Antonio played fast with a bottle and quick with his fists. Of course he knew about his hairy-eared brother and the trapeze queen. Everyone in the carnival knew. The rousties gave Antonio a hard time. Whatsa matter with you fella, that your monkey-man brother gets the girl. After Antonio's reply, the mouth that spoke those words spit broken teeth through a split lip.

One night in late July, Antonio came looking for Luigi. He found him sitting with Tatiana in a boxcar across from the lions and tigers, dangling their feet and gazing at the full moon caught in the weave of a quilted sky. The big cats rumbled and yawned in their train cage.

To Luigi he said, You're not good enough for Tatiana. A little hairy-ears like you. She needs a real man.

To Tatiana he said, Why are you wasting time with this freak? You're coming with me. Now. He pawed at Tatiana's shoulder. She slapped him.

Big man, she sneered. You know nothing. You are nothing. I love Luigi. He is more of a man than you, where it is important for a woman. She laid her hand over her heart.

"I try to walk away with Tatiana," says Luigi, so quietly I can barely hear him. "Antonio, he so drunk he don't know what he do. He try to slap

Tatiana but she lean away. So he punch me, here, in my stomach. Oof. I fall down, my breath is gone."

When Antonio lunged at Tatiana, Luigi stuck out his spindly leg. Antonio stumbled and fell across the tracks, cracking his head like an egg on the iron rail that had brought them all to this time, and this place, and this end.

"This is why I never tell about the carnival, Sophie. It is a terrible time, it is the worst time in my life. Worse than when we work for the Swedish farmer. Then Antonio was my friend. We were blood brothers. So many bad things happen with the carnival. I do bad things, I am so ashamed. I am happy only that my Mamma never know how her sons fight, how Antonio die drunk on the tracks because I kill him. Now you know the truth."

It's a lot to take in. "Lou, you are not responsible for Antonio's death. It was an accident." He's not capable of murder. Is he? It must have been self-defence. My missing uncle Antonio doesn't seem like such a charming rogue now.

"Why did you say you killed Tatiana — my mother?" Alex is calm but there is an edge to his voice. "You didn't end her life, Lou. She did that herself. I saw her fall. You know that."

"After Antonio die, I am so scared and sad and angry, I run away." Lou shakes his head. "I leave Tatiana. She beg me, she say take her too, but I say no. She is better with no Sanzari brother in her life. I think the police, they will come for me. I leave that night, later, when it is raining. I hop a freight train. I don't say goodbye." Lou looks down at his wrinkly hands. "If I take her with me, maybe she is still alive now. But she never tell me she is *incinta*, she is expecting a baby. This is you, Alex. Maybe when I leave she don't know about you?"

He looks hopefully at Alex.

184

"I don't know, Lou. My mother was not a happy person for much of her life." Alex gently shakes Lou's shoulder. "You are not a bad person. Lou. You made a happy life with Rose. And you have Sophie."

Lou's face pinches shut. His chest rises, falls. I watch and say nothing. After a while his eyes close and his face relaxes. "Sophie."

I lean in close. "Yes, Papa? What is it?"

"Don't forget you water the lettuce."

In the hospital cafeteria Alex and I sip our coffees. Double espresso for me. Mint tea isn't doing the job for me these days.

"Alex. The other day, when the nurse asked who was Lou's next of kin?"

"Forget about that. It doesn't matter."

"Yes it does. That was unselfish of you to speak up. I just couldn't. You understand why."

Alex nods. He does not look happy.

"Do you think it's all true?" I ask him, abruptly.

Alex almost spits his coffee.

"Sophie, why don't you believe your own father? I believe him. Why would he lie? Do you realize how sad it makes him when you constantly challenge him?"

"I'm just trying to make sense of it."

"Most of the time, life makes no sense at all," points out Alex, who is becoming irritatingly wise. "Don't fight everything so much, Sophie."

"How can you be so calm about everything?"

He twirls his cup. "My mother was a troubled person. I suspect now she'd be diagnosed with bipolar disorder. She would spend all our money on fancy dresses and silk stockings, living the high life. Then when she was down, she yelled and threw things and broke all the dishes more than once. She hit me sometimes. After those episodes she would go to bed and nobody, not even Marcello could drag her out and make her do her act.

185

Marcello took the whip to her once. I was only six but I — well, I hit him with an iron."

I try not to laugh. It's not funny, but the image of a tiny Alex bopping fat Marcello with a domestic appliance is too much.

"The next day she'd be the most loving, fascinating mother you could hope for. She made life hell, but she was my mother. There were men in her life, they came and went. She never married any of them. So someone had to stay and look out for her. I couldn't even do that, in the end."

I reach out and take his hand in mine. This way of sitting with Alex is beginning to feel familiar, even comfortable.

"It wasn't your fault, Alex. You were only a child. You are not to blame for what happened to Tatiana."

Alex drops his head. "My mother's name was Olga."

For the first time ever, I see him cry.

Chapter 32

Roses for Rose

Everywhere, there are roses; blowsy white ones, dainty damsel-pink buds, yellow bursts like tiny suns. They bloom at the ends of the pews, at the church door, on the altar. Dozens of blood-red roses cover my mother's casket, the same roses she carried in her wedding bouquet. Nico (and Son) has once again emptied his greenhouses for Rose.

What's left of the Sanzari family squeezes together in the front pew of the church; the same church where my parents were married, where Derek and I were married. Alex and I prop up Lou on either side. His elbows and knees poke thin as sticks against the sharply pressed black suit Alex bought for him. Carmina and Margherita sit next to me in black veils and funereal hats, with their daughters scattered around them. Dixie and Jerome are seated behind us, Dixie shushing Jerome, who is as wriggly as a garter snake. Dr Hodges is here too, to pay his respects to Rose and to keep an eye on Lou's twitchy heart.

The church overflows with mourners. I look around, trying to distract myself from the reason we are here. There aren't enough seats, so some people stand at the back. I don't know half of them. There is Rose's long-time friend Anne, who she has known since high school, and some of her retired workmates from the bakery. Mrs Woloschuk is here too, clutching a hankie and wearing a floppy straw hat swathed in black net.

When the minister starts the service I clasp Lou's hand. He starts to sob quietly, and soon we're both weeping. After that I hear nothing the minister says. Not a word, until I hear him ask if anyone wants to say something about Rose. For a moment, no-one moves. My thoughts turn to smoke and drift out of my head. Lou sits frozen to the pew, gripping his carefully handwritten tribute to Rose. Alex puts his arm around my father's shuddering shoulders. I hear him murmuring. Lou shakes his head.

There is a rustling behind me. Dixie strides up the aisle, smiles at the minister, who gazes at her with something like guilty awe, and adjusts the microphone a few inches upward. She has swept up all that dark hair into an Egyptian pharaoh-style beehive hairdo. Her bruised eyes are skilfully camouflaged and she moves stiffly, favoring her left side. Still, she's magnificent. Lou's lips thin. His entire body tenses. Please Dixie, do not make a scene, I beg silently. Not here. Not today.

"We're all here because we loved our sweet and gentle Rose," she begins, "and for a last glimpse of the light she shone into our darkest corners."

I'm so absurdly relieved and grateful I dissolve into a blithering snotty mess. Dixie is relaxed, at ease; the mourners sigh, sniff and even chuckle as she tells story after story.

"My own mother didn't know a cookie sheet from a can opener," she says. "Rose was a baker extraordinaire. If the cookie jar was empty Sophie and I raided the freezer. We thought we were such cunning thieves. Then one day we opened up a container of cookies and found a note at the bottom. "Take as many as you want, cookie thieves,' it said, 'but leave some for Sophie's Papa.' We put them back and never stole cookies again."

"Cookie please, Mommy," cries Jerome into the silence. Everyone laughs, except me. It is such a bittersweet moment I can taste it, thick as blood on my tongue.

Dixie smiles at him, blows a kiss, and tells a few more tales. My mind drifts away until my ears catch the cadence of a poem she is reciting, no it not it's a poem, it's lyrics from a song, one of her favorites. I recognize it straight away. *The Last Living Rose.*

The pain in my heart is so sharp it pierces the breath from my body.

I remember

I remember

I remember

I remember Rose standing in the kitchen with her hands deep in bread dough. Rose in the garden snipping lilacs. Rose taking me to school on my first day. Picking me up out of the dirt when I fell off my bicycle. Walking me to the bus stop in winter in the squeaking snow, both of us cracking ice in the gutter. Rose hugging me so hard I squawk when I tell my parents I'm engaged to Derek.

Rose and Lou, slow dancing on a moon-bright night, under a million glittery stars.

While Alex is walking Lou to the car, Dixie cradles my face in her long, elegant hands. She kisses me. Not mwah, mwah, a full, real, kiss. Scarlet lips on mine. We hug each other, tight tight. I feel the prick of tears again. Down below, Jerome kisses my knees. I freeze. Dixie looks away. I breathe out, bend down and kiss him, too.

Jerome squeals, "Hello Sophie goodbye Sophie hello!"

We walk out of the churchyard together. Dixie holds Jerome by the hand. I hold his other one. The day looks ordinary, like any other day. Cars come and go. Birds sing. There is nothing to show the world what has been lost.

Dixie stoops to smooth Jerome's flyaway hair. "I can't stay, Sophie, we've got to fly back this afternoon. Jerome has doctors' appointments galore. The wretched medics virtually accused me of child abuse for daring to take him away. Plus there's the turtle to feed. We've named her Esmeralda. I don't want to be accused of reptile abuse, too."

"Esmeralda, eh?" How very Dixie. "Not plain old Timmy or Tammy Turtle?"

We both grin. My heart goes ba-boom ba-boom ba-boom —

"Sophie —" Dixie lays a hand on my arm.

"Should we go?" I cut in. "It's getting late. People will be arriving at my house soon."

Dixie opens her mouth, shuts it, shakes her head. Lou and Alex are standing by the black BMW. I feel the Eyes of Alex on us. Granite Grey. He s been watching us the whole time. Dixie stops, turns around and strides up to Lou.

"I'm so sorry," Dixie murmurs to Lou. "Rose was special. We were all lucky to have known her."

She holds out her hand. Lou hesitates, then brushes Dixie's hand aside anc hugs her, hugs her hard, as if he were a drowning man who had bumped up against the only floating log in a turbulent sea.

"Grazie. Grazie mille."

He bends down to shake Jerome's hand. Jerome giggles. "Nice man man man shake hand hand hand." He strokes Lou's neatly trimmed ear. "Soft."

Lou tips his head so Jerome can stroke the other one. My heart slips its fragile moorings. Dixie tugs Jerome away and they climb into the waiting tax .

"Sophie," says Dixie. "Please."

I straighten up and stand back. "I'll call you."

As the taxi pulls away I catch a glimpse of one scarlet-nailed hand floating, ever so languidly, out the window, and two smaller ones, waving goodbye hello goodbye.

Chapter 33

Derek and Sophie, then

There is a photo in the drawer of my bedside table. I have looked at this photo so many times it's gone soft and felty around the edges. Rose snapped this shot on a late September day crackling with bronze and scarlet leaves, the warmth of the Indian summer sun pouring down on my face.

In the photo I am standing in front of my parents' little white house, the house I now own. I'm squinting into the late afternoon rays trying to smile, but not even coming close. I'm holding Jerome in my arms. Jerome, the tiny wee gnome. Even in this faded old photo, it's obvious there is Something Very Wrong with Jerome.

Derek is standing beside me, leaning into me. He is gorgeous, raven-haired, sun-drenched. One arm circles my shoulder. The other arm cradles Jerome.

We are so careless with the hearts we love.

Derek and I met at a high school dance. He was the best looking boy I had ever seen: a head taller than me, panther-graceful, his hair falling over his forehead in an irresistible bad-boy swoop. Eyes so dark they were nearly black. He was funny and spookily prescient and more alive than anyone I'd ever met. I could not believe he had picked me instead of the cheerleaders and snow queens preening around the edges of the school gymnasium.

You're different, Soph, he said, much later. You are who you are.

What did that mean? Even then, he knew more about me than I ever would.

On summer nights we'd go driving in his rusty old Buick down to the river. We'd creep up a set of steps and walk across the rickety wooden train bridge (an act expressly forbidden by every adult who'd done the same in their youth). We never knew when the train would come. You took your chances and hoped it wouldn't come or, even better, it would. We pressed together on the narrow pathway when a train roared past inches away, breathless and electric with adrenalin. Afterward we made urgent, slippery love on the riverbank, branches poking me in the back and a moonlit sky above.

I was hooked. I had never done anything more reckless than ignore my father's lettuces. By the end of the school year I had fallen so hard for Derek I had bruises on my soul.

After I finished high school, we announced our engagement to an ecstatic Rose and a frowning Lou. You too young, Sophia. Who is this boy? What you know about him? So dark, those black eyes, where they come from? He look like the gypsy, maybe Armenian. You wait some years, then you know him better. Plenty of time to marry.

This was not what I wanted, or expected, to hear. Lou had wanted a son; now I could give him the next best thing, a son-in-law, perhaps a grandson one day. Nothing I did made my father happy. And what gave hairy-eared Lou the right to make snide remarks about the color of people's eyes? Lou's guess was astute, though; Derek's father (who he never talked about except to say, he's a jerk, I don't know where he is and I don't want to talk about him) was indeed Armenian and probably a gypsy. Why was an Armenian gypsy worse than an Italian?

All of us were surprised when short, skinny Lou frog-marched a meek and solemn Derek into the garden for a man-to-man chat among the garlic. I never knew what Lou said to his future son-in-law. Take care of my only daughter? Be good to her, be true? Or more likely, *grazie mille* for taking this spoilt child off my hands? All I know is that after their talk Lou thawed toward Derek, but only a smidgeon. When I asked Lou what they had talked about, he said, Men's business, Sophia. For only mens to know. When I prodded Derek, he laughed. We talked about football scores. And basil. How to make the best pesto.

They both lied.

Rose loved Derek almost as much as I did, maybe more. There is no simple way to measure different types of love. Rose treated Derek as the missing son in our family. She fed him, washed his clothes, mothered him in ways that Elvira never did. If Rose suspected something was slightly askew with Derek, she never let on. Rose's only pre-wedding advice was to love each other in good times and bad. If only I had taken her advice. Derek did; Dixie still does.

Our wedding day was perfect. Must I say any more about it? Later, I burnt our wedding photos to blackened dust. When I looked at them, I could not see Derek. I could only see Dixie standing beside me.

In a spasm of extravagance my parents paid for our honeymoon. We booked a seven-day package holiday to Greece. Derek and I drank retsina from shot glasses, licked grilled mullet juice from each other's fingers on the Hania seafront, made love every night in a pension smelling of moldy pillows. The pension owner's wife, a stooped woman wearing black and a conspiratorial smile, ambushed us every afternoon in the stairwell with a tray of olives, cut apples, a ripe pomegranate, tiny clay cups of strong sweet coffee.

The Greek boys were as dark-haired and god-like as Derek. They stared at my new husband with what (in my naive vanity) I took to be envy over his young blonde-haired, blue-eyed bride. Sometimes the Greek boys sat down with us at cafés, boldly uninvited. How are you, where do you come from? Canada, very good country, yes? What is your name? Where you live? Maybe someday I visit you. Sidelong glances at me, while frankly appraising Derek. Years later, after Dixie made her appearance, I understood that look. I have never felt so stupid.

One night I felt ill, after too much retsina on top of too little sleep and some undercooked sardines. Derek went out alone into the sultry Greek night to find something to settle my sore stomach. Some soup. A dish of plain rice. Custard, I begged, if you can find it, with fresh cream and eggs like my mother makes. I waited and waited, peered out the window, waited and fell asleep hungry. Derek came in hours later, closing the door softly behind him. He looked flushed, fuller in the lips, his eyes deep as wells. Where have you been, I murmured, half awake. Are you okay? What happened?

Nothing happened, he whispered. Here, I brought you some soup. Chicken with rice, and an egg stirred in. His hand shook a little when he lifted the spoon to my lips. The soup was cold.

Something had shifted between us. What were we to do? I signed up for an interior design course while Derek — the one with all the artistic talent — peddled vacuum cleaners door to door. After I graduated there were no design jobs. I sold children's shoes in a shop on 2nd Avenue. It was Derek who was hired by an art gallery, Derek who surprised everyone with his flair for shapes and forms that drew the eye, Derek who dug his toes into the design world, lifted off and flew. I wasn't jealous. Not really. Maybe a bit. Actually, quite a lot.

Lou was right. We were too young.

For years we put off trying for a baby, despite Rose's gentle hints and Lou's not-so-subtle complaints about the lack of a grandchild (specifically, a grandson) to warm his aging knees. We had no money. We needed time. It happened anyway. The truth is, I was terrified, given my parent's poor track record in the child-spawning department. When I told Derek I was pregnant, he clutched me so tight I couldn't breathe and broke into an ecstasy of weeping. Perhaps he thought a baby would banish his private demons.

I tried not to think about my worrying lack of excitement. At least I knew what I would do for a while. I quit work. Derek brought me flowers and rubbed my feet and cooked dinner, when 'pregnancy things' gave me an excuse to laze on the sofa reading 'how to be a good parent' books and eat peanut butter and dill pickle sandwiches. Rose and Lou, especially Lou, were thrilled; he had the grandfather rooster-strut down perfectly.

Then the baby was born. Jerome arrived that hellish October night, and the walls caved in. I loathed this little scrap. I despised Derek for not protecting me. I blamed Lou, not Rose, for Jerome's problems — unfair, unfair! The doctors carefully explained the complicated genetics that fingered Rose as the one with the faulty genes. How could it be Rose, not Lou? My father's kinked chromosomes waved at the world from the sides of his head.

Lou's disappointment with this imperfect child, his grandson, was plain. Derek tried to broker peace between Lou and me. He's hurting, too. Be kind to him.

That's right, one freak to another, I spat. It was as close as Derek ever came to hitting me. We both knew I had crossed a line.

The day after Jerome's first birthday I walked out on them both — no, I ran. I ran away from my genetically unlucky baby and my quietly suffering husband and my judgmental father. I ran away to another country and another life. Everything I did, or did not do, was measured and found wanting by everyone except my mother, but especially by Lou. What I had done was unforgivable (although what Derek did later topped the sin chart in Lou's eyes).

Only Rose knew where I had fled to. New York, New York. No-one would find me there. I swore her to secrecy, under threat of my disappearing forever if she told anyone where I was. In New York I met

195

men, some good, some very bad, slept with most of them, and saw Derek's face every time. I drowned Derek and Jerome in oceans of booze. At a design launch party a big name designer offered me a job. I made a fat sum as his design assistant, then creative director and, inevitably, mistress. Five years later it all came to a messy end over an inventively financed inner-city apartment project and an ugly divorce lawsuit. When the project owners and the wife both threatened to name me as accomplice number one in their lawsuits I threw my clothes in a bag, flushed the booze, phoned Rose and took the first plane home.

When I got off the plane in Saskatoon there was no Rose, no Lou, no Derek to meet me. Instead, there was Dixie, this astonishing apparition in white stilettos and a tight black dress, looking sharper and sexier than any New York fashionista. I actually fainted, toppling over my baggage in the airport arrivals hall and smashing my duty-free vodka on the floor. It has been a struggle to find some kind of steadying consciousness ever since.

The only solid truth I know is this: Dixie is a better mother to Jerome than I would ever have been. It is my permanent shame.

My meltdown after seeing Dixie was complete. I raged and cried, abused and accused her. She tried to tell me what I should have known all along. I spat in her face. After that she flew back to Vancouver, to Jerome and out of my life. I found a filthy but furnished basement suite on the west side. My suitcase sat, unpacked, on the cracked linoleum. For weeks I did nothing but stare at the grubby walls and drink to oblivion.

Rose and Lou saved me. They bought their townhouse, crammed forty years of household stuff into it and gifted me their little white house as an early inheritance. I did not want it. With a house came responsibilities. In small, determined ways, Rose forced me to take them on. She gave Sass to me as a surprise birthday gift. I did not want this sleek brown scrap either. Sass was just something else waiting to break my heart. Rose pleaded, reasoned, softly cajoled. Dixie is a wonderful person. Give her a chance, she said, careful not to mention Jerome.

Bullshit, I said, brutally taking sides with Lou against the nightmare that was Dixie.

It took a year of Rose's gentle persuasions and Dixie relentlessly phoning every week until one day I gave in. We have built a kind of simmering, shambolic peace ever since. It's been harder than I would ever have believed.

But I can't imagine life without her.

There are some people we can't stop loving, no matter what. Not mothers, whose love mysteriously begins at the moment we are conceived. Not fathers, with their surprising, infuriating male ways. Not transgender husbands with a capacity for love and forgiveness so wide and deep I am forever caught in its tractor beam. What is left of Derek in Dixie keeps me whirling round and round, a small, cold moon in an endless, dizzying orbit around the brightest star in the sky.

Chapter 34

Lou is surprisingly wise

"Look, Sophie." Lou carefully parts the prickly leaves to show me a late-blooming pink-veined white rose hidden behind a rhubarb bush. "So beautiful. She visit us, my Rosa."

I nod. "Yes, Papa."

Since Rose's funeral, Lou spends most of his days pottering in his garden. He prunes his roses, turns the soil, dozes a little in the late afternoon sun. Often he weeps, and I weep with him. Every day I wake up to the same thought: my mother is gone. I'll never see her again. I can't imagine ever reaching the end of this piercing grief. I can only guess how deep a furrow it cuts through Lou.

A couple of days after Rose's funeral Alex flew back to spring in New Zealand, to daffodils blooming and lambs frisking in green fields. My aunts stayed long enough to help me sort through her belongings. With Carmina and Margherita murmuring encouragement I pulled out every item from Rose's wardrobe, every dress and pair of shoes, and laid them on my parents' bed. I opened her jewelry box and spilled out rings, a few beaded glass necklaces. There wasn't much. Rose was neither a peacock nor a hoarder. I set aside a 1950s blue silk cocktail dress I had seen her wear at parties years ago, and a pair of silver high heels with diamante straps. My tears dripped down and stained the silk. I tried, and failed, to toss out these bits of my mother. In the end, I fled in tears to the kitchen. It fell to Carmina and Margherita to carefully pack my mother's wardrobe, every shoe, every blouse, every skirt, into boxes and call the Salvation Army to take it all away.

Days later I unearthed another piece of jewelry from Rose's dresser drawer. It was a small, shabby brooch in the shape of a daisy. All the gold paint had peeled away from the edges of the petals and not one of the tiny chips of inlaid glass, red, blue and green, had survived beyond the first week.

I had no idea Rose had kept this brooch. I had bought it by mail-order as a secret birthday gift for my mother, with money I'd saved from doing odd jobs for my parents (the much-hated weeding, and taking the rubbish out with only minor complaint and little melodramatic nostril-pinching). On the magazine's page the brooch sparkled, shimmered, gleamed. I was convinced it was real gold set with rubies, emeralds and sapphires. I sent my money away taped to a piece of cardboard inside an envelope, and waited. Six weeks went by, and so did Rose's birthday.

When the much-anticipated brooch finally arrived in all its tawdry cheapness, I cried myself to sleep. The glass lacked sparkle, the gold didn't shine. I had no back-up birthday plan, and no more money, so I gave it to Rose anyway, wrapped with a pretty piece of pink ribbon. She exclaimed on its loveliness and my initiative. She thanked me with kisses. When I tried to pin it on her sweater, the clasp broke. I was inconsolable. This was not the happy birthday scenario I had pictured for six long weeks.

Never mind, murmured my mother, it's the thought that counts. I couldn't agree, and still don't. Thoughts were free; they didn't gobble up $5.99 plus tax and shipping from an eight-year-old girl's hard-earned savings.

Today's task is to sort through an untidy box I found on the top shelf of my parents' closet. Lou waves me away when I ask if he wants to look through it with me. There are newspaper clippings: obituaries, birth announcements — mine, my cousins'. Some Signor Patata ads, letters from friends. Stacks of photos of me, as a squinch-faced newborn, a plump toddler, a shy schoolgirl in new buckle-up black shoes. Here I am wearing my hated Brownie uniform. There are dozens of photos of Rose and me and the rare photo of us all as a family. Here's one of us standing outside the monkey enclosure at the Forestry Farm. I am barely more than a toddler. I pick up the box and take it outside.

"Look, Lou." I hand him the monkey photo.

"Ah, *sì.*" Lou fingers the photo. "I remember this day. After we ask a lady to take this photo, a monkey, he reach through the bar and steal my hat. I am angry. It is a good hat, fits nice, your mother give it to me. Now there is no hat, I look like a monkey too."

"Lou!"

My father smiles. "Don't worry, Sophia. My whole life I have these things, these monkey ears. I am Monkey Man. If I don't laugh, I cry. So I laugh. I have a good life, I make enough money for my family. My Rosa, your Mamma — she love me anyway. She don't care about ears. Other things are important, Sophie. Remember the good. Forget the bad."

He gives me a meaningful look. I have the distinct feeling we are not talking about Lou the Monkey Man, or our Sanzari-Mironescu family triangle.

"Rosa and me, we have problems, but we fix them. We talk and talk, and make the problems go away. If you no talk, the problem gets bigger and then it is so big you don't know how you start to make it small again."

I look up from my box of photos. "You always look so happy together. I don't ever remember you being angry with each other. Maybe once, when she threw the dinner plate at you. What problems did you and Mamma have? What was that fight about? You weren't talking then. I was so upset."

200

Lou says nothing for many heartbeats. It's as if Lou is retreating through time, opening some doors, leaving others closed. Then he clears his throat.

"It is hard to speak about this, Sophia. But you are grown-up now, my big girl. Your Mamma and I, we had the problem making a baby. This is why we fight that day. Two babies before you — they die. Only one baby is born with the breath, a boy, and he die so soon. He have only one day in this life.

"Rosa's Mamma, she blame me. She say to Rosa, I told you, nothing good come from this man. It make Rosa so sad, it break my heart. I am sad, and also angry, not with Rosa, with God. Why he punish us? I think I know."

Tears dribble down Lou's cheeks.

"Sometimes we cry, one time we fight, we say hard words to each other. Rosa, she lose hope for a baby. She is so sad. I am *nella disperazione*. We have the bad time. Then, *piccolo miracolo*, you are born, Sophia. I am very happy for Rosa but in my heart, I have a bad secret. You are smart girl, Sophia. I think you know this secret."

I nod.

"I want so much a boy. I want a son, to call him Antonio. To remember my brother, to make good what I do. *Capisci*? I want a boy so much maybe I go a little bit crazy. I say some things to Rosa about those babies who die, bad things about her and a man she know at the bakery. I am crazy, she is so angry, I think she leave me. I am so scared. If she leave I have nothing, nothing. But Rosa, she has a big, big heart, so much love. She forgive me. I am so happy, I love so much Rosa, and *la mia piccola figlia*. She is so beautiful, like her Mamma. And I forget about having no son, until Alex come. Now I am happy Sophia. I have beautiful daughter, and handsome son, too."

My lips form the words 'DNA test' but my heart isn't in it. I have conceded defeat to Alex. Whatever the test says — and the results should arrive any day — Lou will believe that Alex is his son. Why not, if it makes him happy? My machinations shame me. I am the world's slowest learner in affairs of the heart.

After a while Lou takes my hand. "I make another *confessione*, Sophia."

I'm not sure I want to hear it. There is only so much parental confession I can take. I already feel as though I've been caught peeping through a keyhole into a room full of half-naked people, and some are my parents. There are some things children should never know about their elders.

"Lou, I don't want to know."

"No, no, you listen. This is about your, your friend. About Derek, ah, no, about Dixie." My head snaps up. Lou has never said her name before. He'd rather drink turpentine.

"I am wrong. Dixie is a good, ah, person. Rosa, she know this. *Tuo marito*, Derek, he do something I think is bad, something that hurt you, my daughter, very much and maybe God think so too, but there is good from the bad. Dixie is the good mother. Jerome, he is a nice boy, but he has the hard life. He your son, Sophie. He need his Mamma — and his other Mamma. *Capisci?*"

I'm so astounded I can only nod. *Capisco.* For Lou to even think these thoughts is as startling as if he'd announced he's taking off for Everest base camp on a donkey. Lou and I have never talked about Derek's transformation to Dixie. I thought we never would.

"*Bene.*" Lou pinches an aphid from the pink-veined rose. "*Molto bene.* Listen to your Papa, Sophia. Don't-a wait too long. Don't-a wait for when is too late."

Chapter 35

la vita è bella

There is a sassy new message on Lou's answerphone.

Pronto, you speak to Lou Sanzari, waddaya want.

It has taken Lou a few weeks and several attempts at nonchalance to change his voicemail message. Erasing this last bit of Rose isn't as painful as I thought it would be. It's easier than listening to my mother's quiet greeting from beyond the grave.

"It's Sophie," I say to the sassy machine. "Which salami do you want? The deli is out of that special garlica pepperoni you like. Call me." I add, "Love you, Papa." It gets easier with practice.

Lou is throwing a party of epic Italian proportions to celebrate Alex's DNA test results. My clever plan is an ignominious backfire. I realize now that it was always going to be. Science does not lie. Alex is Lou's son, his own true spawn. There will be no more arguing about it. Lou and Alex are bonded together with Y-chromosome superglue. Without getting my brain bent out of shape over loci and alleles and other genetic tongue-trippers, a telltale bit of Alex's DNA could only have been passed on by Lou. Alex's genetic profile is his own special blend of Olga-Tatiana Mironescu and Luigi Giuseppe Sanzari, not some DNA mishmash from Antonio or another carnival clown. Alex's father is nobody else but Lou.

La vita è bella. Life is beautiful.

I am happy for Lou and for Alex. Yes I am. Lou has gained a longed-for son and Alex has gained a father, although for how long, nobody knows. Lou's heart is repairing itself faster than expected, according to the doctors. He'll be fit enough to board a plane and fly all the way across the planet to New Zealand for Tony and Olivia's seaside nuptials. Of course, I've agreed to Lou's grand journey. I lost the bet, and now I'm paying up. Alex was right. Lou is running out of time. That is the problem with time. There is never the right amount. There is always too much time, or not nearly enough.

Now that the DNA cat is out of the bag, Alex and I have made small but sure progress toward some sort of sibling truce. We chat amiably enough on the phone, and we've met at the Broadway Café a couple of times for lunch. Without Dixie hogging the limelight I manage to have a decent conversation and eat my own burger and fries without her fingers poking around my plate. I tell him stories about Sass the cat, he tells me a little about the places he's lived: Paris and Prague, Sydney and Auckland. There is a reassuring steadiness about him.

Apart from Mrs Woloschuk, Nico, Guido and a few of Lou's card-shark buddies the party will be a normal family affair with my conniving octogenarian aunts, all-female cousins, hairy-eared father, Romanian half-brother, transgender ex-husband and Siderius syndrome son. The only one absent is Rose.

I still can't believe Rose is not lying in her bed like Sleeping Beauty, waiting to wake up. Two years, I'm told, is what it takes to ease this gut-wrenching daily grief. I can't believe it will ever stop. Sometimes I get in the car for my Tuesday visits before catching myself and driving away, anywhere, to park in some lonely spot and cry for my mother. Once or twice I have driven over to see Mel. She misses Rose too, she says, but how can she miss someone she never knew? Perhaps she means she misses the routine of Rose and her hopeful visitors. One day I will stop these visits, and I will miss the routine of Mel.

Dixie and Jerome arrived a few days ago, all elegant raucousness and high-pitched squealing. Sass retreated beneath the kitchen table in hissy indignation, but she was soon seduced by Jerome offering her a bit of fresh chicken and laughing like a drain when her rough tongue scraped his fingers.

We've been to the Berry Barn for saskatoon berry pie and to Wanuskewin to walk the sage-scented paths. Today's excursion is the Forestry Farm, where we admire the hairy yak cooling himself in the shade of a leafy tree and the monkeys screeching and swinging from limb to limb. They stare at us with a fierce, bright cunning. I try not to think of Lou.

In the baby farm animals section, there is a frisky brown and white spotted calf gnawing a fencepost. Jerome puts an eager hand out. The calf sucks and chews his fingers, searching for milk.

"Cows chew everything. That's their way of feeling their world," says Dixie to an astonished Jerome, who sniffs the slobber on his fingers before wiping it on his shirt.

"You'll have to take the next step up from turtle in the pet department," I smile. "Esmeralda just won't cut it anymore after Sass and a yak and a calf."

"You're right." Dixie yawns, watching Jerome stroke the calf's soft snout. "Esmeralda is a thing of reptilian beauty, but she's still just a rock on legs."

Wherever we go, Dixie and Jerome get plenty of looks. It is almost like being zoo animals ourselves. Most are envious gazes/sneak peeks/frank gawps at Dixie, depending on who's looking. Others are pitying/judging glances at Jerome, who is obviously Not Quite Right and never will be. Jerome is blithely oblivious to snubs and slights in a world glued together with Dixie's careful love.

He is a funny little boy, quick to give hugs and slow to pout. His precarious, jumbled view of life and everything in it makes me laugh and wince and sometimes cry. He never questions who I am. I am Sophie, and that's good enough for Jerome. As much as any son with Siderius syndrome can, he looks like his mother. Neither of us has told Jerome that he has two of them.

Back at home I watch Jerome zooming around embracing our knees and tunelessly squeaking out pieces of song.

"It's a shame Rose couldn't be here to see Jerome. She would have loved him."

Dixie purses her pouty Red Devil lips.

"What? What did I say now, Dixie?"

"She did love him, Sophie. She talked to him on the phone every week, until she had her stroke. When you ran off to Pittsburgh or Petula or wherever it was —"

"New York," I whisper.

"— she was the one who got us through. Did I ever tell you about the day Rose first met the new me? No, I couldn't have. You never wanted to talk about it." Dixie scrabbles around in her purse, then remembers she has quit smoking, again, and blows a huge sigh.

"Oh, hell. Got any gum, Sophie? I'm going bonkers. Anyway, I was terrified she'd hate me. She stood barely five feet tall in house slippers but Rose looked way up and gave me her best Rose smile, you know the one that made you feel touched by pixie dust. She said, and I remember this distinctly, 'What a beautiful girl you are, Dixie, I'm so pleased to meet you,' and she kissed me on the cheek."

I reach to touch her but she waves me off.

"That kiss from Rose meant so much to me, Sophie. She helped me belong in the world. Lou, of course, was another smelly kettle of fish. He couldn't forgive me. I guess I don't blame him. I hadn't kept my part of my bargain with you. But you didn't keep yours either, Soph. When you took off, without telling me anything —"

Her face is so full of pain. This is not a conversation I want to have, now or ever.

"Your mother was the rock in our lives, Sophie. Who do you think took care of Jerome when you and I went to Turkey? You never even asked. It was Rose. She loved Jerome to pieces. He misses her. He doesn't understand where Nana has gone. You would have known that, if —" she shrugs, dabbing at her eyes.

If.

If I'd got help when Derek asked me to talk to someone. If I'd gone to the appointments he made for me. If I hadn't run away. Would we have made some kind of family? I have never asked Dixie that question. What would I do if she said yes?

I feel dizzy, as if I've stepped away from plummeting into an abyss. It is unbelievable (almost) that Rose would keep this secret from me. But then, so much of my parents' lives have been secrets. I am even more of an idiot than ever. Of course Rose would love Jerome. He is her flesh and blood, built from her own imperfect genes that she passed to me that I passed to Jerome. Did she feel guilty? I know I did. I still do.

Lou is right. Don't-a wait until it's too late. I blow my nose. Take a deep breath.

"Dixie, I, maybe I'll come out to Vancouver and see you. Both of you. Esmeralda too. I'll bring some juicy Saskatchewan worms. Maybe I could stay for a while." It is a pathetic little concession, over-hearty and glib, but it's a start. I have cracked open the closet door and this time, the bogeyman's not leering back at me.

"When?" When I hesitate, she shakes her head. "Come on Sophie, do it right or don't do it at all."

Christmas, says my heart, before my brain can stick up a warning flag. Why not? Lou will be eating seafood under the trees at his grandson's wedding in summertime New Zealand. I have been formally invited to the wedding, via a sea-blue card embossed with starfish and delivered personally by Alex. I thought briefly about attending the wedding, but I am not ready to see Lou folded into the family bosom of strangers. But the thought of sitting here alone with Sass in my ho-ho-ho hat drinking too much mulled wine is pathetic and scary.

"How about Christmas, Dixie?"

"Christmas? Really? Christmas it is, then, my lovely." Dixie springs up into a little dance. Jerome joins in, a pint-sized dervish. "We'll do it up right. A proper family Christmas, with a fat stuffed turkey. Pumpkin pie, Jerome's favorite. We'll eat like piglets and become festively plump. We'll go to every single one of the Boxing Day sales, darling, and shower ourselves with shoes."

There is so much hope in her eyes. I realize she has been waiting for this moment for years. So have I, if I would only admit it. The feeling of vertigo eases. I stepped into the abyss, and Dixie caught me.

"You'll remember, will you Dix?" I say, trying for jolly. "Should I call you up every day and remind you? And Jerome?" I add, feeling brave.

She picks up my hands, kisses them.

"Darling Sophie. There's plenty of time to remember and forget and remember again. But maybe you should call every day. Just in case."

My little house, my parent's house, where I grew up and where my memory of Rose is still strongest, is ready at last for the big event. My aunts flew in yesterday with my cousins Suzie and Sarah to make sure I am doing justice

208

to their secret Sanzari family recipes. The aunts and I have scrubbed, polished, dusted, cooked and decorated. Jerome tried and failed to blow up balloons with his puny post-pneumonia lungs. Lou sat in my leopard print chair issuing orders in a jungle-king style he enjoyed far too much. Now the Italian feast covers the table, with a few of Mrs Woloschuk's perogies and some vereneky tossed in for those with sturdy stomachs.

Dixie is sinuous and shimmery in a red sequinned evening gown, a white ostrich feather boa and elbow-length gloves. I am frocked and frou-froued too. Dixie forbade me even to think about wearing trousers. She has dressed me up in Rose's blue silk sheath and diamante shoes, topped with a peacock feather fascinator she happened to have stashed in her suitcase.

"It's such fun being a woman, Sophie my sweet. Look at Carmina — eighty-nine and exquisite in that sumptuous georgette frock! Men just wipe the stains off their suits and they're good to go."

Mrs Woloschuk trundles toward me swathed in a muumuu printed with 'Flowers of Saskatchewan' and the same straw hat she wore to Rose's funeral, now bobbing with plastic fruit.

"That hat is a crime against millinery," mutters Dixie. "I'm off."

"Mrs Woloschuk!" I kiss her papery cheek. "How nice to see you! You're looking very, um, festive."

"You like dis dress, Sophia? I make myself, for Florida. Hat, too. Dat a nice dress, Sophie, but you too thin like your fadder, you should eat more perogies. Dat dress is good color for you. When I was seamstress in Kiev–" She stops, looks at me. I wait, smiling.

"When I was seamstress in Kiev I sew da beeyoodeeful dresses for rich ladies, oh my, such dresses you never seen, silk and pearls and sometimes even diamonds. Your friend, she a woman who know how to wear dresses." Eventually she runs out of puff.

"Lou looks happy." I nod to Lou and Alex laughing, Lou is grinning and marionette-twitchy, Alex crinkle-eyed and easy in his skin.

Mrs Woloschuk nods. "Is good to be happy. My Sasha he die many years ago. I em still young woman, good-looking, only sixdy-five. Sasha and me, we are marry for fordy-five year. I em sad for long time. Now, I em happy."

"Don't you miss him?"

"Yes, of course. I miss my Sasha. People we love, we love dem forever. I love him, but Ukrainian mens dey say do dat, cook dis. Now, I don't ask nobuddy. I miss Sasha, but I em happy. I em free." The plastic fruit on her hat dances like Signor Patata the vegetable man.

Mrs Woloschuk grips my shoulders with her hard seamstress hands and turns me to face her.

"Sophie. Is not bad to be happy. Is not crime. You t'ink Lou should be sad always? Your mudder and Lou heff happy life. Dey love each udder. Lou love you, and now he love Alex too, he a nice man, so handsome. Why no? Alex is son of Lou. It is good t'ing for mens to heff a son. Your brudder."

I have a brother. His name is Alex.

Excusing myself to Mrs Woloschuk, I cross the floor and touch his arm.

"Alex. How're you doing?"

He smiles that familiar, neutral curve of the lips. "It's all good, Sophie. Thanks for all your efforts. It's a grand party. Lou is having a great time."

"Is the Sanzari family all you thought it would be?"

He laughs. "Be careful what you wish for." He looks over my shoulder. Then he asks, casually, as if it has just occurred to him, "How long have you known Dixie?"

Prickles in my thumbs. Prickles in my heart. Shivers down my spine.

"A long, long time, Alex. It feels like all my life. It's a complicated story."

"Maybe you can tell me sometime."

210

"Maybe. Or you can ask her yourself." I have no intention of telling Alex one word about Dixie. She can spin any truth or lies she likes. It is not my story anymore. When the heart wants something badly enough it will take it, with no thought for the rest of you, or for anyone else. Blood and bones are carted along for the ride. Entire lives are caught in an emotional snowmelt rushing forever downstream.

Carmina slaps an old Frank Sinatra record on Lou's vintage record player and pulls Alex into a cha-cha. After a short tug of war that Alex was never going to win he dances, effortlessly and impressively, with each of the aunts: rhumbas, foxtrots, even a short, sassy jive with a glowing Margherita. Decades drop off my elderly aunts. This is an exuberant and outgoing Alex I haven't seen before. Change partners and dance. Mrs Woloschuk corrals Guido, who narrowly escapes head injury by plastic fruit. Now Margherita is jigging with Jerome, while Dixie beguiles Alex in a corner.

As the music slows to a waltz Dixie rests one elegantly gloved hand on his shoulder. Alex, calm, cool as a cucumber Alex, turns pink. Chuffed Cerise. They glide around the floor in perfect synch, the cool blond and the raven-haired beauty. The usually boisterous Suzie and Sarah loiter bashful as handmaidens on the fringe madly lash-batting at Alex. It's like being back at the school dance. I don't fancy their chances. Dixie always gets what she wants.

"Sophia." My father is in front of me, bowing. "You look so beautiful. Like your bella Mamma." He holds out his hand. *"Posso avere l'onore di questa danza?"*

I curtsey in my mother's blue silk dress. *"Sì, Papa. Sono onorata."*

I waltz with my father, his hand pressed firmly into my back, round and round, following his steady lead.

211

Alex flew back to New Zealand the day after the party. He will return in precisely nine weeks and three days, according to Lou's countdown calendar. It's no problem, all this flying, Alex tells Lou. He has chalked up almost enough frequent flyer points over the last few months to pay for Lou's ticket downunder.

Lou is overexcited to the point of repeat heart attack at the thought of meeting his grandson (his other, grown-up grandson) and his new granddaughter-to-be. I know Alex will take good care of Lou. If a long-lost Son of Lou had to turn up in our lives, Alex is a better than average luck of the draw.

But before Lou and Alex waltz off into the southern sunset, Carmina, Margherita, Lou and I are all flying to Calgary. Lou wanted to drive, but confinement in a small stuffy car with all of my elderly relatives for ten hours (not counting tea and pee breaks) is more than my life is worth. We are flying to Calgary to see the place where Antonio is buried. Carmina and Margherita, I have discovered, knew about Antonio and Lou all along. The Sanzari capacity for keeping secrets rivals that of national intelligence agencies. I have mixed feelings about visiting the grave of my brutal and drunken mafioso uncle, but it will make Lou happy if I come along, and so I will.

My life has taken some turns for the better. After a social hiatus of many months I have seen two movies, one in the company of an old schoolmate I literally bumped into while furtively squeezing the grape tomatoes at the supermarket. It's a male friend. Victor Chernoff. I remember him being short and quiet and plump-ish. He is now taller and not so plump and not quiet at all. After obliquely trawling for my marital status he asked me out. After a brief attack of nerves and an urge to pee my pants I

212

said yes. I liked the movie. We even had a drink afterward. It was nice. If he calls again, I might even say yes to another date. We are nowhere near the stage where I have to warn him about getting too close to a Sanzari.

Almost as exciting, my bank account is more black than red for the first time in a year. Andy at PaintMe was so enchanted with the Saskatchewan centenary project he passed my name onto a big-name architect working on a commercial renovation on an old department store downtown. The architect wanted someone 'unconventional' to choose the color scheme. I took that as a compliment. Andy gave the guy a huge discount on paint and wallpaper and threw in my services as part of the deal, waving my New York design experience around like a supermarket bonus coupon. The job has been a pleasant surprise. This architect is happily married with three brown-eyed kiddies who scribble felt pen trees and dogs all over the boardroom table when their mother brings them in for lunch.

When I report my news to Dixie she says, "Marvelous, my sweet." After some benign chatter about turtles and little boy's dirty knees, she comes to the point.

"Are you happy, Sophie?"

"Happier."

"Eeyore, Eeyore," she snorts, and I can't help but laugh.

Then there's Lou. What I knew about Lou before Alex appeared in our lives could fit inside a cat food tin. I am beginning to understand that the man who is my father is someone nobler and wiser than I ever suspected or probably deserved. Everything Lou endured — New York poverty, orphan trains, Swedish farmer abuse, gangster crimes, POW lockups, Monkey Man humiliation — all of this he kept locked down, buried so deep it cast no shadows into my innocent, careless life.

If Alex had never contacted Lou, would Lou have told me all of this? Now that I know Lou's story, does it matter? I think it does. Alex managed to crack open a door I never knew existed. I am surprised, grateful, and more often than not, inexplicably sad.

Lou and I still have our bad days, but they are not savage enough to give anyone a heart attack.

Chapter 36

The secret Rose

Rose would have liked Alex. Is that what she was trying to say? I will never know. There are so many things I will never know about Rose. This morning I remembered to have a look at my own DNA results. I had forgotten about them amid heartbreak and heart attacks and confessions and victory parties and new jobs. I clicked on the link to the site, read the words, and re-read them. Then I picked up the phone and dialed the number for the testing company in Pennsylvania. I asked if they were sure they had given me the correct results for the daughter of Rose and Luigi Sanzari. The cool voice on the other end of the phone assured me that they had strict confidentiality and quality control measures in place. There could be no mistake.

I deleted the email. I deleted all traces of this test.

This is one secret my father's ears will never hear.

It was Rose's secret.

Now, it's mine.

About Karen Goa

Canadian-born and -raised, Karen Goa traded a hospital pharmacist's white coat in wintery Saskatchewan for an editing and writing career in New Zealand. She is the author of numerous short stories broadcast on Radio New Zealand National. Her quirky, hilarious travel books have been adapted from print and broadcast on Radio New Zealand.

Karen and her husband live in Auckland, New Zealand. Karen's flying trapeze career was short and shambolic. This is her first novel.

Contact Karen Goa

Please get in touch with your comments and words about life at
karengoawriter@gmail.com
Visit my website www.karengoa.com
and join in the dialog on Facebook
https://www.facebook.com/My-Fathers-Ears-329158303875808/?ref=hl

My Father's Ears is also available as an ebook.

www.ingramcontent.com/pod-product-compliance
Lightning Source LLC
Chambersburg PA
CBHW020109180626
46812CB00006B/2539